Vendetta's Victim

Alex Matthews

INTRIGUE
P R E S S

For information, please contact Intrigue Press, P.O. Box 456, Angel Fire, NM 87710, 505-377-3474.

ISBN 1-890768-14-6

First Printing 1998
First Paperback Printing 1999

Grateful acknowledgment is made for permission to reprint a line from the comic strip *Sylvia* © 1995 by Nicole Hollander. Used by permission. All rights reserved.

For my husband Allen,
Who makes all things possible.

The author wishes to acknowledge the invaluable assistance of Allen Matthews, who tirelessly read revisions and made the computer do what she wanted; Chris Roerden, who provided editing, mentoring, and encouragement; Phyllis Rubin and Sunny Hall, who listened; and Nancy Carleton, Denise Stybr, Jan Fellers, and Carol Houswald, who gave invaluable feedback as critique group members, and Susan Sullivan, who conceptualized the cover and is my life-long best friend.

1

Anonymous Call

Cassidy McCabe glared at the man in the terry robe sitting next to her in the new waterbed. "Zach, please, this is my mother's engagement party. If you don't go, everyone'll think you're an imaginary companion, like Harvey the rabbit."

"Who knows, maybe I am?" Zach searched through the Sunday *Post* spread across the bed and pulled out the Chicago news section. A calico kitten about the size of a large potato attacked his hand. "Any luck finding homes for these bite-sized monsters?" He plunked the calico into Cassidy's lap on top of a sleeping black kitten, then raised the newspaper. In profile his features were smooth and regular, not particularly distinctive, although the fine dark hair, olive skin, and recent scar across his left cheek added an exotic touch.

Damn! I really want him at the party.

Don't nag. You've been living together almost two months and he hasn't cheated on you, lost his job, or broken the law. The man's got a right to say no. This from her proper behavior voice, the one always on her case to do the right thing. Usually, all it did was provoke her rebellious side, in this instance an urge to rag at him some more, retaliate with an onslaught of peevishness.

Cassidy tore the paper out of his hands. "I hate it when you don't listen. It's not like I'm asking you to marry me or anything. All I want is for you to go with me to a big deal family event so that A) Mom and Gran will see that I really do have a boyfriend, B) they won't think you're a major jerk, and C) I don't have to face one more party on my own."

His smoky eyes attentive, he replied, "A) I'm willing to meet your family but not at a mob-scene party, B) sometimes I am a major jerk but I've been trying to curb my innate male tendencies, and C) what about homes for these three house-wreckers?"

An orange kitten crawled out from under the comics page, squawled loudly, and pounced at the crumpled newspaper Cassidy had grabbed away from Zach.

"Why are you being so difficult?" *Who's difficult? Up till now you've manipulated your butt off to keep your mother and Zach apart. Afraid one session with Mom'd send him running for cover.*

Yeah, but going to Mom's engagement party with no boyfriend is too humiliating.

He laid a swarthy hand on top of hers. "I hate parties is all. There's no way out of all the meetings and press conferences, but I'm not about to spend my night off making small talk with strangers."

Don't like parties any better than he does. Maybe I could duck—

Right. And feel guilty for the rest of your life.

The phone on Zach's side of the bed rang. His mouth clamped into a frown. "I was hoping for a quiet Sunday morning." A call on his line usually meant going out to cover a story, then writing it up for the *Post*.

"Moran here." Brief pause. He handed the phone to her.

Cassidy cocked her head in surprise. "Hello?"

The silence went on so long she thought it was going to be a hang-up, but finally a woman's voice responded. "Is this Miss McCabe?"

"That's right." Cassidy clicked into her therapist mode. "What can I do for you?"

"You're a psychologist or something?" The voice was tentative and slightly nasal.

"A social worker actually, but I am a therapist. Are you interested in counseling?" *Not a telemarketer, that's for sure.*

"I got a letter. From Cliff." The pause was loaded with question marks. The caller seemed to expect some kind of explanation.

"Cliff? I don't believe I know who you mean." She tiptoed with her words, certain the line would go dead if she made one false move.

"I thought he was a client of yours. At least, that's what he said in the letter." The woman sounded frightened. "I almost got the idea you were involved in this."

The muscles in back of Cassidy's neck tightened. In a gentle voice, she asked, "Could you tell me something about this letter?"

Another pause. "Why would he say I should see you?"

This is not your garden variety referral. "I wish I had an answer, but I'm as puzzled as you are." The calico began climbing the front of her ancient flannel robe, pulling threads at every step. She had dug the faded plaid robe out of the back of her closet to wear until the kittens were gone.

"I don't understand." The caller sniffled softly.

"Maybe if you explain a little more we can figure it out together."

"No, I can't." Panic in her voice. "For all I know, you could be working with him. Out to hurt people too." The quiet click of the receiver going down.

Hurt people? Oh shit, what is this?

Zach's eyes narrowed. "Who was it? How'd she get my number?"

Cassidy pulled in a deep breath. *Should I tell him?* A still-pending complaint had been filed against her because she had once spilled client information that ended up in a story he had written for the *Post. This woman's not a client. Besides, I need help figuring it out.*

She recounted what the caller had said. "I didn't give out your unlisted number, and I've never had a client named Cliff. I don't believe I've ever even met anyone by that name."

"You remember the names of all your clients?" His voice skeptical.

"You know I've only been in practice four years and I haven't had that many males. I'm certain there weren't any Cliffs. And even if there were, what's this business about hurting people?" She pushed bushy auburn hair back from her face. "And how'd she get your number?"

"I've passed it along to a lot of people. But the rest of it—" He scratched his jaw. "I don't know."

Giving her head a brisk shake, she tried to throw off the mood. "Probably just a crank. Therapists get some weird calls."

She heard paws plodding up the oak staircase outside the bedroom. Starshine, a gaunt calico with swollen nipples dragging nearly to the floor, trudged into the room. Since the cat was licking her chops, Cassidy assumed she had just finished stoking up in the kitchen below. Flopping down in the open space between the waterbed and Cassidy's desk, the calico cooed, calling her babes. All three kittens raced to the side of the bed, poised like Olympic divers, then made a giant leap to the floor. They swarmed over to Starshine, wrestled and clawed for nipples, then settled down to lunch.

From the bed Cassidy had a clear view through the north facing window, one of two tall windows that bracketed her corner desk. Bright light glinted off ice-covered branches. *Glad Zach didn't have to go running off to work.* The waterbed he'd bought because he hated her old mattress made a snug cocoon. The kittens, who climbed on top of each other at nap time, had the right idea. She'd slept alone for three years between her divorce and Zach's move-in, and now it felt good to rub up against a warm body at night, even if the body belonged to a man who refused to accompany her to her mother's party.

She wiggled her toes against his leg beneath the new burgundy comforter he'd bought to go with the bed. "I've finally thought of names for the munchkins. 'Calvin' for the black kitten, 'Hobbes' for the orange kitten, and the calico's going to be 'Sylvia.' You know, after the cartoon characters. You remember that 'Calvin and Hobbes' strip from a couple of years ago?"

He straightened the newspaper she'd crumpled when she grabbed it away from him. "Why names? You said kittens leave home at two months. It's already halfway through January, so where are those surrogate mommies of good character and sound family values you promised to find?"

"Don't worry, I've got some people in mind."

The contented buzz of several bodies vibrating in unison rose from the cat pile on the floor.

⊠ ⊠ ⊠

Two days later snow was coming down when they awoke. Sitting up in bed, Cassidy stared at hypnotically falling flakes while Zach went down for coffee. Her mauve-hued bedroom contained an executive desk against the north wall, an empty space between the desk and bed, and a bureau with TV on top against the south wall.

He returned and handed her a purple mug decorated with a stylized version of a cat. "I better shovel before I leave."

She jerked into alertness. "No, don't." *Can't let him do everything.*

"There you go again."

"Please try to understand. I've been shoveling snow for years. I don't want you just coming in and taking over."

"I'm not any happier about leaving it to you."

Hate feeling like I can't take care of myself. "Look, you've got an office to go to. I don't. You can shovel on weekends, I'll take the weekday shift." Standing, she gave him a hug. "Deal?"

At noon Cassidy clomped out to clear a path for her two o'clock client. Her corner house was handy for back-door access to her home office but burdensome for shoveling. Her sidewalk was half a block long on the north-facing side—*more like half a mile*—and fifteen yards long on the west-facing front.

She cleaned off the back stoop, then tackled the cement walk out to Briar, the side street. Large, gloppy flakes continued to fall, coating her lashes, blurring her vision. *Feels like fifty pounds every shovelful.* Twenty minutes later, having cleared the ten yards of sidewalk between her garage and gate, she dragged the shovel toward the house, arms weak and shaky.

You told Zach you've been doing it for years.

Right—half the job, every time.

Opening the back door, she stepped into her client waiting room, a space divided off from the kitchen by a tall oak closet perpendicular to the outside wall. She'd imparted an air of invitation with fan-backed wicker chairs, a window draped in filmy, raspberry fabric, and a small tea counter next to her office door. Her large, octogenarian house was clearly deteriorating, as evidenced by the kitchen's scuffed linoleum countertop and worn linoleum floor, but she'd done her best to brighten it with warm colors, framed posters, and airy wallpaper.

She stashed her boots and jacket in the closet, then padded into the kitchen to make coffee, feet itchy in thick, wet socks. Inhaling the brew's rich aroma, she gazed through her kitchen window into the kitchen of the house three yards to the south. As she filled her mug, the wall phone next to the dining room doorway chirped.

"So, we finally gonna meet that mystery man of yours?" Gran's chipper voice queried. "The one who's been parking his Nissan in your garage the past couple of months?"

Stretching the cord across the room to the counter, Cassidy dumped cream and sugar into her purple mug. "You've got spies out, haven't you?"

"You betcha. Next thing you know, I'll be bugging your phone. Now stop dodging. Is this Zachary character coming with you Friday or not?"

Cassidy ground her lower lip between her teeth. *Always making excuses. Must be an idiot, living with Harvey the rabbit.* "Not this time." She kept her voice brisk. "He'd rather meet you and Mom without a lot of other people around."

Gran, who was not easily fooled, clicked her tongue. "Well, honey, don't you worry. We've got plenty of time. Besides, you'll probably have more fun without him. Oh, I almost forgot—the main reason I called was to say that your mother's intended is gonna take me out early to that fancy house of his, so you won't need to pick me up. That Roland Mertz may be short on pedigrees, but he sure is long on bucks."

"How're they coming with the prenuptials? Last I heard, Roland's kids were doing their damndest to keep him from marrying Mom." Cassidy moved into the dining room to stare out the wide window overlooking Briar. Noticing that the snow had nearly stopped, she watched a beige hatchback troll east past her house, pull a U-turn, and halt in front of a driveway directly across from where she was standing. *Strange place to stop.*

Gran replied, "Helen says Roland's lawyers have done up a contract leaving everything to the kids. Far as I'm concerned, she'd be crazy to sign a thing like that."

"I agree. What a shame Mom's big moment has to be spoiled by all this Mertz family bickering." A dark-haired woman behind the wheel of the hatchback stared straight into Cassidy's eyes, her features drawn into a fierce scowl. *Do I know her?* Feeling a ripple of uneasiness, Cassidy kept her gaze on the woman until the car rolled slowly out of sight.

✆ ✆ ✆

Starshine slithered between her legs and traipsed across the kitchen to sit beside her dish as Cassidy dutifully piled in food. Sylvia, the newly named calico, and Calvin, the black kitten, skittered over to their mother. Sylvia stuck the entire front portion of her body, legs and face combined, into the bowl, apparently hoping to crowd out everyone else. Calvin leapt at her tail.

Starshine, a glazed look in her eyes, gave up trying to eat and jumped listlessly onto the counter. Cassidy removed Sylvia from the bowl and placed it in front of Mom. As Starshine's head drooped toward the food, Cassidy scratched the cat's raised rump. "These kittens are eating you alive."

Cradling the squirmy children in her arms, she carried them up to the nursery, one of two extra bedrooms that now served as a lock-down for Starshine's brood. She placed them in a nest of old towels and raced for the door, closing it just before they zipped out after her.

Ignoring the kittens' indignant outcries, Cassidy crossed

the hall to her bedroom and pulled out a change of clothes
for her two o'clock client, Ken Leman. She had to get herself
presentable, even though she never knew for sure whether
he would show or not. *Can't figure him out. Comes for four
or five sessions, then disappears. Something not right.*

As she stepped into plum-colored pants, the front doorbell
chimed. She frowned. The client-entrance bell in back was
the one that usually rang. *Nobody comes to the front except
fundraisers and Girl Scouts peddling cookies.* She hastily
zipped up. *Could be kids shoveling snow. If I hire kids, Zach
won't know I wasn't able to finish.* She dashed barefoot down
the cold oak stairs to catch them before they got away.

The air leaking around the front door had turned the foyer
into a walk-in freezer. Cassidy, her feet going numb, opened
up and stared across the enclosed porch that separated her
from the outside screen door. A woman stood on the other
side of the screen, her face framed in long, dark hair. It was
the face that had scowled from the window of the hatchback.
Cassidy's scalp tingled. *What'd I do? Scratch her fender?
Take Zach away from her?* The air behind the woman was
white. The storm had once again intensified, a sharp wind
driving icy pellets against the house.

2

Letter from Cliff

The woman crossed the porch and bore down on Cassidy, who took three quick steps backward. Straightening her shoulders, Cassidy held up outspread hands. "Hey, wait a minute. You can't come barging into my house like this."

"Cassidy McCabe, right?" Several inches taller than Cassidy's five-two, the scowler had intense brown eyes that drilled into her like laser beams.

If she could kill me with those death-ray eyes of hers, she would. In a minute. On the spot.

A piercing gust blew through the open doorway. "If you think you've got some demented reason to yell at me, at least close the damn door."

The brown eyes blinked, as if the weather came as a surprise. She pivoted and slammed the door.

Cassidy folded her arms across her chest. *Toes'll be frostbitten for sure.* "Since you appear to have something on your mind, let's sit down where it's warm and talk like two civilized human beings."

"You're telling me to be civilized?" The husky voice took on a frantic edge. "You know what he did to me, and you want me to sit down and be nice?" The intruder, who looked to be in her mid-forties, had finely drawn features that would have been attractive were her expression not so angry.

"I can see you're mad as hell about something, and maybe you've got a right to be. But unless I know who you are and what this is about, I can't help you."

"You don't think I'm going to give you my name, do you?" Her voice hiked up a notch. "If you get my name, people might find out."

Cassidy began to wonder if maybe she ought to be more scared than she was, maybe ought to be running to dial 911 this very minute.

The woman continued, "Just tell me, what's the deal between you and Cliff, anyway? Why'd he do what he did? And why are you going along with it? You get a kickback or what?"

Cassidy's brow furrowed. "Cliff?" *That woman Sunday— she talked about a 'Cliff.' This one, her voice's different. Not the same person.*

The scowler flipped glossy, deep brown hair back from her face. "You trying to tell me you don't know what this is about? If you're so innocent, why'd he make this big pitch to get me to see you?" She pulled a folded square of paper from her jacket pocket and shoved it in Cassidy's face. "Go ahead, take it. The original's in my safety deposit box. In case I decide to press charges."

At the top was a paragraph from a newspaper clipping; beneath that, a computer-generated message; on the bottom, Cassidy's business card with Zach's number jotted under hers. Her teeth clenched at the sight of her card.

The newspaper paragraph, which had apparently come from a Dear Abby-type column, said:

I URGE YOU TO SEEK PROFESSIONAL HELP. MANY PEOPLE IN SIMILAR SITUATIONS HAVE FOUND COUNSELING TO BE A SOURCE OF GREAT SOLACE. YOU DON'T HAVE TO SUFFER ALONE.

She went on to read the computerized letter:

DEAR DALE,

JUST A NOTE TO LET YOU KNOW HOW MUCH I APPRECIATE YOUR HELPFULNESS IN ACCOMPLISHING MY MISSION. WOMEN HAVE BEEN THE PERSECUTORS, AND NOW THEY SHALL BE REPAID. I CANNOT TELL YOU HOW MUCH IT COMFORTS ME TO KNOW THAT I'VE INFLICTED ON MY ADVERSARIES THE SAME PAIN THAT WAS INFLICTED ON ME.

BUT YOU ALSO DESERVE CONSOLATION, AND TO THAT END I'D LIKE TO RECOMMEND A THERAPIST, CASSIDY MCCABE, A WOMAN YOU'LL FIND TO BE BOTH SKILLED AND COMPASSIONATE. AS ONE WHO HAS ALREADY BENEFITED FROM HER COUNSELING, I CAN ASSURE YOU SHE WILL BE ABLE TO EASE YOUR WAY THROUGH THE TORMENT THAT LIES AHEAD.

ALL THE BEST MY DEAR,

CLIFF CONNORS

Oh shit. Cassidy's chest tightened. *What the hell is this*

Cliff person up to? She gazed into the woman's face. Red veins sketched her eyes. A pulse throbbed at her temple.

Keeping her voice mild, Cassidy said, "Yeah, you do have a right to be mad. But for the life of me, I don't know who this guy is or how he got my card."

The woman, whose name was apparently Dale, raised her right arm, her hand tightening into a fist. "You refuse to tell me what this is all about? You won't explain any of it? You think you can get out of it by simply playing dumb?"

Taking a deep breath, Cassidy forced herself to keep her own arms loose at her sides. "Please tell me what happened. Whatever you say will be entirely confidential. If this guy Cliff did something to you, then sent you my card, I need to know about it."

Dale lowered her fist, then hugged herself. "You're trying to act normal when you're really some kind of sick pervert. Look, I don't understand any of this, but one thing's for sure," her lower lip quivered. "I got suckered once, I'm not about to give either one of you a second chance."

She turned abruptly and stormed out of the house.

Having lost all feeling in her feet, Cassidy ran barefoot onto the porch to try for the license number, but the air was so thick with snow she couldn't begin to make it out. She scurried back inside, sank onto the steps, and stared at the copy of her business card on the sheet Dale had given her. Starshine, who went into hiding whenever there was trouble, poked her head around the corner and gazed curiously at the door.

⊠ ⊠ ⊠

Cassidy stuffed her frozen feet into burgundy pumps and

crossed the hall to the extra bedroom next to the nursery. Zach had turned this room into a minimal office, furnishing it with a fifties-style chrome and formica dinette set he'd taken from the attic of his mother's house when she wasn't home. Since Zach and his mother seldom spoke except to exchange insults, Cassidy understood his reason for sneaking castoffs out of her house without telling her. What she did not understand was why he had left his good oak desk and personal computer, along with most of his other belongings, in his Marina City condo.

When he moved into Cassidy's house, he'd brought with him a couple of suitcases and three boxes containing his camera, several folders of clippings, and a collection of telephone books. The green formica table, extended by two extra leaves to its full length, now occupied the middle of the room. The three boxes sat on top of the table amid a clutter of newspapers and file folders.

Talk about setting it up for a fast getaway. He could be out of here in an hour, disappear like a rent-evading tenant.

Zach wouldn't do that.

Oh yeah? I wouldn't be the first woman he's walked out on.

She dug out the Chicago white pages, carried it to her desk, and flipped to a column of Connors, two of whom had C as a first initial. None were listed as Cliff Connors.

⊠ ⊠ ⊠

Ken Leman, her erratic two o'clock client, arrived on schedule, apparently in an appointment-keeping mood this week. He had gray-streaked ginger hair, a rugged face, and light blue eyes. Cassidy led him into her office, a paneled room with two shabby, black vinyl sofas against the two windowed walls. Leman settled into his usual spot opposite her director's chair.

"Well," she said, "how's it going?"

He straightened the creases in his khaki pants. "Oh, the usual. I still have this feeling—like I don't fit in at work. I'd really like to make some friends but somehow I never have any luck." His chiseled lips stretched in a small smile that seemed at odds with his words.

After Ken left, she waited in her office for the next client. She had four appointments stacked up between three and nine: a battling couple; a depressed woman; a man with relationship problems; a woman at war with her stepchildren.

Hard to focus. All I want is to talk to Zach about the letter.

Zach never comes home till he feels like it. If you didn't have clients, you'd just get bitchy waiting for him to show. So forget your feelings and do therapy.

Nine finally came and her last client walked out into a clear night, the snow-covered ground sparkling with icy crystals. Despite the cold, she stood at the storm door watching until the woman was safely in her car. Cassidy's house was located one block west of Austin Boulevard, the boundary between a high-crime Chicago neighborhood and her own fighting-against-crime Oak Park suburb.

On the other side of Austin, gangs and shootings were routine. On the Oak Park side, the village did its best to keep the influence of an impoverished ghetto from trickling across the boulevard, but the threat of crime was never absent. Cassidy, like all her neighbors, worried about safety but refused to leave, figuring that what the village had to offer in terms of spirit, spunk, and integration made it worth the battle.

She closed the door and hurried toward the staircase at the front of the house. Half an hour earlier she had heard Zach come in. He would be sitting on her side of the waterbed, eyes glued to the television, bourbon and soda in hand. In some ways he was predictable.

Standing at the foot of the bed, she said, "I need to talk. It's important."

Zach's eyes skimmed her face, perhaps checking to see if the "need to talk" meant "angry at him," then returned to the screen. Calvin was attached to his shoulder; Hobbes was draped across his thigh; Sylvia was tucked inside the crook of his arm. Starshine supervised from the highest point in the room, the top of the television that sat on the bureau.

Gritting her teeth at the time it always took him to cut the power, she placed Dale's letter on her nightstand, then took off her clothes. She wrapped up in her flannel robe, pushed Zach over to his side, and settled into her place on the left.

He clicked the remote, took a swallow from his glass, and said, "I'm all yours."

"I've got to tell you what happened. . . . No, fix me a drink. Drink first, then talk."

He smiled lazily, blue-gray eyes amused. "Anything else, princess?"

He can actually say things like that and not sound sarcastic. One of his more lovable traits.

He went downstairs.

A drink for me, another for himself, then how many more for him?

Leave it alone. You've got enough to worry about deciding how you're gonna say what you need to say without getting in trouble again.

Reappearing, he handed her a drink, then sat beside her on the bed. "So, what's on your mind?"

She twisted to face him. "Zach, I need a guarantee you won't use anything I tell you in a news story."

He pulled his head up straight. "You in some kind of mess again?"

"The only messes were the ones you dragged me into. Now promise so I can tell you."

"Don't you think I've learned my lesson?"

She pursed her lips.

"Okay, okay. No stories unless you give me the go-ahead."

Cassidy related what Dale had said, then handed him the letter.

He whistled under his breath. "Now I'm sorry I promised."

"How can you—"

"Just joking. You don't think I'd make that mistake again, do you? This is your housemate and bedpartner, remember? The man who broke his vow of noncommitment to move in with you. I'm a reporter in the office, not in our bedroom."

Starshine dove onto the bed from her perch on the television, landing with a resounding splat and creating a surge of waves that bobbled Cassidy up and down. The kittens, who were piled up asleep, fell over themselves scrambling toward Mom. Starshine sniffed and licked, then rolled onto her side so her babes could relieve her bursting tits.

Zach's brow creased. "Cliff . . . Cliff Connors. Why is a bell going off?"

"That woman Sunday who called on your line. She said Cliff told her to see me. This was a different woman today, but I'll bet they both received the same letter."

"Why write my number on your card?"

Pressing her knuckles into her cheek, she thought about it. "If he's referring women, he wants me to find out what he did to them." She paused. "I think he also wants me to know that he has access to intimate details about my life—who I live with, what your unlisted number is. It's almost like he's telling me he's somewhere close at hand, hovering over my shoulder."

3

Prenuptials

"Now don't jump the gun in making him out to be a serious bad guy. I admit the letter's pretty spooky, but we don't know for sure he did anything worse than jilt a couple of women."

Which, from Zach's point of view, doesn't seem so bad.

"What about 'the torment that lies ahead?' "

"Yeah, but the guy's a fruitcake. Who knows what it means?" He took a bag of pistachios from his nightstand and plopped it between them. The kittens, never very hungry, abandoned Starshine and trotted over in a wobbly line to investigate.

"So, what've we got?" Zach cocked his head reflectively. "Some guy calling himself Cliff did something to two women, then sent a note saying he's seen you as a client and recommending they do the same. Only you don't know any Cliff, although he could be using an alias." He ate a pistachio, then flipped one to each of the kittens, who scooted their prizes across the comforter.

The orange kitten snatched a second pistachio, carried his loot to a tennis shoe Zach had dumped in the far corner, and dropped it inside. Cassidy started to mention it, then remembered his comment about jilting women, and decided not to spoil Hobbes' game by snitching.

Zach stuck a nut in her mouth. "Then there's the question, why you? Is he a fan with an unusual PR gimmick? Or does he have it in for you too?" She saw a flicker of concern in his eyes.

He worried about me? He turns his feelings on and off so fast, I'm never quite sure what he feels.

"You're the shrink. What's his motivation here?"

The cords in her neck tightened. *Hate when he calls me "shrink." Makes it sound only slightly less slimy than "lawyer."* "I don't know anything about the man. No, wait, I do know something. The word 'persecutor' clearly indicates some degree of paranoia, but I can't tell if he feels persecuted by specific women or women in general. Do men feel persecuted by women? You're the male. What's he saying here?"

"Well, sure. A lot of men feel persecuted, but they'd never admit it."

She wanted to ask "Do you?" but therapist-questions usually led to his getting remote, so she settled for the more generic, "Why?"

"Because they need 'em so much. Men need sex and love. They also need admiration—"

Yeah, but they don't want to do anything to earn it. She opened her mouth to protest but he held up a hand to stop her. "Now don't get on your feminist high horse. I didn't say they deserve it—just that they need it. So women have the power to reject guys and cut them off. And guys always feel manipulated."

"Manipulated how?"

"Women want men to change, so they dole out favors. Take us for example." He placed a shelled pistachio in her hand. "You want me to drink less and stop hanging out in bars. To let you know when I'm coming and going, and tell you where I'll be. To be civilized and attend parties."

A knot formed in her stomach. "That's not fair. Women have the same . . ." Chewing on her bottom lip, she thought about what he'd said. "Is it really that bad?"

Wrapping an arm around her, he pulled her up next to him. "I can live with it."

⊠   ⊠   ⊠

Cassidy lay on the bed, Zach's hand around her breast, his mouth raising riot with her hormones. She squeezed her eyes tight as electric bolts jolted through her.

The skritch of tiny claws climbing the comforter distracted her. Opening her eyes, she saw a furry black head pop over the side of the bed. Zach swatted it down, then picked up where he'd left off. *What is this, a bad sit com?* In less than a minute, she heard the same skritch-scratch and an orange head bobbled above the rim. Zach pushed it away, but the black kitten bounced up to take its place. *Gotta be. We've been dumped into the middle of the kind of program I never watch.*

Her eyes met Zach's. She clamped her mouth shut. *Not nice to giggle during sex.* Zach chuckled. Flopping over on his back, he scooted up beside her. They rolled into a hug, laughing until they were out of breath as they scrambled to protect their more vulnerable parts from needle-sharp claws.

⊠ ⊠ ⊠

Cassidy leaned against the bedroom doorjamb, purple mug in hand, and watched Zach dress for work. The gray light filtering through frost-layered windows barely cut the shadows in the room. Zach pulled on jeans, collarless shirt, and nondescript jacket, then thrust his foot into a tennis shoe. "Ouch!"

Cassidy raised her mug to hide a smirk. Zach shook his shoe and a pistachio fell out. Making a noise halfway between a snort and a chuckle, she heard her mother's voice in her head: *Shouldn't laugh at the misfortunes of others.*

His shaggy brows pulled together in a frown. "Where'd that come from?"

"It was Hobbes. He has this really cute trick—"

"Goddammit, Cass, you said you'd find homes but every time I ask, you change the subject. What're you trying to do? Set it up so we get stuck with all three?"

Her neck stiffened. *You were the one said you liked cats so much. If you want them gone, why don't you do it?*

He looked down into her face. "What's this, no answer? That's my game."

She huffed mildly. "I'm just working myself up to be mad 'cause I don't want to admit that my initial attempt failed. When I tacked those adorable-kitten photos on my bulletin board, I was positive clients'd line up to adopt them. But apparently the kitty market's a tad slow right now."

"So what's next? You want me to get rid of them?"

Yes! You do it. Make them disappear in the middle of the night and don't even tell me about it. She pictured Zach in his cube at the office, kittens clambering over his keyboard and monitor. She sighed. "No, I'm the one that insisted on letting Starshine have babies. I'll just have to figure it out."

⊠　⊠　⊠

After Zach left, Cassidy traipsed downstairs for more coffee, three kittens and a wasted mother cat dodging between her feet.

Homes for the wrecking crew. I'm gonna have to hit the phone. And it'll take a full-bore caffeine buzz to do it.

Midway through the living room, her sneaker landed on a slippery little pile. Screeching to a halt, she lifted the offending foot. A vile odor wafted up from the brown goo on the floor. Hopping to the sofa, she perched on the arm and removed the smelly shoe. Four felines crowded around the mess on the floor, nosing the smeared pile and raising curious eyes as if to say, "I wonder who did that?"

Countless paper towels later, Cassidy marched herself upstairs and planted herself in the swivel chair. Her satiny, inlaid executive desk, the size of a small stadium, was one of the many items bequeathed to her by an ex-husband who preferred to travel light. She picked up an unopened envelope, made herself put it down. *You cannot put this off any longer. You have to take the initiative, get proactive. If kitten-takers won't come to you, you'll go to them.*

God, you sound like a sales manager pumping up the troops.

She pulled out her Rolodex and made a list of names, then picked one that seemed easy: Kristi, Zach's sister-in-law.

"Cass, it's so good to hear from . . . " Kristi's silvery voice answered. "I keep wondering how it's, you know, going. With the two of you, I mean. So, you think Zach'll . . . ? If anybody can get him to settle, you're the one to do it."

"Who knows?"

"What's he gonna do with his Marina City . . . ? Put it on the market?"

"Um, I don't know yet." *Not much chance he'll sell it unless he decides to actually move out.* "Look, the reason I'm calling is, we've got an excess of felines over here, and I thought Luke might like a kitten. Cats make really easy pets. No trouble at all." She pictured Kristi's luxurious, designer-perfect house. *Except for climbing, shredding, and missing the litter box.*

"You know, I think . . . He just might be old enough. I love kittens myself. Maybe I'll bring him over, see how he does."

After finishing with Kristi, Cassidy drummed her fist on the desk. *Damn! Wish she hadn't mentioned Marina City.* Every time Cassidy thought about Zach's unemptied condo, it reminded her that he was forty years old and had never been able to stay in a relationship long-term. The one other time he'd lived with a woman he'd felt suffocated and had to leave.

The next ten calls were turn-downs. Dropping to the bottom of her list, she decided to try her mother. Helen was not a good candidate for joining the ranks of the cat-owned, but at least Cassidy could ask without feeling like an insurance salesman.

"Just the person I wanted to talk to," Helen said, her voice fretful.

"What's the matter, Mom?"

"Oh, it's this prenuptial thing. I've been talking and talking and just can't get through to Roland, so I was hoping you could drop by tomorrow and help us sort it out. You're always so good with people, dear. I'm sure you could get him to listen."

Bad idea. Don't get into the middle of this one. "Well, I wish there was something I could do but—"

"Of course you can. That's what therapy is, isn't it? You talk to people and tell them what to do."

"Not exactly." Cassidy drew a sourpuss face in the margin of a managed care form. "Besides, therapists never work with members of their own families."

"Just this once, Cassy, please? I really need your help."

Helen used the same tone Cassidy remembered from childhood: *Please, Cass, don't make trouble, listen to my problems, don't need anything.* She opened her mouth to deliver a gentle no, but an old familiar feeling got in the way: the sense that she was about to do a very bad thing and make her mother unhappy again.

She sighed. "Okay, I'll stop by around two." *Probably not a good time to ask about kittens.* "But don't get your hopes up."

At the end of an hour's phone time, Cassidy had turned up one more lead. Maggie, her best friend and fellow therapist, said that her sister might be in the market for a second cat and promised to check it out. Having done all the tele-marketing she could stand, Cassidy drove to Dominick's, a nearby supermarket, for a bag of peanut butter cups. She hated starting up her old habit again but figured that, if she had to do cold calling, a crutch was warranted.

Sitting inside her frigid Toyota, she unwrapped the first piece. *Just one bag. Just until the kitten crisis is over.*

⊠ ⊠ ⊠

"Okay, Mom, you go first. What is it you want Roland to do?" Cassidy shifted in her mother's overstuffed chair, try-ing to get comfortable on the lumpy cushion. Across the room, Helen and Roland were seated on the sofa, knees touching, bodies angled inward. Sheers covered the window, dampening the light and imparting a claustrophobic feel to the place.

"Well, dear," her mother's voice trembled slightly. "I'm sure you know what the problem is already."

Helen had recently revamped her appearance, and Cassidy was still adjusting to the change. At age five Cassidy's father had taken off, and for the next thirty-two years Helen had adamantly avoided men. Then, three months ago, a friend started taking her to a singles bar for seniors, and Helen had suddenly gone from gray perms to silvery shags, from beige pantsuits to ivory stirrups and tunics.

Tapping her fingers on the chair arm, Cassidy said, "I can't help unless you tell me exactly what you want." She spoke mildly, careful to avoid the note of irritation that sometimes crept into her voice when she talked to her mother.

Roland patted Helen's leg. "That's okay, sweetheart. You just go ahead and tell her."

Cassidy gritted her teeth at his condescending tone. *So what if Mom's got a big, fat diamond on her finger? Better a man who isn't there than a man who goes patriarchal on you.* Roland's voice was hearty enough, but his cheerless, taciturn face undercut the kindly- father image he tried to project.

Helen started wringing her hands. "He's trying to make me sign that awful contract of his. Here he's got this high-priced lawyer and I don't have anybody. If he really loved me, he wouldn't let other people make decisions about our marriage."

"Now Helen, I told you, this paper won't change anything."

"Do you know what it says?" her mother demanded. "If he goes first, I don't get anything. I'll be penniless."

Cassidy drew a long breath. "So, Mom, what would be a fair share of Roland's estate, considering he has five children?"

"At first I thought it should all come to me but I guess his kids ought to get something." Helen removed her clip-on pearl earring. "I just wish you'd tell us what you think, dear."

I think this is why therapists should never work with their own families.

4

New Client

Roland scooted closer to Helen, his hand sliding around her shoulders, his fingers rubbing her upper arm. "Come on, sweetheart, you know how much I want for us to get married. But as long as I can remember, I been telling my kids it'd all be theirs someday. I can't go back on that now."

"It's all June's fault," Helen wailed. "She's the oldest, you know. Her and those other girls, they've been working on him to cut me out of everything." She snapped the back of her earring. Click, click, click. "I could be eighty years old and out on the street for all they care."

No you wouldn't. You'd land on my doorstep. She gazed from the martyrish look on Helen's face to the scowl on Roland's. *What a marriage this is gonna be.*

"I don't think we're going to get anywhere just now."

Cassidy checked her watch. "Anyway, I've gotta run. My client's due in less than an hour."

In the courtyard outside her mother's building, Cassidy pulled the neck of her Kmart ski jacket up tight to keep out the wind. *Doesn't matter how cold, it's a relief to be outta there.*

The courtyard emptied onto Washington Boulevard, where Cassidy turned west and hiked toward her Toyota a couple of cars down. A tall black woman swathed in fur, looking as if she'd just stepped off a runway, walked arm and arm with a scrawny, bantam-rooster white man who resembled Willie Nelson without the scarf. Cassidy nodded as they passed.

She arrived home and went upstairs to check the answering machine. One message.

"My name's Jenny." The nasal voice sounded familiar. "When I called on Sunday you said you didn't know any Cliff, but I think maybe I should see you anyway." Her number followed.

Cassidy dialed and the same voice answered. "Office City Customer Service. How may I help you?"

"This is Cassidy McCabe. You left a message on my machine."

"Oh yes." She hesitated. "I decided I better go ahead and set up an appointment, if that's okay."

"When would be a good time?"

"Any chance you could squeeze me in tonight?" A jittery laugh. "I'm afraid I'll lose my nerve."

They set an appointment for eight.

Cassidy was always eager for new clients to build both

her bank account and her practice, although the pressure was off now that Zach was pitching in more than his share, more than she actually wanted him to. But with Jenny it was different. What she hoped to get from this new client was the key to Cliff.

✉   ✉   ✉

"I guess it wasn't the easiest thing, coming here tonight," Cassidy said to the heavyset woman seated on the black vinyl sofa in her office.

"That must sound silly." Jenny laughed briefly. "I mean, there's no reason to be afraid of a therapist, is there? Except that," her smile wavered, "I've never talked about any of this before." She had oatmeal-colored hair loosely curled around a broad, no-makeup face. Her baggy pants made her large body appear shapeless and lumpy. Everything about her was designed to avoid drawing attention except her glasses, owlish plastic frames brightly speckled in yellow, pink, and blue. Her watery gray eyes hid behind them.

Cassidy said, "Most people are nervous the first time they talk to a therapist, so let's begin with the basics." She wrote Jenny's address and phone number on the legal pad in her lap. "You can say whatever you like. You don't need to tell me anything until you're ready."

"Okay." Jenny huddled into herself, holding her body still except for her hands, which never stopped moving. Her fingers brushed the seat of the sofa, tracing the square edges of a piece of plastic tape that covered a hole where a button was missing. "Guess I should mention I'm an only child. My mother—she's dead now. When she died, that started the whole thing." She croaked out a small laugh. "Here I go, wandering all over the place as usual."

"Don't worry, just say whatever comes to mind."

Her colorless eyes sent Cassidy a grateful look. "Well, anyway, Mom was always sickly, and Dad, he got real frustrated with her being in bed all the time. So then, when I was sixteen, he got a divorce. Mom was so mad about it, she didn't want me even mentioning his name." Her voice, stiff and tense when she started, gradually grew more animated. "But that's not important. The important thing is, I was always the one who had to take care of her, and somehow I knew I'd never get away. I'm thirty-nine now, and I never dated more than one or two boys until . . ." The nervous laugh again.

God, what a miserable life. Groomed to revolve around her mother from the beginning. Studying Jenny's face, Cassidy saw a flush rise on her pale cheeks. *Embarrassed. Probably not used to anybody looking at her.* Cassidy shifted her gaze to the black window stretching across the room behind the sofa. The brass fixture cast a strong light, but opaque windows, paneled walls, and dark corners made the room less than cheerful at night.

Jenny straightened her shoulders. "First time I ever saw Cliff was at my mother's wake. She died, let's see, it's been two and a half years now. Cancer, you know. Suffered something awful. Actually, it was a relief to see her go, even though I was really scared of being alone for the first time, what with the house and all." She paused to stare at the floor.

Cassidy noticed a broken stem on the coleus that resided on the wicker table between her chair and the sofa. The waiting room radio played faintly in the background. "Slip, slidin' away . . ."

Jenny took a deep breath. "He came up to me at the wake, said his name was Cliff Connors, and that he'd known my mother from church. She was a devout Catholic, you see."

Cassidy heard the back door creak. Zach. A small sense of warmth spread across her chest.

Jenny went on. "Well, anyway, I didn't think anything about it that first time. But then I bumped into him again at the post office and he invited me for coffee. He talked about this divorce he was going through. Said it was pretty messy, his wife was kind of crazy-weird. So anyway, he said he wanted to see me again. Just to talk, you understand. And that he'd call me but I couldn't call him because of his wife. So then we started meeting for coffee, and after that it was dinner and a movie."

Tears welled up. Removing her glasses, she pressed her thumb and index finger against her eyes. Cassidy reached for the tissue box half covered by the unpruned coleus and inched it closer to the sofa. Jenny shoved her glasses back on. "This seems really stupid now, but at the time I thought . . . well, I thought Cliff was my reward for being a good daughter all those years." Plucking a tissue, she laughed bitterly.

"Did he hurt you?" Cassidy asked.

"I let him . . . " Jenny dabbed at her nose. "He talked me into having sex. At first it seemed like a dream come true. Like we were living out all my fantasies." Dropping her head, she ran a hand through her curls. "Then it got bad." Her voice flattened.

A prickle of dread. "How was it bad?"

"I don't want . . . I can't talk about it. Not yet. All I can say is, on the last night he was pretty rough. He told me . . . he said he was HIV positive. And he . . . injected me with blood. To make sure I got it too." Two tears spilled over and trickled in wet lines down her cheeks.

"Omigod!" Cassidy's outspread hand pressed against the base of her throat. A sense of horror came over her, then her feelings clicked off, disconnected by the internal circuit breaker that kept her from getting sucked too deeply into other people's experiences. But she knew Jenny needed her to stay emotionally engaged. She drew in a lungful of air and forced herself to step inside Jenny's skin. "What a terrible thing. I don't know how you got through it."

Behind the glasses Jenny's moist eyes blinked. Relief flooded her face. Grabbing another tissue, she wiped the damp streaks. "You must think I'm really stupid, letting somebody I just met, who's not even divorced yet, talk me into . . . well, you know."

"I think you were just unprepared to protect yourself against a man like Cliff. I mean, who would know how to deal with somebody that vicious?"

Jenny smiled weakly. "I wasn't even sure I'd be able to tell you."

"This Cliff person sounds really disturbed. When you phoned Sunday, you mentioned a letter. Did he say in the letter to call me?"

Jenny nodded. "He said you'd helped him with it."

"I can't think of a single person by that name and I haven't

worked with anyone who's tested positive. Could you tell
more me about the letter?"

Jenny slumped back on the garage-sale sofa. "It came a
couple of weeks ago. At first I was really upset and confused
and didn't want anything to do with it. But I couldn't stop
thinking that maybe you could help me make sense out of all
this. Especially if you knew Cliff and could tell me why he
did it."

"I'm afraid I never heard of the man before your call on
Sunday, although I suppose it's possible he saw me under
some other name. Do you have a picture?"

"He never let me take any."

"Maybe if you described him I could tell whether I know
him or not."

Jenny scrunched her forehead. "He was quite a bit taller
than me, must've been around six feet. Seems like he was
fairly solid, you know, thick in the chest and shoulders. I'm
sorry, I'm not very good at this. He said he was forty, but I
think he probably lied a lot so I don't know if that was the
truth."

"Did he look forty?"

"It was hard to tell. The main thing was, he was completely bald, but I thought he was really handsome that way.
He loved movies and science fiction, especially Star Trek.
Anyway, he said he liked being bald because it made him
look like Jean Luc. He said Jean Luc was actually shorter
than he is but on TV it's hard to tell."

"Jean Luc? You mean the captain in the Star Trek series?
Did he look like Jean Luc?"

"You know, the funny thing is, it's hard to remember. He

talked about it so much I started to see him that way, and now I'm not sure if he really looked like Jean Luc or I just wanted to believe it."

Shaking her head, Cassidy frowned slightly. "If only I had some idea . . ." *This woman needs help. You can worry about Cliff later.* "But that's not what you're here for. What about the HIV? Do you know for sure you've contracted it?"

Jenny mumbled. "I'm sure."

"You've been tested?"

She shook her head. "I just know. Even though nothing's happened yet, it's there inside me, growing like crazy, hiding out and waiting to take over."

Cassidy leaned forward. "It's really important to see a doctor. Even though you feel certain you've got it, it's possible you don't. And if you do have it, you should find out about medication. From what I hear, AIDS may not be necessarily fatal anymore."

"I know. I read everything I can get my hands on." Staring at her ceaselessly moving fingers, she was silent for several moments. "This'll probably sound crazy, but living a longer life doesn't seem worth having to see doctors and take pills all the time. Even before Cliff, I used to lay in bed at night wishing I could go to sleep and never wake up." She laughed her jittery laugh. "Those few months with Cliff—that was the only time I ever had anything that made me happy. I know the sickness'll be awful, but at some point it'll all be over and I can have some peace." She looked up, her moist eyes begging Cassidy to understand.

Cassidy's throat thickened. Swallowing, she said, "So you're saying your life is so empty you want it to end—even though it means having AIDS." *If I can get her to feel better about herself, maybe she'll change her mind. Don't wanna get pushy in the first session.*

Jenny nodded, then gazed into her lap again.

"Okay, I can accept that for now. But I still think at some point you ought to consult a doctor."

✆ ✆ ✆

When Jenny was gone, Cassidy sat in her darkened office, gazed through the east window, and thought about what she'd heard. From her director's chair she could see a filigree of tree branches and, at the far end of her yard, the peaked roof of her garage.

A man who claims to be your client is infecting women and referring them to you. What are you going to do about it? Her feelings churned.

My duty as a therapist is to maintain confidentiality and provide the best therapy I can for Jenny. My duty as a human being is to prevent Cliff from racking up any more victims. So, what are the options?

You could forget Cliff and just work with Jenny.

Except I couldn't live with myself, since I'm the only one who knows what he's up to. Who has any chance of stopping him.

You could launch your own investigation and keep Zach out of it.

I need someone to bounce ideas off of, someone more experienced than I am. On two previous occasions, Zach had talked her into working with him to solve cases. The idea of tackling a psychopath all by herself was overwhelming. *This is over my head. My chances of nailing Cliff go way up if I bring Zach into it.*

A blast of loud rap, probably from a car parked beside her office, jolted her briefly, then stopped. She heard two combative voices moving off toward Austin Boulevard.

Okay, how about you include Zach but give him minimal information and no names? Turning it over in her mind, she tried to imagine how it would go.

Doesn't feel right. She bit the inner lining of her lip. *If I'm constantly screening, we won't be able to do the free-wheeling kind of brainstorming that needs to be done.*

So how bad would it be to lay it all out, tell him everything that might pertain to the case? She cringed at how bad some of her colleagues would consider it. *But would it hurt Jenny or anyone else if one other person has the same information I do?* She stared at the garage roof, the exact replica of a small pyramid. The one other time she'd confided in Zach he'd misused the information, but she knew he felt guilty and wouldn't do it again. As a reporter he often had to maintain confidentiality, just as she did. He would not slip up.

Okay, that's it then. I'll tell him. She sighed and felt calmer. It was not a good decision but the best she could do, and if it blew up on her, she'd take the consequences. *Why is it so much of life is trying to figure out the lesser of the evils?*

Climbing the stairs, she was surprised not to hear the television. She found Zach sitting on the nursery floor, knees bent, back against the wall. Three kittens climbed on his body; a can of cat treats lay next to his hand.

She leaned against the doorjamb. "Just when I think I have

all your moves down pat, you do something different. You and Starshine always keep me guessing."

"Took some pictures." He jerked his head toward a camera on an old bureau in the corner. Before its current incarnation as nursery-cum-jailhouse, the space had served as a junk room, accumulating the bureau, a four-layer pile of boxes, and other assorted castoffs.

As Calvin climbed out of Zach's lap, Sylvia jumped down from his shoulder to attack her brother. Zach said, "Now that you're serious about finding homes for these guys, we've gotta get to it and finish up their baby books."

Baby books? He's as big a sap as I am.

She dropped down beside him, knowing she'd be sorry later for exposing her violet wool skirt to ruinous cat claws. But at the moment she was too distracted to care. Folding her arms across her knees, she rested her chin on them.

Zach rubbed her scalp. "Tough session?"

"I discovered what Cliff's doing and it's worse than I ever imagined." She shivered slightly. "I have to figure out who he is and I need your help to do it."

"That's what the police are for. Your job's to do therapy."

"The police don't know he exists."

"Take your client by the hand, drive her to the station, and sit with her while she lays it all out."

She stared at Zach in amazement. "In the past, you've always come up with some excuse to avoid the police."

"In the past, I was chasing a story." She saw a glimmer of regret in his eyes. "Since Cliff's off limits in terms of the paper, there's no reason not to give this over to the police. They've obviously got more resources than we do."

"The reason not to take this to the cops is that my client won't do it. She absolutely refuses to disclose to anyone other than me."

Rolling on top of Calvin, Sylvia bit his throat. Zach said, "You can work with her, get her to change her mind."

Cassidy considered what a relief it would be to hand Cliff over to the professionals, then sighed, realizing she couldn't do it. "She's too fragile. I can't pressure her to do anything that might be harmful."

"Well, then, there's nothing more to be done. I can't write a story, she won't go to the police. And you," he gave her a straight look, "would have to be crazy yourself to go after a warped, potentially dangerous psycho like Cliff."

Where's that old reporter's drive to chase down bad guys? He can't exploit somebody for a story? He doesn't care?

Now stop, insisted the part that was hooked on him. *How cynical could anybody be who makes baby books for kittens?*

She furrowed her brow in irritation. "This is just a ruse, right? You're really itching to go after Cliff but since it's my idea this time, you're playing hard to get."

Instead of pursuing the topic, Zach took a treat from the Pounce can and held it out to Hobbes. The kitten ignored Zach's offering and scuttled across the room to climb on a dumbbell laying under the window. Hoisting the front half of his body over the bar, he dangled all four feet off the ground. Sylvia popped out from behind a guitar case standing in the corner and attacked his tail. The dumbbell and guitar had been left behind by her ex-husband Kevin, whose attention span was not much greater than the kittens.

"What's going on?" Cassidy demanded. "Those other two times you insisted we had to investigate. Dragged me in kicking and screaming."

A glint of amusement came into his eyes. "I decided not to do that anymore."

"What?"

His face grew serious. "After those Halloween shootings, I realized I had no business getting you into dangerous situations. From now on, I'll handle investigations, you stick to therapy."

Cassidy picked Calvin off her skirt and stuck him on Zach's chest. "That seems a little strange, considering who rescued whom."

"Yeah, but it got pretty bloody at the end, and I don't think you're emotionally finished with all of it yet."

He knows when I'm done? She spoke through clenched teeth. "I'm fine." *If you're really fine, why so pissed he brought it up?* "What're you doing, trying to be the therapist again?"

"Living with you's ruining me." Grinning, Zach snatched the orange kitten just before he started climbing her skirt. "I'm getting sensitized. Before you know it, I'll be too soft to ask obnoxious questions and prey on the innocent. The paper'll can my ass. I'll have to sponge off you. I'll end up sinking into hopeless dependency."

5

Personal Ad

Cassidy pushed unruly cinnamon hair back from her cheek. "Stop trying to distract me. Look, we have to track down Cliff. He's doing something really vicious, and I'm involved because of the letters. Plus he spied on me to get your unlisted number."

Zach said in his laconic voice, "First you tell me you're gonna take on a psychopath, then you say I've gotta go against my basic philosophy and do something purely altruistic."

She frowned. "You mean, if there's nothing in it for you, it doesn't matter who gets hurt?"

He laid his arm across her shoulders. "Okay, we'll do it. But I meant what I said. I don't want you getting into anymore situations where you have to play pistol packin' mama."

'Specially if you can't get your byline on the front page.

Oh come off it. What's wrong with his wanting to protect you from your own insane urge to play Rambo?

"So, you gonna fill me in on what your client said?"

Picturing herself stepping over a bright red line emblazoned with the words PROFESSIONAL ETHICS, she felt her stomach wrench. "Okay, here goes." She told him Jenny's story.

He watched her closely. "You feeling guilty about telling me?"

"Yeah, but I don't see any better way."

"Situational ethics are okay by me." He shrugged. "Well, let's see what we can come up with." Gazing thoughtfully into space, he said, "What does it mean that he mailed out the letters a couple of weeks ago? It could be somebody you just met or it could be somebody from the past. Maybe you've known him a long time but he just got this new idea and now he's adding another sadistic turn of the screw."

"No strange men've entered my life recently so he must go back a ways." She caught her bottom lip. "We don't even know for sure he's got the virus. It's possible the guy's delusional and just thinks he came up positive."

As Starshine trotted into the room, her children crowded around her. She touched noses with the orange kitten, then rolled him on his back, scrubbing the base of his tail while he chewed her ear. Smacking him soundly, she flopped down to nurse.

"I can't think of anyone who fits the description." Cassidy shook her head. "Especially the bald part."

"Could've shaved his head to disguise himself."

"I suppose that's a possibility. He might've used a Jean Luc approach with Dale and Jenny, then grown out his hair before coming in as a client. If that's his game, he's succeeded in leaving me with a total blank as to which of the thirty or so male clients I've seen thus far might be Cliff. There's certainly nothing distinctive about the rest of the description." She spent several seconds trying to visualize the men she'd seen in therapy in the past four years. "There're probably five or six who'd fit Jenny's description in terms of age, height and build."

"And to make matters worse, we can't even be sure he ever was a client." Zach rubbed the back of his neck. "Considering you've never treated anybody who admitted to testing positive, he could've just made the client part up. In fact, given that your face appeared all over TV last Halloween, he might be a Hinckley type who's picked you to play Jodie Foster."

"I refuse to expand the search to people I don't know. Dealing with all the approximately six foot males I've ever met is bad enough."

"What I'd really like to know is how many women he's done this to. What percent do you think would follow up on a letter like that?"

Starshine struggled to her feet, knocking the kittens off balance, then jumped to the top of the stack of boxes. Cassidy replied, "My guess is they'd all be torn between curiosity, anger, and shame. The majority probably wouldn't do anything. They'd make the same assumption Dale did, that Cliff and I are in cahoots. But I expect they'd all have some ambivalence—like Starshine with her kittens."

"If I were to publish Jenny's story and ask the other women to call in anonymously, there's a good chance we'd hear from most of 'em. We could get a more precise description, lay out a timetable. I wouldn't have to use her name, you know."

She pulled away. "Don't even think of it. Remember the complaint that got filed against me because of that other story you wrote? The hearing's still months away and God only knows what the penalty will be."

His face reflected something akin to guilt. She knew he was sorry, and in all fairness, it was more her fault than his.

The sound of crying kittens distracted her. The children had gathered at the bottom of the pile of boxes to make pathetic noises and claw at the cardboard. They seemed to be on a fifteen-minute feeding schedule.

Mowr! Starshine glared at Cassidy.

"Maybe she's mad 'cause I haven't gotten rid of them yet." Mad, just as Dale had been. Dale was so mad she'd burst in to yell at Cassidy and demand an explanation. The other women might want to yell at her too but perhaps were too timid to push their way into her house. If they could talk anonymously, however, they might be happy to do it.

"How about an ad?" Cassidy asked. "We could take out a classified ad directed to all the women Cliff's had contact with."

"Let's see . . ." Zach cocked his head. "Desperately seeking someone. Any someone who's been seduced by a walking persecution complex named Cliff is instructed to call Cassidy McCabe. You can wail on her all you want, free of charge."

"No, seriously." She jabbed him with her elbow. "We could put his name up front in bold type. 'Cliff Connors: Cassidy McCabe wishes to talk to anyone who has information about this man. All calls anonymous.' He's referring clients, I need to know why."

"A front page story'd get more coverage."

She lowered her brow. "No stories."

He shrugged. "Okay, we'll go with the ad. I'll submit it tomorrow to both dailies and the *Free Chicago*, which means it'll show up Sunday in the major papers, Saturday and Wednesday in the giveaway. We probably oughtta run it a month."

"Here's hoping they're all as pissed as Dale and can't resist an opportunity to tell me about it."

Zach scratched his jaw. "Think I'll hook up a recorder to the phone—"

"No you don't. I'm willing to tell you everything relevant to the case, which—as long as you keep your journalistic promiscuity in check—shouldn't be a problem. But I won't go one inch further."

⊠   ⊠   ⊠

On Friday evening Cassidy dressed for her mother's engagement party, then headed west on the Eisenhower Expressway toward Roland Mertz's family home out in the farmland beyond the suburbs.

Zach had not appeared before she left. *No surprise. He*

knows I'll be out. Bet he's happy for an excuse to go boozing. Must be as many alcoholic reporters as alcoholic cops.

You trying to change him, like he said?

Just a few improvements.

Exiting the expressway, Cassidy drove through Bloomingdale and out into the sparse countryside beyond. Although she'd never visited Mertz Manor before, her mother had talked about it so much she felt she knew its entire history. Roland's father had built it as a simple farmhouse, and thus it had remained until after Roland's wife left. At that point he'd brought in an interior designer and had everything redone. Helen, hugely impressed by the idea of a designer, claimed the house was now a veritable showcase, which probably meant it resembled a picture out of *Family Circle* magazine.

Following her mother's instructions, Cassidy turned right onto Chippewa Road. *Eight miles north, five miles west, and I'm there.* Trees hugged the two-lane road, branches merging overhead to form a narrow tunnel. With thick woods on both sides and a cloud cover on the sky, there was no light at all inside her encapsulated aisle, not even the ghostly reflection from ground snow.

She'd known Roland lived in the hinterlands but wasn't expecting anything as empty as this. It was almost as remote as the southwestern forest preserve where she'd followed a lone pair of taillights last Halloween. The forest preserve where the shootings occurred.

Her stomach felt twitchy. As if there were worms in it. *That's disgusting. Where'd that come from?* She clenched her teeth and tried to bend her mind toward something else.

Zach, for instance. *Should be here with me. If he won't do anything he doesn't want, I'd be better off without him.*

What? You always have to get your own way? You put on this big show of independence, why wouldn't he think you could go to a party by yourself?

I can. Just don't want to is all.

Her headlights were a grainy runner of light. Other than that, darkness. Dark as the inside of a stomach. Dark as Halloween. That wormy, twitchy feeling up and down her spine.

Shouldn't have to do this. Shouldn't be out here in the forest preserve all alone.

This isn't the forest preserve. That was Halloween, when you followed the Caddy deep into the woods, aimed the gun, pulled the trigger. And then all that blood.

Suddenly, half a mile ahead, two points of light appeared out of nowhere. She blinked, uncramped one hand from the wheel, rubbed her eyes. *What's that? The car I'm following? The Caddy?*

Her mouth went dry, her lungs closed. The taillights faded. A gunshot sounded in the back of her brain.

She gasped, trying to fill her lungs. Her throat constricted. Her heart ticked faster, too fast, a bomb ready to explode.

Turnoff up ahead. *Get off this road. This road's going backward, taking you back in time where you don't want to be.* She tapped the brake, cut the wheel. Her forehead was damp, her eyes gritty. Maybe she should stop, rest a little. Maybe she should go home.

Have to get to the party. You don't show, Mom'll never

*forgive you. Can't go around being afraid of the dark, afraid
of memories.*

She took a deep breath. Fewer trees now. Open fields,
snow covered ground. Releasing one fist from the wheel, she
wiped her sweaty forehead.

Good God, what's happening to me?

*You know what this is. You've heard clients talk about it
often enough.*

Oh shit. I'm having an anxiety attack.

✆ ✆ ✆

Driving slowly, feeling disoriented and staticky, she finally saw a wooden sign that said MERTZ MANOR, and
beneath that, ROBERT * ROLAND * RONALD. Roland was the
fiancé. Robert was Roland's father, founder of the family
business that had brought in the money Helen and the kids
were now squabbling over. Ronald was Roland's son, the
male child who had taken five tries to conceive. Roland
admitted to having exerted extreme pressure on his wife to
keep popping out babies until she finally got it right: a son
to maintain the Mertz bloodline and business.

Cassidy turned into the drive, a two-lane road leading to
a tall house aglow with lighted windows. *Still shaking.
When's it gonna stop?* As she stepped out of the car, her
vision tilted and she lurched forward. *Anxiety attack—a lot
worse having than hearing about.*

She gulped cold air to clear her head but it was still
buzzing as she climbed the porch steps. Peering through the
front window, she saw a room crammed with people.

*Feel so weird. How can I face that mob? I try talking, I'll
sound like an idiot.*

Just slip in quietly, have a glass of wine, wait till you get normal.

Inside, she glanced around a wide entry hall, living room to the right, dining room to the left, the hall leading to open french doors at the rear of the house. Maids in black dresses and white aprons moved through the crowd. One took her coat. Another held out a tray of plastic glasses. Clutching one, she sagged against a wall and chugged what tasted like bargain basement chablis. *All that money, he buys cheap wine.*

The alcohol went to work, warming her stomach, loosening the muscles in her neck. As black-and-white flitted past again, she deftly exchanged her empty glass for a full one.

Gotta pull yourself together.

Right. Another bottle of wine, I'll be fine.

Smoke stung her eyes. Dishes clattered, voices yelled. Squinting through the haze, she searched for Helen and Gran as she checked out her mother's version of showcase. Heavy fabric draped the high ceiling and tall windows, creating an air of sophistication. But the impression shifted jarringly as her eyes dropped to ground level where glimpses of boxy plaid sofas and chairs were visible in the gaps between bodies. *Should've skipped the designer, bought the whole works from Ward's.* A giggle bubbled up in her throat. *Hysteria . . . does that go with anxiety attacks?*

Eventually she spotted her mother and grandmother beside Roland and his cronies at the far end of the room. *Expects me to go stand next to her, be the dutiful daughter, let her show off what a good mother she is. And not a word about living with a renegade reporter who won't show his face at family functions.*

Why can't you ever just be nice? Give her what she wants?

She gritted her teeth. The thought of maneuvering through packed bodies and shouting out a conversation with Roland's friends made the static in her head rev higher. *Have more wine, mellow down first.*

A maid moved toward the dining room on the other side of the hall. Following after her, Cassidy snagged a full glass and watched people milling around a table laden with food.

Need something to eat.

You kidding? Mouth's so dry, stomach's so jittery, you'd never get anything down.

Cassidy sipped wine, then realized the alcohol was not helping the fuzziness in her head. *Shouldn't drink unless I eat. Can't eat unless the anxiety goes down.*

All I want is to go home. But how'll I ever be able to drive back through that long, dark tunnel without totally losing it?

6

Party

Cold water, Cassidy thought as she set off down the hall in search of a bathroom. Inside, she gazed at a lace-edged towel and washcloth. *Should have a DON'T TOUCH sign like in museums. What are people supposed to use, toilet paper?* Soaking the washcloth, she buried her face in it. *There goes the makeup.* She glanced in the mirror, then looked quickly away, not liking what she saw.

Back in the hall, she followed the sound of a pert female voice through open french doors and into a paneled den. Three people sat on yellow plaid furniture in a rectangular arrangement. A large blonde woman bathed in rosy half-light from the overhead fixture waved a beckoning hand.

The woman presided in an armchair, the short side of the

rectangle, with two men on sofas at either hand. Each held a plate in his lap. Cassidy sank onto the nearest sofa.

The woman, an attractive, wide-bodied figure who looked a few years older than Cassidy's thirty-seven, gave her a bright, welcoming smile. "I'm Louise Mertz, last in line of the girls. And this handsome guy over here," she gestured toward the sandy-haired man on the opposite sofa, "he's my kid brother Ron. But don't get your hopes up—this is the only happily married man I know. Course his wife *is* over two thousand miles away, and I certainly don't stay up nights checking to see what time he comes in."

She pointed to the dark-haired man on Cassidy's sofa, "This other good-looking guy is Patrick Larkin. He's one of my best friends," she smirked slightly, "and he's not available either."

"Hey, let the lady get a word in." Ron, the brother, leaned forward. His good-natured voice held a note of amusement. "You'll have to excuse our Louise. She's a competitive talker."

Cassidy glanced from one to the other, trying to get the two men straight. *Ron, male heir, seems like the sort who'd wear pocket protectors to work. Patrick, best friend, sharp looking, doesn't let anybody overshadow him—not even Louise.*

Patrick, who had curly hair and a neatly trimmed beard, gave her an encouraging smile. They all looked at her expectantly. *S'posed to do something.* If only her head weren't so blurry. *Oh yeah.* "Cassidy McCabe. Helen's daughter."

Patrick nodded. "Oh sure. We've heard all about you."

Ron added, "All good."

Louise's round, pretty face gleamed with delight. "I'm so glad to meet you."

Cassidy said, "Uh, me too. I mean, I've been wanting to meet you too." Her mouth was still dry so she sipped more wine. *Roland's kids? Supposed to be all pissed off 'bout the marriage? Wouldn't know it by the way these two are acting.*

Patrick said, "The Mertz family grapevine's been all atwitter since Roland's big announcement. Louise insists on passing along every little tidbit."

"I'm relentless." Kissing her fingertips, Louise flicked them in Patrick's direction.

Ron said, "Relentless, as in nosy." He had light brown, shaggy-neckline hair and deepset eyes that receded into near invisibility behind his rimless glasses. Although Cassidy knew he had only two years on her, his harried expression made him seem older. He caught her looking at him and broke into a cozy smile. "Dad says you've solved a couple of mysteries and Lou's dying to pump you about it."

Oh shit. Not up to talking "Um, look, it's really not very interesting." She sipped wine and searched for an alternative topic. "Ron, I understand you're here from, uh . . . Seattle, and you're here to help your father with the business. How long you planning to stay?"

His worry lines deepened into a frown. "Hard to say. I've been cluttering up Lou's condo three weeks already, and the wife's getting sick of it. But Dad's reluctant—"

"Reluctant?" Louise jerked upright. "Roland's putting on the screws full force to coerce little bro here into becoming the next pres of Mertz Enterprises. Dad's always been hell bent that the kid has to take over when his majesty steps down."

"Lou!" Ron raised his hands to ward her off. "We just met this poor woman. You don't need to dump on her like this."

"You know better than to try and stop me." Louise shook her finger in his face. "If Cassidy's gonna be part of the family, she needs to hear the lowdown."

"Lou's right about Dad." Sighing, Ron intoned, "The Mertz family business must go to the male heir." Then, in his own voice, "An electric motor warehouse operation. How could I resist?"

Patrick stroked his bearded chin. "Don't let Roland push you around. Just do whatever you like."

"Easy for you to say," Ron shot back.

"Now boys, don't fight." Louise plucked a brownie from Ron's plate, popped it into her mouth, and blissed out. She was one of those outsized women who made the most of her buxom appearance by going for larger-than-life elegance. In contrast, her brother had a regular-workout build, but the good looks nature had bestowed were undermined by the limp dress shirt, scuffed shoes, and tight face of someone with too much on his mind.

"What do you think of the decor?" Louise dabbed a napkin to her perfectly outlined, carmine mouth.

"Decor?" Cassidy swallowed wine and tried to concentrate.

Patrick chuckled. "Now Lou, that's not nice."

Louise replied, "He's right, it's not fair to put you on the spot like that." She pressed the fingertips of both hands together, displaying red nails that exactly matched her lipstick. "You see, Patrick's an interior designer, so when Dad decided he wanted to take the unprecedented step of remodeling the old homestead, I recommended my friend here."

"She threw me to the wolves." Patrick's voice deepened in mock disapproval.

"The wolfman," Ron added.

"Anyway," Louise continued, "halfway through the job, our father found out what the bill was going to be and tried to sue."

Ron, mimicking Roland's rough baritone, said, "I don't need any Goddamn faggot telling me what furniture to buy."

Louise laughed boisterously. "Right, Dad. You sure do know your furniture."

Ron shook his head. "The only reason he redecorated in the first place was to get back at Mom. She always wanted to fix the place up, but he wouldn't spend the money. So after she left he did it out of vindictiveness."

This is the man my mother's marrying?

Patrick said to Louise, "I thought Roland was going to have apoplexy when you walked in on my arm tonight." He turned to Cassidy. "Lou made me come as her escort so she could stick it to the old man."

An impish look came over her face. "Tomorrow he'll call to yell at me for being a fag hag."

Gesturing around the room, Patrick said, "Needless to say, I'm not eager to have my name associated with the final product here. Now if you'd like to see what my design concepts really look like, you can come to my house and I'll give you the grand tour. We're practically neighbors, you know."

Ron explained, "He's got one of those Oak Park mansions. Rattles around in it all by himself."

Hearing footsteps, Cassidy turned to see a tall man coming through the doorway behind her. Sinewy and lean, with wavy blonde hair, a deep tan, and diamond studded earlobes, he reached out to touch her shoulder. "There you are, Cassie." His voice was light and musical. "I've finally tracked you down."

"Um, do I know . . . ?" She blinked, trying to get his face into focus. "It can't be!"

"Yes it is."

"Not Mark. Marky, is that really you? What are you doing here?"

He laughed, a bright, airy trill. "What kind of greeting is that for your favorite long-lost cousin?" He perched on the arm of her sofa, angling his body to face the three at the opposite end. "I'm Mark Sanders. Cassie and I grew up together but we haven't seen each other in what? Twenty years? So this is our big cousinly reunion."

Cousin Marky. Finally get to see him again.

That's great. Unless, of course, you have to speak. In which case you'll be lucky to get out three coherent words.

Patrick stood and made introductions.

Ron cocked his head at Cassidy. "You mean, you really didn't know he was going to be here? This is all a surprise?"

Mark replied, "Nobody did except our mutual grandmother. I'm out in L.A. now, and I had this business trip that happened to coincide. So I decided—what the hey—I'll show up unannounced and see if my used-to-be best cousin recognizes me after all these years."

"What a dirty trick." Louise waved a hand sharply downward. "Anybody snuck up on me like that, I'd demand retribution." She looked at Mark. "You should be penalized by having to wait till we're done before you get your turn at Cassidy."

"Sorry, but I have every intention of whisking her away." Bouncing to his feet, he tugged at her arm. "We've got some serious catching up to do."

That mean I have to stand up?

Cassidy started to rise, realized she had a half full glass in her hand, and tipped it up to empty it. Mark tucked her arm through his and moved her toward the door.

This is good. He's holding me up. Now if he does all the talking and I hang onto him, maybe nobody'll notice.

As they headed down the hall, Mark said, "Let's go sit on the stairs like we used to when Gran had parties. Remember how she'd let us get away with things when our mothers weren't around?"

"Uh huh."

Mark steered her around the newel post and onto the staircase. "You haven't even asked how I happened to have a trip planned to Chicago. I didn't fly halfway around the country just for Auntie Helen's engagement party, you know. Although I do have something I really need to talk to you about, but we'll deal with that later."

"You do?"

"Now pay attention. This is important." They sat together on a step near the top. "I finally got my big promotion! I've been at this fashion house for years, and at long last I've been moved into a slot where I get to fly around purchasing fabrics. Just imagine, this month I shop Chicago, next month Paris." He stopped talking and peered down into her face. "Hey, what's going on? Are you okay?"

"I'm fine," she said without conviction.

He looked doubtful.

"Well, I'm not fine." *God, this is so embarrassing.* "I had an anxiety attack coming out here, then I drank too much wine trying to get over it, and now there's no way I can drive back. The last thing I want is for Mom to find out. She'd never let me live it down. Only, I don't know how I'm going to get home."

He patted her arm. "Don't worry, this's a gig we've all been through a time or two. You just let me handle it." Two beats of silence. "Here's what we'll do. I'll take you home and Gran can drive your car."

"I can't ask Gran to—"

"She'll love it. Nothing she likes better than pulling off some stunt behind Helen's back."

⊠ ⊠ ⊠

As Cassidy gradually came awake, the white-hot pain in her forehead sharpened. *Keep your eyes shut, don't move, wait till it goes away.*

A damp nose bumped her cheek. The nose pulled back, then a small, furry body twisted itself in her hair. She pictured the calico kitten snarled in her red-brown tangles.

How had she gotten home? *Oh yeah. Mark drove. Nattering on about needing to talk, let's do lunch. Opened the garage for Gran to park the Toyota, walked me to my door.*

If the Toyota were here, she wouldn't have to tell anybody. After all the ragging she'd done about Zach's drinking, it would not be fun to explain why she'd been driven home.

She heard his footsteps on the stairs. *Keep your eyes shut, don't move, wait till he goes away.*

"Hey, party girl. Don't you have an eleven o'clock?" Zach's voice, disgustingly cheerful. Her head pounded. A coffee mug thumped down on the nightstand. Blinds rustled. The phone shrilled.

"Zach Moran here." Brief silence. "Somebody named Mark. Should I get his number?"

"No, I'll talk." Wobbling to her desk, she dropped into her chair. "Hello?"

"Morning, sunshine. How you doing?"

Why did everyone have to be so damned cheery?

"I'm fine. Haven't had my morning coffee yet so I'm a little groggy."

"Well, sweetie, I just called to set up lunch. You remember—something we have to talk about?" A pause which she did not fill. "Tsk, tsk—you really did have a bit too much of the grape, didn't you? But that's okay, I'll tell you all about it when we meet Monday at noon. There's a decent restaurant in my hotel, the Mexicali Rose. That's the Belvedere on Ohio. You got that?"

Pushing back her rat's nest hair, she reached for a pen. "Uh, would you run that by me again?"

⊠ ⊠ ⊠

Cassidy was getting dressed when the phone rang a second time. Her mother's voice said, "I'm so sorry I didn't get to see you last night. But Gran explained you were afraid you'd spoil my evening if you told me you were sick."

That's me, ever thoughtful. "Well, I didn't want to worry you." She tapped her forefinger against the wine bottle that sat on her desk to collect loose change.

"But I was disappointed I still didn't get to meet that Lawrence boy you've been dating. I just can't get over the fact that you're involved with Mildred Lawrence's son—the girl who didn't know I existed when we were in high school. Him and you've been seeing each other all this time," her voice turned snide, "and isn't it strange how we've never been able to get together."

Dating, she says. How delicate. "It's 'Moran,' Mom. He's got his father's last name. And the reason he didn't come is, he didn't think a party was the best place for a first meeting."

A long silence. "I don't exactly get the idea he wants to meet me."

⊠ ⊠ ⊠

Her doorbell rang and Cassidy went downstairs to greet her client. Mira eased onto the taped-up vinyl sofa, a cold glare from the window backlighting her piquant face and close-cropped jet hair. A twenty-eight-year-old MBA married to an attorney ten years her senior, she had started therapy six months ago because her husband's sexual addiction had pushed her into serious depression.

Cassidy took her place in the director's chair on the opposite side of the wicker table. She had popped two aspirin and was beginning to feel normal. "Well, how's it going?"

"It's been a long week." Mira raised a manicured hand to cover a yawn. Her lean, boyish figure was sheathed in a black jacket and short skirted yellow dress. A black beaded necklace descended from her neck.

"Oh, you know something?" Mira's usually spirited voice was mumbly from exhaustion. "Jake's started growing a mustache and beard. I've told him over and over how I feel about facial hair, but apparently my opinion doesn't count."

Not considering Jake's beard a fruitful line of inquiry, Cassidy asked, "Why so tired?"

She gave a delicate shrug. "I've started working with a personal trainer and the only time we could fit it in was five a.m."

Cassidy shook her head. *The woman fits into a size four with room to spare and she sees herself an ounce away from obesity.* "Every time you start some killer diet or exercise routine, it only lasts a few weeks, then you backlash. You know we've talked before about going for moderation instead of these huge pendulum swings."

Mira's defiant eyes met hers briefly, then slid away.

No point pushing. Just makes her defensive. "So," Cassidy said, her voice even, "what do you hope to accomplish with all this early morning torture?" *Besides sleep-depriving yourself into zombiedom.*

Mira tugged the jet beads out to the side. "I know you're right about the exercise and dieting. But sometimes when Jake goes out at night I catch myself sneaking an entire half gallon of ice cream out of the freezer. And then it comes back to me, what I looked like as a teenager." She shuddered. "If I ever put on weight like that again, I'd shoot myself."

Cassidy sipped tea from her purple mug. "You hoping that firmer thighs or buns of steel'll keep Jake from wandering?"

"I know it's stupid." She lowered her dark, wavy head. "You've told me a hundred times that the sexual acting out is Jake's problem and there's nothing I can do to change it. But I can't get over the feeling that if I just looked better, if I could think of the right thing to say, he'd come to his senses."

"So the reason Jake has a sexual addiction is because you haven't said the right thing yet?" Cassidy crossed her legs, her violet pump nudging the wicker table.

"I may not know the right words, but I'm absolutely great at spitting out the wrong ones." She coiled the necklace around her fingers.

"I suppose Jake took offense at something you said and used that as an excuse to go out on the prowl."

"Not exactly. Variation on a theme." Mira's finely drawn lips pulled back in a grimace. "All last week was pretty bad. He was in that mood when he doesn't talk—you know, sullen and angry. And I was doing what I always do—fixing special dinners, renting movies I thought he'd like, anything to keep him from going out, only it never works."

He has gourmet meals at home, dessert elsewhere. And then got the nerve to be pissed.

Mira's winged brows drew together. "Then, after work on Friday, he was totally different." Her slender fingers picked at the square of tape covering the hole where the sofa button was missing. "He gave me this big hug when he came in, then started telling me about his cases. After dinner he lit a fire in the fireplace and we snuggled on the couch." She shook her head. "I can't believe I could be so stupid, but I was actually thinking—maybe he's finally realized how much I love him and he's going to clean up his act." Glancing at Cassidy, she said bitterly, "Fat chance."

"What happened?"

"I spoiled it." She smacked a hand to her forehead. "I can't believe how stupid I was."

Cassidy waited.

"I asked where he'd been the night before. He'd gone out around nine and didn't get home until two. Of course I knew where he was, and I also knew he didn't want me bringing it up." Her liquid brown eyes looked beseechingly into Cassidy's. "So why did I do it?"

Because you're tired of being walked on. Because you can't stand letting him get away with it. Because you're mad as hell and not gonna take it anymore.

And who should know better than you, after all those bad old years with Kevin?

Mira dropped her eyes to her hand, which was picking at the tape again. "Then he went into that cold, stony mood of his, and he said, if I really wanted to know he'd tell me. So I had to hear all about everything—the pornography, the prostitutes, the gay sex. It's like he wants me to know, wants to rub my nose in it."

Cassidy sat straighter. *Like Cliff wants me to know.* A sense of alarm began growing in the back of her mind. "Jake doesn't like your seeing me, does he?"

Mira cocked her head, surprised at the sudden turn. "No, of course not. He resents it that I talk about him. He gets really angry, says I'm violating his privacy by telling you what he does."

"Has he ever expressed any feelings about me?"

Soft rose suffused her cheeks.

"It's okay, I won't take it personally."

"Well, one time he said you were a ball-busting bitch who hated sex because you weren't getting any yourself."

Sees me as the archetypal, castrating mother. So why would he send his victims to me? Rub my nose in it too?

Cassidy's eyes narrowed. *Find out what he looks like. Ask if he ever shaved his head.*

Yeah right. She may not be so smart where Jake's concerned, but she's smart enough to notice if her therapist turns wacko detective on her.

⊠ ⊠ ⊠

Coming through the kitchen after her session, Cassidy saw Starshine on the counter next to the sink. She automatically filled the cat's bowl, but Starshine took a cursory sniff, then sat erect and fixed luminous green eyes on her human housemate.

"Not hungry? What is it then?" Leaning against the sink, Cassidy scratched behind the cat's black ear. "I bet you're just looking for adult conversation. I hear mothers get desperate to have some mature dialogue with other grown-ups."

Starshine's eyes took on a contented look, her body vibrating in a throaty purr.

"As a matter of fact, I do have something I need to consult with you about." Cassidy stopped scratching and snagged a bag of peanut butter cups out of the cupboard. "I'm having this little problem of overidentification with Mira." *When you were with Kevin, you got just about as nutso as Mira is with Jake. Which makes it hard to be objective.*

Mwat. Starshine batted Cassidy's hand as she unwrapped the candy, a reminder that she had not yet fulfilled her car-scratching duties.

Quickly stuffing a Reese's in her mouth, she resumed stroking the cat's sleek pelt. "Anyway, Mira's session reminded me that after Kevin my greatest fear was that I might make the same stupid mistake—or some other stupid mistake—all over again." *God knows, when you first met Zach you figured him to be the biggest mistake around.* "So I thought it'd be a good idea for you and me to do a quick inventory here."

Starshine nipped her finger, then pulled herself up tall, wrapping her tail around her hindquarters.

"I take it you'd prefer not to raise any questions where Zach's concerned. You have this mad crush on him and don't want me interfering. Sort of the way Mira feels about Jake." *But it's your job to ask questions—of yourself as well as clients.*

Starshine's eyes gradually shifted from green to amber, an indication of her increasing disdain for the topic at hand.

Cassidy took a step back, hooked her thumbs into her skirt waistband, and plunged on. "The first red flag was irresponsibility. Based on the fact that he let his plants die and he'd cut himself off from his family, I figured him to be as unreliable as Kevin."

Then you learned more about his family and realized a cutoff was the only option. "He may not come home as early as I'd like, but he always gets here. So I guess I'd have to give him a C plus on responsibility."

Starshine blinked slowly.

"I don't care if you're bored. I can't be a therapist and not analyze relationships." She shifted her weight to one hip. "Okay, so here's the next red flag—boundaries. It used to drive me crazy, his barging into my bedroom. But the interesting thing is, when I stopped shoving him away, he got a lot less intrusive. Which leads us to control. He was way too pushy at first, just stepped in and took over."

Hardly surprising, considering his mother'd make Margaret Thatcher look like a wimp, and he's always had to exert extreme force to keep her from swallowing him up.

"Actually, we've both got a fairly high need to have things our own way. Guess I'd give him a C on boundaries and a C minus on control." *You wouldn't do much better on the control score yourself.*

Raising her haunches in a long stretch, Starshine sprang onto the refrigerator. She gazed down disinterestedly and uttered a Mrowr, which Cassidy took to mean, "Why don't you give it a rest?"

Standing with feet apart and arms crossed, she said defensively, "We only have honesty and commitment left to go. When we first started, I was really scared he'd turn out to be a liar and a cheat, same as Kevin." *No evidence he's playing around, and whenever you back him into a corner you get the truth out of him.*

"I'd have to give him a B plus on honesty." She ran her tongue across her upper lip. "But commitment—that's the biggie." *You pick men who leave and Zach's a leaver. Man scared of attachment, woman scared of abandonment. Now there's a winning combination.* Her forehead began to throb again, followed by a hollow feeling in her stomach. "If anything's gonna be a deal buster, it'll be commitment."

As Starshine leapt to the floor and stalked out of the kitchen, Cassidy headed for the aspirin in the upstairs bathroom. The calico jumped onto the vanity to watch as Cassidy washed down two tablets.

Now that Cassidy had stopped subjecting her to unwanted conversation, the cat purred loudly, her eyes hopeful, an expression Cassidy had seldom seen outside the kitchen.

"Now what?" She could hear the skittering of tiny claws in the nursery next door. "The kittens? You're obviously not racing in there to be with them, so what is it?" She noted again Starshine's look of exhaustion. "I'll bet you want a little peace and quiet." She closed the door. "I guess a lot of mothers hide out in the bathroom."

Sloshing water on her face, she glanced in the mirror. Her cheeks were sunken, her deep-set, hazel eyes bleary. Hangovers did not become her.

Mwat. Starshine used the scratchy, begging tone that meant she wanted petting, so Cassidy hoisted the cat onto her shoulder and rubbed the loose skin at her neck.

A high-pitched squeal penetrated the door, a sound indicating that the fangs of one kitten had punctured the anatomy of another. Starshine dropped to the floor.

"Duty calls, oh well." Trailing Starshine into the nursery, Cassidy sat on the floor and watched as mother cat examined each of the tumbling bodies with her nose, then sprang to the top of her pile of boxes.

You had an anxiety attack. You need to do something about it. That from the voice always pushing her to do the right thing.

Do what? Go back into therapy? Costs too much money. Takes too much time. Don't want to think about it.

Scooping up Sylvia, Cassidy held the kitten in her palm, one fingernail scratching behind the small ear.

Least you could do is tell Zach. He had some kind of problem, you'd want to know.

Her gut twisted, a clear NO. *Don't want him thinking I'm some needy, dependent female, can't drive to a party without clutching up. That'd push him away faster than anything.*

No secrets allowed. That's what you always tell clients. If everything's not out on the table, the relationship's doomed.

The phone rang and she dashed into the bedroom to get it, happy for an interruption to the bickering voices in her head.

An unfamiliar woman's voice responded to her greeting. "I saw your ad about Cliff. And I thought I should call. I made a terrible mistake, and I thought I ought to pass the information along in case there's anything you can do to stop him."

7

Lunch

"Please tell me everything you know," Cassidy said into the receiver. Sitting in her desk chair, she grabbed a pen and paper.

Zach came into the room with the Sunday edition of the *Post*, which he always picked up on Saturday afternoon, and settled on the bed to listen to her end of the discussion.

Hanging up, Cassidy swiveled the chair to face him. "Her name's Irene."

"Cliff did her too?" Zach's voice was clipped, the way he sounded when pursuing a lead.

"Story's almost identical." Kicking off her violet pumps and flexing her toes, Cassidy crossed her right ankle over her left knee. "Cliff first approached at her mother's wake a year and a half ago, then ran into her again at the library.

Said he was in the middle of a nasty divorce, wife was crazy, just looking for a friend. He then, of course, proceeded to seduce her. The last time she saw him, he told her he had HIV and injected her with his blood. She didn't hear from him again until the letter a couple of weeks ago."

"She get tested?"

"She's positive." A feeling of heaviness settled over her. "There goes my last hope it wasn't for real." She glanced out the window between the desk and bed. Only four o'clock and the outside light was already grainy. "Irene's stronger than Jenny. She's forty-three now, been on her own since her twenties. Even lived with a guy once, although I get the impression she lacks confidence in the man-woman department. I'm sure Cliff looks for women with insecurities where men are concerned."

"Same description?"

"You were on target with your shaved head theory. This guy wasn't bald and he wasn't wearing a wig." Gripping her nylon-covered ankle, she pulled it in toward her body, jostling her violet skirt up to the base of her thigh. "By the time he met Irene, Cliff'd grown out a healthy head of hair. Dark brown, shoulder length. He wore it in a ponytail and billed himself as a Liam Neeson lookalike. And, of course, after hearing his routine a few times, she also started seeing him as Neeson's twin—evil twin after that last night."

Zach clasped his hands behind his head. "So the deal is, each victim gets a different movie star. You know, that's not half bad. Given the Rashomon theory of perception, there's a good chance Jenny or Irene—or even you—could look right at him and not recognize him, since each of you is looking for a different persona."

I ever have any movie-star clients? A few John Good-mans, but no Jean Lucs or Liam Neesons.

She said, "The rest was pretty similar. A little under six feet, broad-shouldered, muscular." Her eyes skimmed Zach's burly chest, the usual faded black tee straining across it. "I get the sense he's a little leaner than you, but basically the build's similar. Irene thought he was forty-two. That's a couple years older than he told Jenny, but not far off." She nibbled her little finger. "Oh shit. What if Jenny sees the ad?"

"You'll think of something."

Oh, Jenny, didn't you know? Catching Cliff is part of the therapeutic process. But don't worry, I won't expect more than twenty percent for getting you on Oprah.

Zach asked, "Did Irene say what got her to call?"

"She'd like to see him caught. She also assumed that I knew him and could explain why he did it."

He rubbed his jaw. "Odds are you do know him—you just haven't figured it out yet."

"Zach, I thought of somebody. I hope to God I'm wrong, 'cause if I'm not, my client Mira—this nice young woman whose only crime is being in love with a jerk—is seriously at risk. The reason she came into therapy is this guy she's married to is an honest-to-God sex addict. I've read about this kind of thing, but I've never known anyone as certifiably addicted to all sorts of bizarre sexual stuff as this guy is. He does almost everything—massage parlors, prostitutes, even anonymous gay sex in restrooms."

You just told him all about Mira's husband without even flinching. Losing your ethics is almost as easy as losing your virginity.

"And to top it off, the guy's an attorney." Cassidy shook her head. "Although, considering all the sleazy lawyers in the world, I guess that shouldn't come as a surprise."

"You say his wife's your client? What about him? They ever come in as a couple?"

"Unfortunately, I've never laid eyes on him. He's even more anti-therapy than you. He's also got a real grudge against me. Hates it that Mira's telling me all his dirty little secrets. But the odd thing is, he seems to enjoy bragging about his exploits to his wife."

"Is that the connection? The sex addict wants his wife to think he's a stud, and Cliff's sending his women to you for the same reason?"

Her brows pulled together in concentration. "It's more like he does it to spite her. He tells her about his acting out when he's angry, to hurt her. And since he's so pissed at me, I thought he might want me to know how bad he is for the same reason. At least, when I was sitting there with Mira it all made sense. But now I'm not so sure. From what his wife says, this guy's got a real thing about privacy. Doesn't want anybody except the two of them knowing what he's up to. So if he hates having his wife talk to me, it seems a tad unlikely he'd want all his other women reporting in."

"From the tone of his letter, I get the impression Cliff is a real fan of yours, which this guy obviously isn't." Zach shook his head. "But we're trying to apply logic to a nutcase, which is probably a waste. Since this is the only guy we've come across who's obviously at risk for AIDS, I vote we check him out."

"I suppose." She caught her lip between her teeth. "But I haven't a clue how to follow up."

"All we have to do is find out," he ticked them off on his fingers, "if he's the right size, shaved his head a couple of years ago, and has HIV."

She crossed over to sit beside him on the bed. "Well, how?"

He ran his hand up her thigh. "I ever tell you how much I hate pantyhose?"

She pushed his hand away. "C'mon, help me with this. How do we find out?"

"Ask his wife if he ever shaved his head."

"She's only known him a little over a year. Whirlwind romance." Cassidy frowned. "So what else is there? The best thing would be for me to get a look at him, see if he fits the description. Maybe he came into therapy under an alias and I'd be able to recognize him. I suppose the easiest way would be to look him up in the yellow pages and schedule an appointment. I could turn the tables and see *him* under a phony name."

"Too risky." Zach shook his head. "The last thing you need is an attorney who already has it in for you discovering his wife's therapist snooping around his office." He laid his arm across her shoulders. "But I could go. I'll make an appointment to . . . uh, draw up a will. If he's five-three we can forget it. If he's physically in the ballpark, I'll wait in the car with my zoom lens and get a shot of him leaving the office." He leaned closer, his face touching her hair. "I'll get on it Monday morning."

"I guess there's nothing we can do till then."

Reaching under her skirt, he grappled with the waistband of her pantyhose. "I wish you'd take these things off."

She tugged her hose down and tossed them on the floor.

Zach placed his hand on her thigh again, bringing up a wave of heat. "You haven't said a word about the party. How was it?"

"Oh, pretty stuffy." *You should tell him.*

"You know this morning when you didn't get up?" Amusement percolated in his voice. "If I didn't know what a ringer you are for Carrie Nation, I might've suspected a little overindulgence."

Sonuvabitch's gloating. She gritted her teeth. *He's not getting one word outta me.*

✉ ✉ ✉

Although Sunday passed quietly, Cassidy slept fitfully that night, dream fragments chasing through her head. Behind the wheel of the Toyota, pursuing two points of light as she cut through heavy darkness in the forest preserve. Slumped in the seat of Mark's Porsche, his voice droning in her ears. Driving inbound on the Eisenhower to meet Mark for lunch, icy worms nibbling at her spine.

Eyes opening abruptly, she felt her stomach getting twitchy again. She slid quietly out of bed and padded down to the kitchen, where a voracious horde awaited breakfast.

Anxiety attacks aren't over.

Starshine, bounding first to the counter, then to the top of the fridge, fixed large black pupils on Cassidy's face. She was clearly in her tiger mode, a predatory state she had not mustered the energy for in a long time. Cassidy turned to watch, glad to see there was life after motherhood.

"I'm supposed to meet Mark for lunch, but if the dreams and my stomach are telling me anything, it's—'This is not an auspicious day for car trips.' "

Mrowr. Starshine flipped inside out and backward to catch her tail, nearly lunging over the edge of the refrigerator.

"What are you doing? Getting hysterical to remind me what anxiety attacks are like?"

The cat dove to the floor, then streaked out of the kitchen, the kittens careening after her.

Cassidy read a Sylvia cartoon taped to the fridge. Peering into a crystal ball, a turbaned woman said, "You'll fall out of a thirteenth story window into the arms of your demon lover."

Bad omens all over the place. Don't go.

Crazy thinking. Anyway, you can't cancel. Not when you haven't seen Mark in twenty years.

So don't drive.

She imagined herself walking to the garage, getting in the Toyota, backing out. Her stomach flip-flopped.

All right. Stupid as it is, I'll take the el. The el meant leaving an hour early, transferring three times, waiting interminably in below-zero weather. *Still better than driving.*

With a sense of relief, Cassidy headed into her office and pulled Mira Sheffield's folder from the file cabinet. When Zach came down, she was seated at the dining room table, a Chicago phone book and pad of paper in front of her.

He poured coffee and sat at the foot of the table. "What're you doing up so early?"

"Remember Jake, the sex-addict attorney? He's got a one-man office on Lawrence and he concentrates on civil law."

"Solo practice, huh? Odds are his name's not big enough so they'd know him in the courts." Dark hair, normally combed to the side, fell across his forehead, making him look younger. Although he was in no way uptight or rigid—sometimes, in fact, he went to the opposite extreme—he nonetheless remained so habitually in control that even small lapses such as uncombed hair imparted an odd sense of vulnerability.

Cassidy laid her hand on his arm. "Even though it's a solo practice, he probably has a secretary. So I thought we could wait until ten, give her a chance to settle in, then call and ask if he's ever tried the skinhead approach to fashion."

Zach looked skeptical. "You just going to come out and ask?"

She smiled benignly. "I've got it all figured out."

"Okay, you give it a shot, then I'll call later and make an appointment."

✉ ✉ ✉

Just before ten Cassidy settled into her desk chair, Zach observing from the waterbed behind her. She could feel her heart thumping. *Should've let Zach do it. Lying to get information's no problem for him. Me, I'm the kind polygraphs were made for.*

You're the one said you wanted to find Cliff Connors. You

start asking Zach to do everything, you'll end up a dependent little mouse.

She punched up the numbers.

"Jake Sheffield, attorney at law." Female, fast-paced, just a hint of black.

"Hi." *Nice day today. How ya doin'? Whaddaya think of them Cubbies?* "I'm trying to track down this guy I met on vacation. I think his name's Jake Sheffield but I'm not exactly sure, so I thought maybe I could check it out with you and—"

"He's not here now. Let me take your name and number. I'll give him the message."

"No, wait." She drilled her fingernails against the pad. "I don't really want to talk to him. I mean, it would be too embarrassing if I've got the wrong guy. I just want to describe him so you could verify if it's the same person, then I could leave a message. He was about six—"

"Look, lady, I think you better ask him yourself."

"It was two and a half years ago. He had his head shaved back then. I don't know if he still—"

"Can you hold a minute? He just walked in." The voice got muffled, a hand over the earpiece. "Hey, Jake, I got this ditsy woman on the line. Thinks she met you on vacation a couple of years ago."

A man's voice. "Here, give it to me."

Go ahead, ask. What's the worst that can happen?

Haven't you learned anything? The worst always happens, and it's always even more hideous than you imagined.

Cassidy eased the receiver down and swiveled toward Zach. "You'll just have to go ahead with the appointment and hope he's not five-three." She thought about Mira. "No wait—hope he *is* five-three."

⊠ ⊠ ⊠

Cassidy pushed open the glass door and walked inside the Mexicali Rose. A cloud of warm, humid, chili-laden air blew over her. Blinking back tears from the cold, she stuffed her gloves into her bag and rubbed her hands together. Sunshine streamed through windows along the south wall. Widely spaced blonde tables stood on a glossy hardwood floor, giving the place a light, airy feel.

Seeing Mark wave from a window table, she broke into a wide grin. *Can't believe it's been twenty years. Way he chattered coming home from the party, like we'd seen each other yesterday.*

"Heavens, sweetie, you look half frozen." Mark gave her a quick hug.

"Have you been gone so long you forgot what Chicago winters are like?" She draped her coat over the back of her chair and sat down.

"I thought you'd park in the hotel lot and stay warm. If I'd known you were going to freeze your little buns off, I would've driven out to Oak Park."

"Good to see what the real world's like. Makes me feel even smugger about my daily commute from the bedroom all the way downstairs to my office." She gazed into his sky blue eyes. "My God, what a gorgeous hunk you've grown into." Wavy, golden hair formed a deep widow's peak above his finely boned face.

"You're not half bad yourself, cutie pie."

She plunked an elbow on the rose tablecloth and rested

her cheek on her hand. "So, what is all this secret, important stuff you want to talk to me about?"

"We'll get to that later. Save the worst till last."

That worst thing that always happens again? A chill ran along her spine. She scrutinized his clear eyes, healthy tan, dazzling smile. *Can't be too bad.*

He went on quickly before she could interrupt. "First we have to catch up on all the news. Did I tell you I finally caught myself a 'husband?' "

"Hey, congratulations! So, how do you like married life?"

The waitress, her mascaraed, charcoal-shadowed eyes devoid of expression, set a Dos Equis beside Mark's plate and took Cassidy's order for coffee. Mark tilted his glass and poured. "It has its ups and downs. This guy I'm with, he's a psychiatrist, name's Bill. Do the men in your life ever complain that being a therapist gives you an unfair advantage? That therapizing means you know all sorts of sneaky little tricks to play?"

"Mostly they complain that I ask questions all the time."

"Bill and I bought a house a little over a year ago. The place is fabulous but I'm not so sure we should've moved in together."

"What's the problem?"

"Those men're right—you are nosy. Of course, I love talking about myself, so it's okay by me. But that's what I don't get with Bill. He's just not interested enough to ask questions, and when he does, he can't be bothered listening to the answers. What it comes down to is, I don't get enough attention. And believe you me, sweetie, I want my share of air time."

A psychiatrist who doesn't listen. Why am I not surprised? "So what's keeping you together?"

"What do you think, babycakes? He's got a scrumptious bod." He waved breezily. "We better take a quick peek at the menu before that raccoon-eyed mannequin comes back."

Cassidy's olfactories had decided for her when she first stepped inside the door. "House specialty: Hearty bowl of our zesty chili garnished with sour cream, onions, and cheese."

She laid the menu down and let her gaze drift out to the street. The table was set on a diagonal with the window, and her view slanted off to the west. A few hardy pedestrians trickled past on the sidewalk outside. Beyond the sidewalk, four lanes of cars, all moving east on the one-way, no-parking street, bumped ahead in sporadic bursts of motion. A white limo, blue minivan, green sedan rolled and stopped, rolled and stopped into her line of vision. *Maybe getting my nose iced on the el's not so bad.*

"Well, sweetie, I know what I'm having."

She smiled at him briefly, then something dragged her eyes back to the street. Something about the sedan. Her brows pulled together. A tingly feeling, like a cold draft on her neck. She squinted at the green car as it rolled and stopped to a point directly in front of their table, a sidewalk's width away.

Mark said, "The black bean, goat cheese pie. Just listen to this—it sounds divine."

A break in the stream of pedestrians afforded her a clearer view. Through the driver's side window she saw a black ski-masked face. *Drivers don't usually—*

"Layer of black beans, simmered in garlic and cilantro, over a tortilla crust topped with—"

The sedan's window slid down. A barrel came up, hands steadied the barrel, the ski mask tilted behind the hands. Fire flashed from inside the round, black hole.

"Pop!" A bullet pierced the plate glass window, leaving a small hole.

"Omigod!"

Blood spurted from Mark's head as he fell sideways. Dropping to her knees, she ducked her head and wrapped her arms around it as objects fell on top of her. The sounds of broken plates, stampeding footsteps, and high pitched screams came from all directions.

Mark lay face down on the other side of the table, his muscles jerking. Assaulted by the stench—coppery blood, acrid urine and feces, she turned her head. *Gotta get away. No, can't leave.* Gritting her teeth, she forced herself to look at him again, then began to crawl over cutlery and broken glass to the place where he lay. As she made her way through the maze of fallen chairs, she briefly noted a sting in the palm of her left hand.

Reaching Mark, she rose onto her knees. Beer dripped from the edge of the table onto his body. His neck was twisted so that the right side of his face was uppermost. Blood gurgled from a small hole near the temple, matting his golden hair, streaking his tan face. One light blue eye stared blankly.

She touched his cheek. His skin felt warm and alive. *Maybe he isn't dead, maybe . . .* She tried to clean off the blood with the sleeve of her sweater but all she did was smear it. Yanking her hand away, she folded her arms tightly beneath her breasts and began rocking from the waist.

8

Aftermath

Cassidy continued rocking for a stretch of time that seemed neither short nor long. Then she heard a calm, female voice behind her right shoulder. "We need for you to move now."

Twisting to look, she saw a woman with a pleasant face and kind eyes.

"I'm going to put my hands under your elbows and help you up." The woman had amber-flecked brown eyes, rounded cheek bones, and a firm chin.

She got Cassidy to her feet, then guided her away from Mark's body. People were everywhere. A man flashing pictures. Three men talking loudly next to where her cousin lay. A couple of uniforms off to the side.

"Only one shot. Since the window didn't shatter, the bullet must've been—"

"You got somebody talking to the staff?"

"Back in the kitchen."

The woman walked Cassidy to a table across the room, sat her in a chair, then took a seat opposite her. "My name's Emily Barowski. I'm a police detective and I need some information. You feel up to talking?" Her honey-colored hair was jaw length, her trim body clothed in a crisp wool blazer and skirt.

"You were at the table with the man who got shot? Can you tell me his name?"

"Mark Sanders. He's my cousin." Her voice sounded flat and metallic. *Maybe I've turned into a robot.* No, that wasn't right. A robot was filled with mechanical gadgets. She had nothing at all inside, just hollow and empty.

Emily had taken out a pad. "And your name?"

"Cassidy McCabe."

"McCabe? Now where've I heard that name before?"

Cassidy stared into the pleasant, kindly face. She didn't know where the detective had heard it so she didn't say anything.

"Excuse me a minute, will you? I'll be right back." The detective was gone for a while, then returned and sat down again. She continued asking questions and making notes.

Cassidy glanced at her hands. Sticky and red. A tiny cut on her left palm. She tried wiping her hands on her sweater, but the sweater was sticky and red also.

More time passed, Emily asking, Cassidy answering.

Then she noticed a man approaching off to the left. Zach. *What's he doing here?*

Sliding into a chair, he laid his hand over hers. "You okay? Shit, that's a stupid question. Of course you're not."

She blinked. *How'm I gonna explain I've gone robotic on him?*

Emily tilted her head at Zach. "She's in shock. Perfectly reasonable, considering. But she did manage to give me everything I need for now."

"Hey, Emily, I really appreciate your giving me a call." Emily's eyes smiled back at him.

✉ ✉ ✉

Walking her into the bedroom, Zach instructed her to raise her arms so he could remove her sweater.

Cassidy clamped her arms against her sides. "What're you doing?" *Oh, I sound like me again.*

"First you're going into the shower, then into bed."

"I can take off my own clothes."

Standing back, he gave her an appraising look and nodded. She stayed in the shower a long time. When she returned in her flannel robe, the pile of bloody clothes was gone. Zach was sitting on his side of the bed, Starshine curled up next to him, no kittens in sight. Cassidy sank down beside him.

Zach put his outspread hand on her thigh. "I fixed you a drink. It's on the nightstand."

"I don't want a drink."

"You definitely need something. Since you refused the Xanax the E.R. doc tried to give you, you'll just have to get tranquilized with bourbon."

She took a swallow. Strong. Glancing at the window, she saw the light was almost gone. Only five-thirty. *Too early to get drunk.* She gulped some more.

Zach said, "I'm gonna cancel your clients for the next couple of days."

"I never cancel clients. Besides, it isn't necessary. Really, I'm okay now."

"That's nice but I'm still canceling your clients." He said it matter of factly, no question at all, a done deal.

Her shoulders stiffened. "You don't know who they are so you can't." Swallowing deeply, she felt the alcohol burning in her stomach. As the tension eased, an image of Mark falling sideways flashed through her head. She ground her teeth, pushing it away. "I have to call Gran." She let out a long sigh. "God, that's gonna be tough. They've always been close, even though he's lived in California all these years." She raked both hands through her heavy, damp mop. "No, I can't call. I've gotta do it face to face."

"I'll drive you over as soon as I cancel tomorrow's clients."

"I'm a full grown, adult person. I can make my own decisions, and I've decided not to cancel."

Walking around to face her, he stood beside the bed, his jaw tightly set. "Goddamnit, Cass, I'm getting pretty sick of this. Whenever you think I need straightening out, you don't hesitate. But even when it's obvious as hell that you need help, you always fight me."

"I'm not fighting. I just—"

"I'm bringing your calendar over here, and you're gonna

write down the names and numbers. Then I'm going to reschedule your Tuesday clients."

She pulled her legs up tight, curled her arms on top of her knees, and buried her face. *Whenever he tries to do anything for me, I go all out to stop him. What's wrong with me?* Starshine wormed her way into Cassidy's lap and purred adoringly.

Feeling Zach's hand on her head, she looked up.

"You gonna write out those names and numbers for me?"

He gave her the calendar and a notepad, then waited as she scribbled the information. When she handed it back, he settled in beside her.

"How you doin'?"

Gazing upward, she pictured the lithe, blonde teenager Mark had been. What'd always struck her the most about him was his spirit, his aliveness. *He can't be dead.* Her throat thickened. "Remember, I told you Mom and I lived at Gran's till I was fifteen? Well, Mark used to bike over all the time. I didn't have many friends, and he was like the big brother I never had. When nobody was looking, he'd let me ride on the back of his bike to Peterson's and feed me hot fudge sundaes, which were way cooler than peanut butter cups."

She dropped her head and Zach massaged the back of her neck. Clearing her throat, she continued, "Then his dad got transferred. Just about the time they were scheduled to move, Mark came out to the family—I think he wanted to talk to us about it before he left." She sighed. "My mother, who is clearly living in the wrong century, freaked. By then we were in our own apartment, and she said I had to stay

away from him, which I, of course, ignored. Then the day
before he left—"

Her eyes filled. "The day before he left, I told Mom I was
going over to say goodbye. She had a fit just as I was heading
toward the stairs. I turned to yell back, stumbled, and fell
down the whole flight." She sniffled, rubbing her nose with
the side of her hand. "So I ended up in the emergency room,
Mark moved away, our mothers stopped speaking, and I
didn't see him again until the night of the party."

Tears ran down her cheeks. She grabbed a handful of
tissue from the nightstand and covered her face. Shoulders
shaking, she gasped and sobbed. Zach stroked her hair. She
crawled into his lap, rested her forehead against his chest,
and cried herself out.

⊠ ⊠ ⊠

The dry rasp of a shovel scraping cement pulled her from
sleep the next morning. She awoke with a crying hangover:
achy head, stuffy nose, fuzzy brain. Not surprising after her
crying jag the night before, followed by Zach's canceling
her clients, the two of them driving to Gran's to deliver the
news, then crying herself to sleep afterward.

She dragged downstairs to find Zach in the kitchen,
pancake batter mixed and ready to go. He turned on the
burner under the skillet. "We've got the whole day free and
I think it's time to break out of our normal routine. You need
fresh air, exercise, and snow in your face. I need time out
from having to be such a sensitive guy."

"What're you talking about?"

"I drove over to my mother's house early this morning
and dug my old toboggan out of the garage."

"I don't like zooming downhill without brakes."

Zach's mouth tightened.

Would it kill you just for once to be agreeable? "Okay, I'll go."

⊠ ⊠ ⊠

Pulling off her soaked gloves, Cassidy rubbed chapped hands together in the stream of warm air coming from the Nissan's vent. They had put in a long two hours at a toboggan run in the southwest suburbs, the only hill in their flatland vicinity high enough to go down, and now were driving north on Harlem. A light flurry of snowflakes splatted against the windshield.

She said, "The big question is why?"

"Why what?" Zach stopped behind a half block line of cars waiting at the Windsor Street railroad crossing. "Why train tracks cut across all the north-south streets west of Austin?"

"Why Mark was killed. He just happened into the wrong place at the wrong time? The shooter missed me and got him by mistake? There's some tie-in between him and Cliff?"

"I talked to the police this morning. Since the shooter fired only once, Mark was probably the designated hit. If he'd been after you, he would've tried again. Least that's how the cops read it."

Envisioning yesterday's meeting between Zach and Emily, she replayed his voice as he thanked the detective and suddenly realized he'd spoken in the warm, burry drawl he usually reserved for the bedroom. She ran the tip of her tongue across her upper teeth. "Cops? You mean Emily, don't you?"

"I've been mulling over the possibility of a Cliff-Mark connection. First you have a guy who has HIV claiming he's a client. Given that he's infected, there's a good chance he's either bisexual or gay. Then your gay cousin gets shot. Seems unlikely two such bizarre events'd be purely random. But it's hard to come up with any kind of explanation to tie them together."

They passed a tavern, a Bohemian restaurant, an Elks Lodge, and a sports bar.

She furrowed her brow. "Maybe Cliff got to bragging. Somebody in the gay community could've heard he was sending clients to me and passed the word on to Mark. Maybe that's what Mark wanted to tell me."

Zach shrugged. "The shooter was driving a stolen car. Pedestrian got a plate number that matched a vehicle taken just a couple of hours earlier."

Which you found out when you called Emily. Cassidy turned her back and stared through the side window at wind-surfing snow flakes. She held out a full minute, then swiveled to face him. "How did Emily know that I'm your current girlfriend?" *Current? Guess that's bitchy enough.*

His voice tightened. "I told her."

She waited, hoping he would elaborate. When he didn't, she asked, "And how did you happen to tell her?"

"This the third degree?"

"Yes."

Zach snapped the radio on, punching up a rock station which he knew she hated. But at least he twisted the volume down to a mere background throb. "Emily and I had a thing going some time back. Couple months ago she broke up with

her new boyfriend and called to see if I was available. I told
her about you."

"You tell her over drinks? Dinner maybe?" *Or, considering that bedroom voice I heard, maybe you stopped by her
place.*

"Look, this has nothing to do with you."

"As in, none of my business?"

"Right."

She crossed her arms. *Why wouldn't he want to go back
to Emily? She's definitely prettier and probably just as
smart.*

Cassidy pictured herself and Emily on a beauty pageant
runway with Zach in the judge's stand. Next to Emily's
disciplined hair, softly rounded face, and tall, well developed figure, Cassidy appeared short and saw-toothed. Although she had a slender, whiplash body, there was no
bountifulness to it, no amplitude. Her face was too narrow,
her hazel eyes too deepset, her mouth too thin. Her only
abundant feature was her hair, which tumbled in wayward
curls around her neck and shoulders.

Why on earth would Zach want me instead of her?

Now wait a minute, her therapist voice interjected. *You
know damn well most people don't hook up on the basis of
looks. Zach obviously picked you 'cause you're so irritating.
The man likes a challenge.*

After several moments of silence, she said, "I think I have
a right to know about women from your past who cycle
around and call you again. Especially when you're gazing
into each other's eyes right in front of my catatonic face."

"Emily knew who you were. Doesn't that tell you where things stand between us?"

"Well, okay." Cassidy dropped her hands into her lap. "I don't mean to be so accusatory. It's just that the way you sounded when you talked to her made it seem like something was going on. In the present."

Clicking the turn signal, he pulled into the right-hand lane, preparing to heading east on Madison Street. "I don't like this jealousy, Cass. I'm not Kevin. You don't have to worry about what I'm doing when I'm not with you."

Jealousy? Was that it? Her shoulders hunched. More like unclear signals, missing information. "It's not that I don't trust you. I really do believe you're not gonna cheat on me." *He wouldn't bother to cheat—he'd just leave.* "But I need you to fill in the blanks. You and Emily obviously have some history, and I don't wanna have to guess what it was."

"But that's just the point. It's history. I shouldn't have to explain."

"You *do* have to explain. This is a relationship, remember? When you have a relationship, you catch each other up. You explain the past."

⊠ ⊠ ⊠

Cassidy was crossing the bedroom when the phone rang. She stepped over to her desk and picked up.

"I'm calling because . . . I was looking through a *Free Chicago* and I saw Cliff's name." A woman's voice, high-pitched, a little hyper.

Cassidy dropped into her chair and took a pen from the ceramic mug penholder. "Did he send you a letter with my card?"

"I just about went crazy when I got it. Not that I had far to go. I mean, I was half crazed already just knowing about the AIDS. But that letter, that was the real corker."

Cassidy yanked out a legal pad. "Would you mind giving me your first name?"

"Lorianne."

After asking every question she could think of, she thanked Lorianne and hung up. She rotated to face Zach, who leaned against the doorjamb. "That's number four."

"Same story?"

"Only the actors are changed to protect the guilty." She pressed the heel of her palm against her forehead. "Why am I making lame jokes? This whole situation's a nightmare."

"Who'd he look like this time?"

"Bruce Willis in *Die Hard*. Sandy hair, flattop. Age thirty-nine. Twenty-six months since he first approached her. At her mother's wake, of course."

"Not hard figuring how he finds 'em."

"The obituaries. He looks for women in their fifties or sixties who have daughters with the same last name."

Starshine drifted into the bedroom followed by Calvin, who skulked behind her in a low-slung, stalking position. Noticing how concave the calico's sides were, Cassidy was reminded of the emaciated appearance of AIDS sufferers. Calvin made a huge leap and attached himself to Mom, forepaws clutched around her neck.

Cassidy frowned. "What a rotten kid. She's so starved she can hardly stay on her feet and he goes for the jugular."

Shaking her head, Starshine dislodged the kitten, but

before she could jump onto the desk he'd wrapped his body around her hind leg.

"Hey, your light's blinking." As Zach punched PLAY, Cassidy peeled Calvin off his mother and shut him out of the bedroom.

Three messages. The first two were from Cassidy's mother offering to sit by her bed and play nursemaid while she recovered from Mark's shooting. The third was from Gran checking to see how she was. Cassidy glanced at late afternoon sun slanting through the west-facing window. "Guess I ought to let Mom come over." *He met Gran last night. No problem there. Mom's another story.* Her voice dragged. "You two'll finally get a chance to meet."

He gave her a long look. "I almost get the sense you'd rather we didn't. However, at this point I don't see any way out. So what say we take your mother and grandmother out to dinner?"

"Dinner?" Zach would insist on paying. Since she'd already fought him about canceling clients and explaining Emily, she couldn't pick a fight over who paid. But she could go for cheap. "All right, dinner at Clancy's."

9

Dinner

Cassidy sat on the cold hardwood floor of the nursery, Calvin draped across her lap, relaxing to the rumble of his body-shaking purr. She heard a soft thunk from somewhere below. Could be Zach, who'd gone out to shovel the front sidewalk, which she'd neglected because clients did not come in that way. Or could be a cat noise. Odd sounds had become less threatening since Starshine co-opted her space.

Some time later, Zach yelled from the foot of the stairs. "Hey, Cass, we need to get moving."

Time to expose Zach to your mother.

All these months Mom's been thinking he's the problem. Too snooty, too disinterested to meet her. Now she's worked up this big grudge against him. Should've gotten it over with back at the beginning.

Right. Like you should tell somebody you've got herpes on the first date. No point putting yourself through it unless you're headed toward the bedroom. And no point putting Zach in the same room with your mother unless you've got some reason to think he's going to stick. Which you still don't have much of.

Cassidy went downstairs. Trotting around the room divider, she saw Zach near the back door buttoning his sheepskin jacket. Something flagged her attention, something out of place. Glancing at the small counter next to her office door, she spotted an envelope propped against the hot water pot. "What's this?" Tearing it open, she pulled out a computer generated message. "Omigod! It's from Cliff." Zach moved closer so he could read over her shoulder.

DEAR CASSIDY,

     I APPLAUD YOUR INGENUITY. THE AD IN THE FREE CHICAGO WAS EXCELLENT.

A tremor ran down her arms. "He was here. Right here in our house."

"Shit! He walked in while I was out front shoveling."

     YOU SEE, I HOPED YOU'D HAVE THE OPPORTUNITY TO SPEAK TO EACH OF THE WOMEN WHO'VE HELPED ME ACCOMPLISH MY MISSION, BUT I REALIZED NOT ALL WOULD COMPLY.

     HOWEVER, YOUR CLEVERNESS WILL INCREASE THE NUMBER YOU HAVE ACCESS TO, WHICH DELIGHTS ME NO END. PERHAPS IT WILL HELP YOU TO KNOW THAT I BEGAN MY CRUSADE NEARLY THREE YEARS AGO, AND DURING THAT TIME I'VE SELECTED SEVEN WOMEN TO SERVE AS UNWITTING

ACCOMPLICES IN CARRYING OUT MY MISSION. THESE WOMEN
WILL SHARE MY FATE. THEY'LL DIE FOR THE SINS OF WOM-
ANKIND, JUST AS JESUS DIED FOR US ALL.

                    WITH INCREASING RESPECT AND AFFECTION,
                              CLIFF

"Just look at this letter." Cassidy shoved it toward Zach.
"There are seven women he's done this to. Seven women
living with a potentially fatal disease."

"A fucking crusade." He returned the paper to its envelope, slid it into a plastic bag, and stuffed it in his jacket
pocket. "We'll keep this for evidence." His brow furrowed.
"At least now we have some idea how he got my unlisted
number. Probably went through the bedroom and took it off
the phone."

He studied her face, his eyes worried. "Look," he grasped
her upper arms, "the last thing you need right now is to be
thinking about Cliff. Just put this out of your mind and let's
go have dinner with your family."

                         ✉ ✉ ✉

"I haven't been here in ages," Gran said. "Not since the
early days with your grandfather. We used to come here for
hamburgers and a pitcher on Saturday nights." She patted the
table's dark, polished wood surface. "Always did like this
place."

Clancy's was one of a string of bars in a nearby blue collar
suburb. The air was smoky, the lights dim, the half-dozen
patrons middle-aged and older.

Helen pulled a napkin out of a metal dispenser and wiped
the tines of her fork. She stared across the table at Zach, her

gaze fixing on his scar. "I understand you live at Marina City."

The muscles in back of Cassidy's neck tightened. *Oh shit, here she goes.*

A spark of amusement flickered in Zach's eyes. "No, as a matter of fact I live in Oak Park with your daughter."

"Better watch out, Helen," Gran warned gleefully. "Looks like this new S.O. of Cassidy's isn't gonna give you an inch." Gran was tiny, wrinkled and wiry. A wild blonde wig framed her squirrel-like face.

Helen said, "But I guess you've still got that condo of yours in the city. I suppose that's so you can head back downtown when you've had enough of life in Oak Park."

"Why're you doing this, Mom? I thought you wanted to be nice. Feed me chicken soup." She pictured Helen waving a broom in Zach's face and shouting "Shoo!" *Mother hen protecting her chick? More like little mutt yapping at big showdog 'cause the showdog's higher up the social ladder than she is.*

Zach sent Helen his most unflappable smile. "What makes you think I haven't settled in for a nice long stay?"

Helen's lips tightened, creating little clefts at the corners of her mouth. "When people can't be bothered to attend family parties, I'd guess their ties don't go all that deep."

He boomed out a hearty laugh. "You and my mother oughtta get together. When it comes to family-loyalty sins of ommision, she'd be happy to cite chapter and verse."

Mom can guilt trip me all she wants. She won't get anywhere with Zach. He's trained with the masters—his own family.

"You never did know when to quit," Gran said to her daughter. "I don't know why you're giving this good-looking guy such a hard time. Now that you've got Mr. Big Bucks Mertz on the string, you oughtta be happy that Cass's got a studmuffin of her own." She cupped her hands around her mouth and stage-whispered to Cassidy, "What do you think of that one? I got it out of a book."

Zach's glance lingered on Gran's gnarly face. "You're pretty hot stuff yourself."

"It's the Farrah Fawcett hair." She straightened her wig. "I don't like to give my girls here any serious competition, but I know Cass can hold her own."

Doesn't matter how old Gran gets. She'll always be a babe. Poor Mom—overshadowed her whole life.

Zach raised his glass toward Gran. "If I weren't smitten already, I'd run off with you in a minute."

Gran chugged the rest of her beer, banged the mug on the table, and wiped her mouth with the back of her hand. "How 'bout another round?"

He waved the waitress over.

Gazing across the table, Cassidy had a sudden memory of sitting with Mark in Gran's kitchen, laughing until her sides ached at her cousin's clowning. She swallowed, carefully realigned the silverware, then brought her eyes up to meet Gran's. "I know you were pretty devastated when we told you the news last night, but do you think you could manage to talk about it now?"

Gran's face sank. She suddenly looked every one of her eighty-four years. " 'Course I can. Mark was a great kid and I'll miss him, but I'll be okay."

Helen drummed her fingers on the table. "What I'd like to know is, whatever made him show up at the party? I couldn't believe it when I heard this—well, you know—this strange person calling me 'Aunt Helen.'"

Gran glared at her daughter. "Don't you dare say one word against him. I kept my mouth shut twenty years ago when you made that big stink about his being gay. You were such an awful brat! Your very own sister stopped speaking to you, and I sat by and didn't do anything. But now he's gone, and I wish to heaven I'd turned you over my knee back then, like you deserved."

Helen's face turned dark red. "Mother!"

Cassidy rested her hands on the table, fingertips pressed together. "He had something to tell me but he never got the chance. You have any idea what it could've been?"

Gran shook her head. "When he came by Thursday morning he was talking a mile a minute 'bout his job and his boyfriend and that house they got together. He brought over this notebook computer of his and showed me how to go online and talk dirty to all these perverts around the country. But I don't recall anything special."

The waitress brought hamburgers, onion rings, and more drinks. Helen took a dainty sip of white wine and stared morosely at the sloppy hamburger on the thick ceramic plate. She muttered, not quite inaudibly, "Guess Clancy's safe enough if you're embarrassed to be seen with the people you're with. No chance of running into any of your fancy, country club friends at Clancy's."

Propping her elbow on the table, Cassidy lowered her forehead onto the heel of her hand.

Zach said to Gran, "You got any dates lined up with those e-mail perverts?"

"Not yet, but who knows? I told 'em I was a twenty-year-old stripper lookin' for some action. You wouldn't believe the offers I got. Mark left it at my place so I could tinker around, and now I suppose I might as well keep it. That e-mail is sure gonna give my imagination a workout."

Zach's voice turned crisp. "You've got Mark's notebook?"

✉ ✉ ✉

Dropping Helen off at her apartment, Zach drove toward Gran's south Oak Park bungalow. "What was that crack your mother made about country club friends?"

Cassidy pulled her knit cap lower over her ears. "Mom's convinced the only reason you didn't rush right over to meet her is that your family's blood runs a lot bluer than ours. According to her, nobody who grew up in a north Oak Park mansion could possibly be serious about a peasant-type like me."

"Boy, will she be disappointed when she gets to know me."

Gran spoke from the backseat. "Helen always took it so to heart that we were blue collar kind of people. I tried to help, but back then the class system at Oak Park High was pretty fierce. She just never got over the feeling that people like your mother look down on her."

"My mother looks down on everybody."

✉ ✉ ✉

As they pulled up in front of Gran's bungalow, Zach said, "I'd like to take a look at that notebook."

"Sure thing." Gran hopped out the rear door before Zach could open it for her.

They trooped into the dining room, a track-lighted space dominated by the bleached oak table in the center. A slim plastic case sat at the head of the table, stacks of books, newspapers, and magazines piled around it. Tossing his jacket over a chair back, Zach picked up a coil of wire and headed through the kitchen doorway in search of a phone.

There he goes, wandering around other people's houses just like he did with me when we first met. She mentally shrugged, noting with surprise that it didn't bother her so much anymore.

Gran dumped her coat on the table. "While you're warming that thing up, I'll just fix us some drinks." She sailed into the kitchen, her exit followed by the sound of rattling ice.

Zach sat in front of the notebook and began moving the cursor while Cassidy watched over his shoulder. *Everywhere I go, people start babbling this foreign computerese. Makes me feel like a lone Cro-Magnon being pushed into extinction by hordes of tool-wielding Homo sapiens.*

WELCOME TO AMERICA ONLINE came up on the screen, then a box labeled SCREEN NAME, and inside the box, GRAN-MUFFIN.

Holding a tray of drinks, Gran positioned herself behind Zach's other shoulder. "That's me, 'Gran Muffin'." She handed glasses to Zach and Cassidy, taking the last herself.

Zach clicked GRANMUFFIN, and the words DRESSMAN, TOPPER, and ARTBOY popped up beneath it.

Cassidy asked, "What're you looking for?"

"Mail. Soon as I decipher the password, I can access his outgoing and incoming mail."

"You two planning to track down that shooter?" Gran's voice bubbled with excitement. "Remember, Cass? Last time you were on a case you said I could be your assistant."

Cassidy took the chair kitty-corner from Zach's. Looking at Gran, she said, "One thing I'm definitely going to do is call Mark's partner. You have his number?"

"Here you go." Gran pulled a slip of paper out of the mess.

Zach folded his arms on the table. "Did Mark say anything about his password? Or mention anybody he's corresponding with?"

Gran sat across from Cassidy. "Let's see now . . . I asked if I could read his mail and he said I couldn't 'cause it was naughty. Then I said that was even better, but he wouldn't budge. He did tell me he'd been e-mailing somebody in Chicago. I asked what his boyfriend thought, and he said he didn't see any need to bother Bill with it."

Cassidy leaned forward. "He have plans to meet this e-mail buddy of his?"

"He met somebody." Gran's face knotted in concentration. "He told me everything he was gonna do, and I think he said he'd come in a day early so he could get together with some guy on Thursday night. It could've been the e-mail guy, but it also could've been this old friend he mentioned."

Zach rubbed his jaw. "What'd he say about the old friend?"

"Something about a buddy from high school he'd stayed in touch with." Gran twisted her glass on the table. "But I didn't catch any names, and I don't know if he was gonna see both guys or just one of 'em."

Cassidy pictured her cousin as a sprightly teenager standing next to a shorter, more solidly built boy whom he'd referred to as his best friend. Tears stung the back of her eyelids. "I remember this kid Mark used to hang out with. I saw them together several times." She tried to sharpen her image of the friend but couldn't get his face into focus. "Damn, I can't bring up either his name or what he looked like. How 'bout you, Gran? You remember Mark's friend at all?"

Gran shook her head. "Sorry, I just don't recall anything about it."

"Well," Zach tapped the edge of the keyboard, "I guess all we can do is hack our way into his e-mail."

Cassidy asked, "So, how long's it gonna take to break the code?"

"Depends on how devious his mind was. Well, Gran Muffin, here's your first assistant detective assignment. Get me his address, birthdate, and social security, plus anything else you can dig up regarding his hobbies, interests, and sexual proclivities. Although one of the latter's right in front of us."

Cassidy scanned the screen names. "What? Topper?"

"Yep."

⊠   ⊠   ⊠

A soft weight landed on Cassidy's foot, waking her up. A fang penetrated her big toe. The assailant was Starshine, whose latest trick was burrowing under the comforter and attacking her feet. Cassidy kicked the cat away but she returned a moment later to jump the other foot. Hauling herself upright, Cassidy chased her out and closed the door. Why was it she kept leaving the bedroom open at night? Oh yeah, she didn't want Starshine to feel rejected.

Three a.m., of course. The time Starshine liked to play. The time Cassidy could never get back to sleep.

She replayed the scene at Clancy's.

Mom always knows how to get to me.

Her Marina City comments wouldn't bother you so much if you weren't trying so hard to ignore it. The condo's a backdoor escape route, ready and waiting.

So what if he leaves? Kevin left and it didn't kill you.

Not quite.

She tried to imagine what it would be like if Zach did what Kevin had done. Like a permanent rainy day. Like living with chronic fatigue. Thinking of Zach brought a warm, melting sensation into her chest, but she avoided putting a name on the feeling. Naming it would make her even more scared. It was safer to keep herself vigilant by dwelling on his unemptied condo.

⌧   ⌧   ⌧

She awoke to the growly sound of Zach's new snowblower. His purchase of an expensive household item without prior discussion had not pleased her. *I did fine all these years without any damned mechanical shovels. What's he gonna do when he moves back to Marina City? Snow blow his balcony?*

At ten-thirty Cassidy headed toward the rear of the house to prepare for Ken Leman, the client who frequently failed to show. Although iffy about Leman's appointment-keeping ability, she did not want him to arrive and find the door locked. Ever since Cliff's letter, Zach had been making sure the door was bolted whenever he went out. Her jaw tightened in irritation at Zach's diligence at lock setting.

You know he's right.

Yeah, but what if some client finds the door bolted, assumes he's got the wrong time, and leaves? Or comes early and I have to run open it in my dustbowl grubbies? Or when I'm in my panties and bra and can't get downstairs for fifteen minutes?

All of the above are better than Cliff walking in on your shower. She pictured herself as Janet Leigh, a menacing shadow visible through the shower curtain. *Norman Bates, Cliff's real movie idol.*

Midway through the kitchen three furry bodies started doing kamikaze runs at her feet. Throwing himself beneath her burgundy pump, Hobbes sent up a piercing wail, then raced around the room divider as if she'd just proven herself a certified kitten killer. The moment she stopped moving Calvin planted his front paws on her pump to gaze beseechingly into her face and Sylvia tried to climb her pantyhosed leg.

"How thoughtless of me to assume that a couple of breakfasts plus snacks from Mom would hold you till lunch."

She picked up the two beggars and carried them over to the bowl in the corner, then scurried to put down food before they had time to get a clawhold on her legs. The calico dived in head first, the black kitten bumped his head against her shoe, and the orange kitten came squawling from the other side of the divider.

Starshine plodded into the kitchen, sides especially hollow as her body stretched in walking. Glancing at the crowd around the bowl, she leapt onto the counter, apparently too weary for competitive eating.

"You've got to stop nursing. Those little terrorists of yours are sucking you dry."

Mrowr. Starshine eased over on her side, the only comfortable position for chapped nipples and swollen mammaries.

Scratching behind the cat's ear, Cassidy elicited a low-pitched thrum. "I thought they'd be gone by now. But it looks like they're gonna be with us for a while, and it also looks like you're powerless over your urge to pump out milk. So I guess it's gotta be my job to save you from yourself."

She grabbed all three kittens and carried them off toward the stairs. "I now declare this day one of the enforced weaning program."

10

Cat Control

Ken Leman took a sip of tea, then placed the blue and white mug on the wicker table between the vinyl sofa and Cassidy's director's chair. "Cute kittens on the bulletin board. I'd take one myself if the building didn't have a no-pets clause." He placed his hands on his thighs and sent her a smile that lasted an instant too long.

He'd do small talk the whole hour if I let him. Almost like he's trying to schmooze me. This just normal avoidance or something else?

Crossing her leg, Cassidy smoothed her rose skirt over her knee. "Last session you were telling me about your difficulty making friends at work." She dredged up from her memory the fact that he was business manager for the Melrose Park Health Clinic.

He shook his head slightly. "I don't get it. They act like I don't exist." His gray-streaked, ginger hair was immaculately styled; his crisp cotton shirt and khaki pants had an expensive sheen to them that probably meant they'd been purchased at stores she never set foot in.

Looks like he's supposed to look, talks like he's supposed to talk, but something about him never quite seems real.

"I'm basically a nice guy. I take showers and change my underwear. Why would they want to be so unfriendly?"

"Unfriendly how?"

He ran a palm over the top of his sleek hair, managing not to create the slightest ruffle. "It's a subtle thing, really. Hard to describe. The docs're all pretty cliquish, which isn't surprising. But I would've expected the nurses to be more sociable. I go up to them all the time, ask about their families and boyfriends. Usually I get these short responses, then they make some excuse to disappear." The corners of his mouth curved into a small, secretive smile.

I've seen that smile before. Always a little unsettling. This time, downright incongruent. "Most people'd be hurt if they got that reaction, but when you talked about it just now, you started to smile. What do you suppose that smile's about?"

"I wasn't aware I was smiling." He immediately grew serious. Without the odd smile, his rugged face was quite attractive.

The smile could mean that he's putting something over on me. Or that he secretly wants to get rejected. Maybe the way Cliff wants women to reject him so he can blame them for his being gay.

Cassidy glanced through the window at a pearl-colored

sky, then moved her eyes back to Ken. "What about your social life? You've always been a little vague about relation-ships." *Been assuming he was straight but don't even know that for sure.*

He sat taller and took a sip of tea. "Dating's not a problem. I guess I look okay." The smile reappeared, slightly smug now. "I may not've met the right person yet, but I seem to get plenty of action."

"You mean, the only time you run into this negative response is at work?"

"I just don't seem to fit in at the clinic."

Cassidy wrapped her hands around her knee. "So what do you think the problem is?"

"Maybe the fact that I'm the only nonmedical person aside from the clerks." His light blue eyes appraised her coolly. "If you look at it that way, I suppose I really am an outsider, so it's not surprising they'd treat me like one."

Cassidy blinked. *Did I miss something? First he can't understand why they're so unfriendly, then it's obviously because he's nonmedical.*

Cocking her head quizzically, Cassidy asked, "Have you always been in health care?"

"Oh no. My degree's in business and I've had lots of different jobs. I've worked for an appliance distributor, a manufacturing company, a motor warehouse. God, that was a miserable situation. The old man was a tyrant."

"Did you have any problem making friends in those other places?" *He'll say it's just the docs.*

"Only since I moved into the medical field."

The hour moved slowly, but eventually her clock chimed twelve, announcing the end of the session.

"Well," Ken regarded her warmly, the way Starshine did when her stomach was full. "Very enlightening. Same time next week?"

He's gonna blow off the next session. "That'll be fine."

He handed her a check. "I'd like a receipt for that."

She placed the check on top of her calendar and made out his receipt.

As he stood to leave, Cassidy eyed him closely, trying to gauge his height. Only five-two herself, she judged most people to be either *tall* or *taller.*

Said he was forty-one. Probably around six foot. Well built, obviously works out. Could fit Jenny's description.

Ask him if he's ever shaved his head.

Right. And while you're at it, tell him you're Sergeant Friday in drag.

He raised his hand in a parting gesture. "Take care now."

She saw him to the door, then returned to the office to get her calendar and check. What was it she didn't like about the phrase "Take care?" *Overly solicitous.* She pictured a used car salesman, shoulders bowed, hands rubbing unctuously. *Unctuous, that's how he comes across.* Except for the secretive smile.

What exactly do you have here? Guy who appears to be straight but you can't tell for sure. Talks about work, avoids discussing relationships. Feels his co-workers reject him. Drops in and out of therapy.

Somebody you've been feeling not quite right about from the beginning.

So why'd it take you so long to tumble to Ken as a suspect? Kept looking for sex and dating issues. Gotta start thinking outside the box.

She picked up her calendar, glanced at the check on top, then gazed at the blanket of fresh show that lay across her backyard. Her subconscious tugged at her, pulling her eyes back to the check. Classic design, vaguely Grecian, blue shading into mauve. His signature in order. Nothing unusual.

Wait. There is something. Good old subconscious, never lets me down. His name was printed in the left-hand corner, but there was no address or telephone number beneath it.

She pulled his file from the metal cabinet in the corner and sat in her chair to go through it. *First session eleven months ago. Said he wanted to increase confidence, raise self-esteem.* She grimaced. *Now that's about as generic as you can get.* After the initial hour, he'd appeared for six weeks with an occasional missed appointment, then pulled a no-show and failed to return her calls. Fifteen weeks passed before he resumed therapy. He picked up as if nothing had happened, came regularly for five weeks, then disappeared again. After another long hiatus, he'd started on his third round, now into the fourth week. Each time he returned, she'd tried to pry an explanation out of him for the previous dropout but was never able to break through the man's evasiveness.

In the first session he had given her an Oakbrook address. Then, when he started up again four weeks ago, he'd left a return number on her machine that, if she remembered correctly, had a Chicago area code. She flipped back through her calendar and found the number jotted next to his appointment time. *If that's his home number, he's obviously moved. Which fits with the no-address checks. Guess there's nothing sinister about moving and not getting checks printed with a new address right away.* She felt mildly disappointed that her subconscious had led her astray, making more out of a nonaddress than was warranted.

But the lack of address and the Chicago number still bothered her. *Didn't say anything about moving. Along with a lot of other things he didn't say.* Deciding it was worth a call to reverse directory, she took his file up to the bedroom. She was headed through the dining room when a feline disturbance from above penetrated her consciousness. As she neared the stairs, the cat noises became more distinct: the kittens' high-pitched squeals, Starshine's throaty wail, the rattle of the nursery door.

Oh shit. The weaning program's gonna be tougher than I thought.

Upstairs, Starshine lay beside the door, one front leg shoved all the way under, both hind claws digging at the wood. Small black and orange paws poked under from the other side. She clamped her hands over her ears at the combined screech. Starshine's huge mournful eyes reminded her of the saucer-eyed children paintings. Noticing that the cat's claws had cut white grooves in the door's oak finish, Cassidy dragged her away from her post.

She oughtta be grateful they're out of her hair for a while. Fat chance.

Carrying Starshine into the bedroom, Cassidy closed the door and dropped her on the waterbed. The cat jumped down instantly and threw her body against the barricade.

"I know you're uncomfortable, but all you have to do is tough it out a couple of days. Mothers need to know when to let go."

Wham!

"It's like giving up cigarettes or peanut butter cups. You have to endure a little short-term pain."

Wham!

"Okay, okay." She opened the door and Starshine zipped across the hall. "If you're determined to batter immovable objects, I'd rather you do it out there."

Starshine stood on hind legs to rattle the nursery door-knob.

"Oh great. All I need is for you to learn how to open doors."

Doing her best to tune out the din from across the hall, Cassidy sat in her swivel chair, dialed reverse directory, and punched in Ken's Chicago number. A mechanical voice gave her his address.

Well, what do you know? East Roger's Park. She pictured garbage strewn yards, graffiti painted buildings. Rogers Park was a catchall for a wide array of ethnic groups—Vietnamese, Native Americans, Appalachians—with poverty the only common denominator. *That's why he left off the address. So nobody'd know where he hangs his Michigan Avenue clothes.*

Staring at her notes, her eyes fastened on his work number. He had to be telling the truth about his job, since that was the main thing he talked about. *Can't be sure of anything.*

She dialed and a woman's voice answered. "Melrose Park Health Clinic. How can I help you?"

"Ken Leman please."

"Sorry, there's no one here by that name."

What? Why'd anybody come to therapy and bitch about a job he doesn't have?

She took out a pad and drew a time line showing Ken's two absences from therapy. The first had extended nearly four months, the second a little over three, both long enough for Cliff to have completed his seduction routine. And if Ken were Cliff, it would make sense to assume that he'd quit therapy during periods when he reinvented himself as a movie star lookalike so that his therapist wouldn't question the radical changes in appearance.

If that were true, his lapses would correlate with two of his mission-to-infect relationships. Unfortunately he had started therapy less than a year ago, and the three women Cassidy had talked to so far went further back. But there were four others whose time frames she didn't know.

If any of those other women had a Cliff-encounter that fell exactly within the brackets of a therapy-absence, I'd be ready to do around-the-clock surveillance the minute he drops out again.

She needed all the time frames. Her ad would appear in the *Free Chicago* again today. Maybe another woman would call.

Or maybe you can get Cliff to tell you.

Cliff had responded to the ad. He wanted her to know as much as possible about his mission. *Why? Is he an insecure Don Juan, needs someone taking notes on his studliness? He setting himself up to get caught?*

She dialed the *Free Chicago* and dictated another ad:

CLIFF: GOOD TO GET YOUR LETTER. IF WE'RE GOING TO BE
PEN PALS, MAYBE YOU COULD PROVIDE SOME INSIDER TIPS.
WHY ME? WHAT ARE ALL THE DATES? WHAT NAME WOULD I
KNOW YOU UNDER?

Next she dug out the California number Gran had given
her for the home Mark shared with his psychiatrist-lover Bill.
She dialed and a curt male voice answered. "Dr. William
Mackey."

"I'm Cassidy McCabe, Mark's cousin. I was having lunch
with him the day he was killed." She ran her fingers up and
down the coin-filled wine bottle.

"Yes, I know. His grandmother told me about it, but I still
can't believe it's true. This is the last thing I ever imagined
would happen to me."

The image of Mark falling sideways flitted through her
mind. She closed her eyes briefly. "I'm still having trouble
with it myself."

"You have no idea how difficult this has been." His voice
caught. "I'm sorry, I shouldn't be going on like this. I don't
know what's the matter with me. Every time anybody calls,
I just start talking, can't seem to turn it off." He paused.
"Mark said you were a therapist, so maybe you'll understand.
I'd spend my whole day listening to other people, then come
home and Mark'd listen to me. Now I open my door and
nobody's there."

"You must feel so alone." She thought of the glow that
came over her when she saw Zach at the end of the day.

"Mark said he had something to tell me, but he never got it out. I thought you might know what it was."

"So many things got left unfinished. I just can't get over the suddenness of it."

A tad self-absorbed, but I guess he's entitled. Speaking slowly and distinctly, she asked, "Did he explain what he wanted to talk to me about?"

In a low voice, he said, "I don't know." A pause. "We were having some problems over his trip to Chicago."

"I realize this may be hard to talk about," she chose her words carefully, "and I wouldn't ask if I didn't really need to know, but could you tell me what the problems were?"

"I shouldn't be discussing this." He sighed. "But I guess there's no harm, and since you're a therapist I trust you won't be passing anything along." She heard him take a deep breath. "This was his first business trip, and it was making me damned uneasy. You see, he'd started e-mailing these guys from around the country, and one of them lives in Chicago. I was afraid the situation'd present more temptation than he could handle. So anyway, we were never able to talk about his trip calmly, which is why I don't know too much about his agenda with you."

"He told Gran he had an old friend here, and he also mentioned somebody he'd met online. You happen to know if he was meeting either of those guys?"

"He said he wasn't planning to see anybody outside of family." He paused. "But who knows?"

"He tell you the high school friend's name?"

"He probably mentioned it but I can't remember. I have

to admit, I was so agitated about the e-mail buddy, I wasn't paying attention to much else."

"I was really hoping his friend might be able to explain what Mark wanted to talk about. Maybe you could send me the names of everybody he knew in Chicago."

"Everything he had is in one of those damned computer files, and as much as I've racked my brain over it, I can't come up with the password."

Cassidy gritted her teeth in frustration. "Well, if you do break the code, I'd appreciate a call."

"Sorry I haven't been more help." He gave a ragged laugh. "Seems like I ought to be able to answer some of your questions, considering we've lived together for over a year."

What was it Mark said? He didn't get his share of air time? "The main thing I needed was to find out why Mark set up our lunch date. Please, can you remember anything at all?"

"Let me see . . ." A long pause. "I think he had a message to give you. A message from somebody else."

11

Rape and Bondage

Cassidy's right heel started drumming the floor. "Who from?"

"I wish I could tell you but . . ."

After they hung up, Cassidy propped her feet on the radiator and gazed at a layer of sparkling, cut-glass ice covering the window. *Guy's really torn up. But he showed minimal interest in Mark, outside guarding his sexual property rights. No wonder Mark got so involved with those e-mail buddies.*

She could see how listening to clients all day might leave a therapist feeling empty. She pictured herself rattling on to Zach until his eyes glazed over. *God, I hope I never turn into Bill.*

Talking to Mark's partner had stirred up her own sense

of loss, and she felt a sudden urge for chocolate to tamp those feelings down. As she left the bedroom, Starshine stopped banging and fastened betrayal-filled eyes on Cassidy as if to say, "Why are you doing this to me?"

She sighed and opened the nursery door. Starshine pushed her emaciated body through a melee of bobbing fur, rolled on her side, and cooed.

✉ ✉ ✉

She was standing in front of the sink unwrapping her second Reese's when Zach called. "I had my appointment with the sex addict attorney this morning and there's no obvious reason to rule him out. He's a little shorter, a lot thinner than me, but the descriptions you have are pretty inexact. I got a couple shots of him leaving the office, plus his plate number."

Leaning against the dining room doorjamb, she gazed out at snow- covered roofs on the other side of Briar. "I suppose he made you pay up front."

An edge came into Zach's voice. "Hundred and twenty before he'd even talk to me, and all I got in return was a lot of legal gobbledygook. Oh well, if we bust him it'll be worth it." A pause. "I'll pick up a pizza and be home by five so we can eat together before your evening sessions."

Never leaves before five. What is this sudden attack of homebodiness? He can't be that eager to show me the pictures.

You know what it is. Thinks you can't handle Mark's death. Patronizing you, assuming he has to be around for you to lean on, even though he wouldn't accept leaning privileges himself if his life depended on it. No right treating you like you're this little porcelain doll. You've gotten through plenty of crises on your own—father's leaving, Kevin's bailing, client's death, those Halloween shootings.

She wanted to be insulted and angry but then remembered the anxiety attacks. *Okay, so maybe I'm having a little problem with Halloween, but the rest's all taken care of.*

By five o'clock, when Zach came in with a flat box wafting tomato-oregano aromas, she'd decided she could endure being patronized as long as he brought pizza. He put the box on the dining room table and handed her two snapshots, each a close-up of Jake Sheffield's face, his overcoat collar pulled up around his ears. She studied the tightly curled, gray-tinged hair above a high forehead; the deep-set eyes partially hidden behind wire-rimmed glasses; the newly grown beard and mustache obscuring his mouth and jaw.

"I don't think so." She chewed her bottom lip. "But I can't be a hundred percent sure. Maybe he's started losing weight with the HIV and his face has thinned out. Maybe I knew him when he had a different hairstyle, no beard or glasses." She shook her head. "I never feel totally confident about faces."

Zach hung his coat in the room-divider closet. "The fact that you can't ID him doesn't mean much. Could be you do know him but he's changed his appearance. Could be he picked you 'cause you're his wife's therapist and the whole deal about being a client is pure fabrication."

Cassidy set plates and napkins on the table. "On cop shows the victim usually goes flipping through mug shots, then points to a photo and says 'He's the one.' If it were me, the best I'd ever be able to do would be 'I think maybe it might be him.' " She placed two cans of cola next to their plates.

Zach looked at the table. "Where's the beer?"

"You're asking me?"

He got out a Red Dog, then sat at the teak table.

Although the pizza fumes had her stomach gurgling, Cassidy held off long enough to tell Zach about her conversation with Bill and her plan to communicate with Cliff through a *Free Chicago* ad. Taking a large bite, she waited for Zach to admire her cleverness before relating the Ken saga.

"I've created a monster." Grinning, he snagged a pizza slice. "You're getting to be such a great little snoop, you won't need me anymore."

She ran her fingertips down the arm he had slung across the table. "Even if I don't need you for detective lessons, I can still think of a reason or two to keep you around."

Dropping a rim of crust on his plate, Zach took a second piece. "Getting back to the sex addict attorney, I have to tell you, if I were gonna pick somebody to be HIV positive, Jake Sheffield'd be at the top of my list. What an asshole."

"What'd he do to qualify as an asshole?" She ripped off a large piece with strings of mozzarella dripping from the sides.

"His attitude more than anything. I've been accused of arrogance myself on occasion, but I'm a piker compared to Sheffield. Seeing him makes me not want to be arrogant any more."

She swallowed a mouthful, lingered a moment over the

taste, then said, "Here you're rooting for Jake to be Cliff, and I've just come up with another candidate. A client, name of Ken." She pulled off another chunk of pizza, separating the cheese strings with her fingers, then went on to tell Zach about Ken's lapses from therapy, his Rogers Park address, and the job he didn't have. *Talking about clients is like having sex. It gets easier all the time.*

Zach cocked his head thoughtfully. "Much as I like Jake for our serial killer, I have to admit the contradictions in Ken's life are very intriguing. The downside is, all we've got on Ken is an address. Why don't you give it to me and I can nose around, see if his neighbors noticed anything."

"Is Cliff a serial killer? I don't think deliberately infecting someone with HIV meets the criteria for murder, although to my mind it's almost worse. Cliff may not have taken those women's lives—that is, if they can maintain the cock-tail regimen— but he's certainly doomed them to living out their days according to the clock and the pill." She rubbed her hands on her greasy napkin, now nearly shredded, then tossed it in a ball on the table. Reaching for the unused napkin beside Zach's plate, she finished wiping her fingers. *Something unnatural about a man who can keep his hands clean while eating pizza.*

She pressed curled fingers under her chin. "Legally, Cliff's guilty of rape plus the intentional spread of a fatal disease, which ought to get him put away for a long time. That is, if we ever identify him. And then, even if we do, we won't be able to turn him in unless we have a victim brave enough to go to the police."

Zach grabbed the last piece, saving her from herself.

"You having doubts about whether or not we'll get him locked up? This psycho is not gonna continue terrorizing women." His voice tightened. "You and I will find a way to nail the sonofabitch."

☒ ☒ ☒

The last client of the evening was Jenny. Struggling against her pizza-induced stupor, Cassidy led the large woman into her office. "Remember how confused I was about Cliff claiming to be a client? Well, it occurred to me that he might've disguised himself by shaving his head and that might be why I didn't know who he was."

Jenny's eyes darted around the room. Clasping her hands, she jiggled them in her lap.

Cassidy observed her client closely. "Is it upsetting to hear me talk about trying to identify Cliff?"

"Well, I guess I would like to see him caught. As long as I don't have to do anything."

"Whatever you say is confidential." Cassidy got a sick feeling in her stomach. "But I'm worried that he might hurt somebody else, which makes it important to find out who he is. Actually, I've thought of a person who might do what Cliff did. Now this man doesn't resemble your description, but if his head and face were shaved, he might. Anyway, I've got a couple of pictures and I'd like you to look at them."

"I suppose." Her voice was doubtful.

Feeling threatened. You're contaminating the therapy.

Gotta do it. Can't save Jenny, gotta save whoever's next in line.

"You don't have to." Cassidy held her eyes. "But it would help to know if this might be the guy."

Jenny pressed her fist into her cheek. "You're sure nobody will find out about me?"

The sick feeling returned. "I'm sure."

"Okay, you can show me the pictures."

Cassidy handed them over. Jenny glanced quickly, then away. Slowly she moved her gaze back to the photos, relief spreading across her broad face. "Didn't I say he was bald and looked like Jean Luc?"

Totally blocked what I said about using a disguise. "It's possible he wasn't really bald, just shaved his head. So, if you imagine this man with no hair, is there any resemblance at all?"

"Oh no, this couldn't be Cliff. Cliff didn't look anything like this."

Too certain. Not trying to visualize Cliff looking any different.

Don't push. She's scared to death of seeing his face, probably could've looked at Jean Luc himself and said no.

"Okay, Jenny, thanks for trying." She tucked the photos into her calendar. "So, where would you like to begin?"

Jenny's mouth twitched into a nervous smile. "There're a lot of things I was scared to tell you last time, but now I'd sort of like to get it over with. It's just, I'm not sure anybody'd want to hear it. I mean, it's not very . . . nice." She blurted out a raspy laugh.

"I want to hear it." *God, I wish I could make it all go away.*

"Remember, I told you at the beginning it was like a dream come true, but then it got bad? Well, the first time I slept with Cliff, he was as gentle and sweet as he could be. I was pretty scared, but he made it seem like what we were doing was the purest, most honest kind of love." Jenny raised the garish glasses to the top of her head and wiped a hand across her watery gray eyes. "During the whole time, even when he wasn't so nice anymore, I really thought he loved me."

"You needed to believe in him."

"I wanted that feeling to last so bad. But of course it didn't." She laughed bitterly. "And what I thought was love turned out to be something else."

Cassidy's throat tightened. "We all want to be loved."

A nerve-jarring shriek came from the kitchen. Jenny's shoulders jumped.

Cassidy grimaced. "One of the kittens. Hobbes, actually. I know it sounds like he's being killed, but he just does it for attention."

"Oh." Jenny gave her head a little shake. "I saw those kittens on your bulletin board. Really sweet." She wrapped a curl around her finger. "I was gonna tell you about Cliff changing, how it started with just small things at first. I hardly even noticed." Jenny sighed heavily. "But it kept getting worse until he wasn't the same anymore at all."

"How did he change?"

"In the early days, he was happy with everything I did. But then I started making mistakes, and he let me know about it." She began wringing her hands in her lap. "He'd get mad because I wasn't home when he called, or because I couldn't meet him right away, or because I didn't say what he wanted. I kept thinking, if I just tried harder I'd get it right." Ducking her head, her eyes skimmed Cassidy's face. "Now I realize he was just setting it up so I'd do whatever he said." She choked out a brittle laugh. "I can't believe how stupid I was."

"Are you blaming yourself for what he did to you?"

"I always feel like everything's my fault. Well . . . I'm getting to the hard part again." Lowering her head, she took a moment to prepare, then raised her eyes and looked straight at Cassidy. "He told me he'd always had this fantasy of tying a woman up and raping her. He swore he'd never do anything to really hurt me." She shook her head disbelievingly. "And I fell for it. Geez, what a dummy."

"You were in love with him."

She laughed. "And look where it got me." She crossed one leg over the other. Her tennis shoe had a loose thread on top where the stitching had come out. "What he did was— Well, he had me lay spread-eagle across the bed, then wrapped my ankles and wrists with loose rope and pretended to rape me. It felt really weird, but he kept saying it was just a role play, there wasn't any harm to it. When he first asked, he acted like he was afraid I'd reject him. Well, I know what it's like to get rejected, and I didn't want to hurt him, so I agreed."

Cassidy's scalp tingled. "Just a role play."

"He kept gradually making it more true to life, and then, on the last night, he brought some boxes with him." Dropping her head, she wrapped her arms beneath her billowing chest and hugged herself tightly. When she looked up, her face was ashen. "He told me I had to lie on my stomach. I didn't want to, but he just kept at me, and finally I did. Then he got out the ropes, and this time he tied me for real." She started shaking. "Oh God, I'm so ashamed. I don't think I can go on."

"You don't have to tell me anything you don't want to." Cassidy's voice came out dry and scratchy.

Jenny closed her eyes behind the glasses, then opened them slowly. "I've gotta get it out. Anyway, I couldn't see what he was doing, but he said he was setting up a video camera to record everything. And then he . . . did something that really hurt a lot. I started to scream but he grabbed my pantyhose and stuffed it in my mouth. I could hardly breathe, and the pain—I thought I was gonna die. But I didn't get off so easy." She laughed harshly.

"Oh God, Jenny, I can't believe what he put you through."

"Afterward he took the pantyhose out of my mouth and put them somewhere. I never saw them again so maybe he took them with him, I don't know. Then he stood there and talked. Something about his mission. After that, he looked me in the eye and said he had AIDS. I was so scared from being raped that the AIDS part didn't even register. The next thing he did was pull out this big syringe. He said he was gonna inject me with his blood and that if I was a different type I'd probably get pretty sick afterward, and he sure was right about that. I watched him put the needle in his arm, fill it with blood, then—" Her hand flew to her mouth. She gagged hoarsely and ran into the bathroom next to Cassidy's office.

⊠   ⊠   ⊠

After Jenny recovered from her nausea and was calm enough to leave, Cassidy went back into her office. She turned off the ceiling light and stared at the mauve-blue sky, giving herself time to return to her own reality.

She gradually eased Jenny's story into a box in the back of her mind, then went upstairs. Zach was seated at the green formica table in his office, Mark's notebook open in front of him, Starshine stretched out beside it.

Coming up behind him, Cassidy looped her arms around his neck. "How's it going?"

The calico attempted to walk across the keyboard but he pushed her away. "Any luck with the pictures?"

As she slipped into the chair beside his, the kittens darted through the doorway and attacked her feet. "She took a quick peek and said no. She's very resistant to the whole idea of catching him. Afraid she might get pulled into it. Or, at the very least, hear about it on the news and have to relive it. I doubt she'd recognize any picture unless we came up with an exact replica of the way he looked before."

Zach put his hand on her knee.

"Cliff persuaded Jenny to act out his bondage-and-rape fantasy. Then, on the last night, he did it for real."

His steady gaze held hers. "Guess that's not surprising, given what we know about him."

Cassidy pressed an outspread hand against her forehead. "Every day that goes by increases the odds of his assaulting another woman before we catch up with him. I hate thinking somebody I know may be doing this and I can't stop it."

Zach reached over to massage the cramped muscles at the back of her neck.

She said, "I've thought up one possibility for checking on Ken. He talks about the Melrose Park clinic in such detail,

I think he has some history there. Anyway, to follow up on a long shot, I'm going to waste some time at the clinic tomorrow looking for somebody to tell me why Ken doesn't work there anymore."

"Wasting time." He frowned and clicked off the monitor. "That's the biggest part of any investigation." Closing the notebook, he led the way into the bedroom, Cassidy, Starshine and the kittens following behind. As Cassidy took her place on the bed, the kittens climbed the comforter to join her.

Zach sat at her desk to go through the mail. He had started sneaking off with the bills and paying them before she could get to it, which caused her considerable frustration. He said, "Your friend Maggie called to say she's coming by tomorrow to pick up one of our housewreckers for her sister."

Calvin curled into Cassidy's lap, purring rambunctiously. Sylvia stalked Hobbes, who was pouncing on wrinkles in the comforter. Starshine watched from atop the television. Stroking the black kitten, Cassidy said, "I wonder which one? And how Starshine'll take it?"

Zach turned to send her a pointed look.

Sharp claws dug into her arm. Sylvia had sidled up from behind and pounced on her hand, which was foolishly moving. The small calico wrapped herself around Cassidy's wrist, front claws hooking in, back claws digging grooves in her flesh. Cassidy removed the kitten, then grabbed a handful of tissue from the nightstand to sop up the blood. She moved the wastebasket up close to the bed to toss in used tissue as blood continued oozing through the scratch marks.

Calvin stalked away from her lap and threw himself on
Hobbes, who let out a penetrating howl. Starshine sat up tall
on the television, then dove onto the waterbed, separated the
combatants, and sniffed the kittens anxiously. Satisfied that
both were still breathing, she bounced back up to the TV.

Zach swiveled the desk chair to face her. "After meeting
that attorney today, there's something I wanted to ask. You
said his wife—what's her name? Mira?—knows about his
screwing around, which means she's aware of the risk to
herself. Now that I've seen the guy, I can't understand why
she puts up with it. It's not like he's a charmer or anything.
So what's the matter with her?"

Cassidy pictured her slender, dark-haired client twisting
a jet-beaded necklace around her fingers and saying, "I
know it was stupid." Her eyes flitted to the opposite wall
where an arrangement of family photos hung. One was of
her ex-husband Kevin looking gorgeous as he stood on the
bow of a boat, a picture she'd never been able to part with.
*How'd you like it if one of Zach's old girlfriends was staring
at you from the wall? Definitely should've thrown it away
before he moved in.*

She said, "What's the matter with Mira? I expect there
are people who'd ask the same about me. Why did I stay
with a philandering, con-artist husband all those years?"

"So what's the answer?"

"Women do that kind of thing." She sighed. "Not all, but
some. Some men do it too."

Zach watched her, his gaze relentless, the expression that
came over him whenever he was trying to make sense out
of something he found incomprehensible.

"Okay," she jerked her head in a small nod. "I think I can explain about Mira. Just don't ask about me."

"So why does she stay with the asshole?"

"Because he's arrogant. Jake acts superior, and Mira buys into it. She considers him a prize, although objectively speaking, he's not only not a prize, he's downright dangerous. But Mira can't get past her first impression of Jake as a blue-ribbon kind of guy. The problem is, she grew up with a Cinderella fantasy, which a lot of women have. If she could only get some prince to see her as his princess, she'd finally feel lovable. It isn't Jake she's hooked on, it's the fantasy. She can't give up the hope that someday she'll say the magic words, Jake'll realize she really is princess material, he'll be transformed by the power of her love—meaning he'll quit acting out—and they'll live happily ever after."

Zach shot her a skeptical look. "That's crazy."

Hobbes sat alone in the middle of the bed, the other two having jumped to the floor. He gazed up at his mother on the TV set, stretched his neck, and emitted another screech. Snapping alert, Starshine once again leapt down to the waterbed. After conducting a cursory sniff, she grabbed Hobbes' scruff, the kitten curling to create minimum drag, hauled her loud-mouthed son to the side of the bed, leaned forward, and dropped him into the wastebasket.

Cassidy and Zach let go with a burst of laughter. She said, "What every mother'd sometimes like to do with an aggravating kid."

Hobbes knocked the basket over and skulked away, head and tail down, clearly embarrassed.

Cassidy wiped her eyes. "On a more serious note, after

realizing what a great candidate Ken made, I started think-ing—if I were to list every approximately forty, approxi-mately six-foot male I've ever known, we'd have more suspects than we could handle."

"I think our best bet is to go with your intuition. Limit ourselves to the guys who set alarm bells ringing."

Cassidy stared into space for a moment, then sighed and moved her eyes back to Zach. "I get this nagging feeling there's one more. Somebody who's a major bell-ringer. But I can't put my finger on it."

12

The Clinic

Zach crossed to stand at the foot of the bed, the photo arrangement on the wall behind him. Resting his rear on the dresser, he folded his arms across his chest. "How about your philandering ex?"

"Huh?" Her eyes strayed to Kevin's picture just above Zach's right shoulder.

The lines running downward from Zach's hawkish nose deepened. "Doesn't Kevin have all the makings of a good psychopath? I've been wondering if you'd get around to bringing him up, but from our discussion tonight, I get the impression you're not about to. Why not Kevin? From what you say, he's got years of bed-hopping under his belt and he's slicker than shit."

"Because Kevin would not rape women and infect them with HIV, that's why not."

Zach's level eyes appraised her. "I'm going down for a drink. You want one?"

"Well, okay." As he left the bedroom, her gaze slipped back to the photo. *Zach's never met Kevin, never even mentioned the picture. Maybe he doesn't know who the guy on the boat is. Maybe he hasn't noticed.*

There isn't much Zach doesn't notice. I gotta get rid of that picture.

✉ ✉ ✉

The white globe above the waterbed was unlit but a gloomy light pervaded the room. Cassidy lay spreadeagled on the bed, her wrists and ankles tied. She could sense her attacker sitting in the desk chair but did not turn to look. Anxiety jangled along her neural pathways, small explosions sputtering at the ends.

Starshine plunged down from the TV, setting off a sharp cascade of waves that rose and fell beneath Cassidy's flattened body. A telepathic message emanated from the cat's large green eyes: "He's here. He has a newspaper in his lap but he's not reading it."

A worried look crossed the triangular feline face. Her eyes communicated: "I have to stop him."

The calico lunged, her sinuous body enlarging from house cat to tiger as she flew across the room. Hitting the desk, she hovered over the faceless man who looked up in terror from his chair. The cat leaned forward, closed her jaws over the man's neck, and dragged him from the room.

Cassidy opened her eyes and checked the clock on the

bureau. Nine a.m. Zach usually brought coffee when he arose at seven but this morning he'd deliberately let her sleep in.

Still coddling me, still thinking I'm whacked out over Mark. Maybe he wants to be Tarzan, trying to make me be Jane.

Nah, not our Mr. Noncommittal. He's definitely not the type to look for a clinging-vine Jane. Besides, if it's dependency he wants, he'd never've picked me.

She rolled out and went downstairs for coffee, stepping carefully to avoid the kittens who raced beneath her feet as fearlessly as drunken adolescents playing chicken with two tons of metal.

Standing in front of the sink, she tried to concentrate but the continuing edginess from her dream jumbled her head.

Forget coffee. You're wired enough already.

It's morning. I can't not have coffee.

She started the machine, went into her office, and closed the door, ignoring the kittens' indignant squeals. As she sank into her director's chair, a memory began to take shape.

A man sitting on the sofa opposite her, his hair dark brown, longish, swept up into a small pompadour. The square face displayed hooded eyes, a broad nose, and thin-lipped mouth. *Donovan, that's the name. Henry Donovan.* He leaned back, knees apart, a newspaper spread across his lap, his right arm hidden beneath the paper.

The final minutes of her last session with Donovan came back.

"I didn't want this divorce in the beginning, you see, but now that it's over, I realize it's the best thing that could've

happened." He slid his left hand inside his armpit and
scratched through his limp dress shirt. "All those years I
wasted with Beth. God, what a cold fish. Sex with her was
about as exciting as checkers. Now I'm seeing how it is."
His heavily lidded eyes regarded her slyly. "There are chicks
out there who appreciate a good time."

Cassidy's stomach churned, the uneasiness that always
came over her in sessions with Donovan. Trying to nudge
him in a different direction, she asked, "What else was
wrong with your marriage?"

"Mostly it was sex. You see, the amazing thing is, all
those stories I used to hear really are true. Here I am at
thirty-five having an easier time getting babes into the sack
than I ever did ten years ago, last time I was single."

"What's the payoff in changing partners all the time?"
Although she tried not to look at his lap, her eyes slipped
downward and fastened on the newspaper covering his right
hand and crotch. *What's he up to, anyway?* Her imagination
kept providing an answer she didn't like. *He can't really be
doing what I think he is, can he?*

"What's the payoff?" His voice was incredulous. "That's
pretty obvious, isn't it?"

She felt her face heat up. "What I meant was, why do you
want to sleep with all these different women instead of
developing a relationship?"

"A man gets out of jail, why would he want to go back
in?"

"What is it about a relationship that seems like jail?"

His thin lips widened in a smile that made her stomach
even more jittery. "You see, it's like this. All that time I was

married I felt half dead, see? Now, as long as I keep moving, I can have it whenever I want, as much as I want, and it's never dull. It's like snorting coke every night without the crash or the addiction."

She was not able to follow his words. Her attention kept straying to the newspaper.

This is simple countertransference. You're just reacting to the changing-partners routine 'cause it reminds you of Kevin.

Every time I move him away from sex, he rubberbands right back. He's getting off on this sleaze.

"Let me tell you 'bout this girl I met last night. Maybe then you'll understand why the freedom's so important." Donovan looked away, shifted his body slightly, then brought his gaze back to her face. "I meet this chick at a bar, see, and she's really hot, so we have a few drinks, then she asks me up to her place. And once we're in the elevator, she backs me up against the wall and sticks her hand inside my pants." His voice took on a slow, dreamy cadence. "Well, let me tell you, my cock got so stiff, I thought it was gonna break off."

Cassidy stared at the newspaper, which seemed to be moving.

You cannot let this go on.

What if he's not doing anything?

You have to get him out of here.

Clearing her throat, she said in a hoarse voice, "Henry, I'm sorry, but I can't continue this session."

"What?" He looked genuinely puzzled.

"I get the sense that your real agenda here is to talk about sex, not do therapy."

Deep lines furrowed his forehead. "If all I wanted to do was talk dirty, I'd call a friggin' nine-hundred number."

"I suggest you try a male therapist. I can give you a referral if you like."

Folding the paper beneath his arm, he got to his feet. Her gaze riveted on his crotch. His wool pants fit smoothly across his abdomen with no sign of a bulge. *Oh God, I was wrong. Doesn't matter, you still can't work with him.*

He glared from a distance of three feet. "What're you doing? Throwing me out? You take my money for six sessions and now you wanna dump me? Isn't there some kind of law you can't just blow clients off like that?"

She clamped her mouth to stop abject words of apology from pouring out. A slight tremor ran down her arms. Struggling to regain control, she said, "I would like you to leave now. I'll send you a full refund."

He spent nearly a minute trying to stare her down, eyes glittering with malice. When she refused to discuss it further, he finally turned and slammed his way out.

⊠　⊠　⊠

So "Henry Donovan" was the name she'd searched for the night before. She pulled his file and took it up to her bedroom. He had come to see her more than three years ago, during her early days as a therapist when she was too inexperienced to know how to handle a player like Donovan. He would be thirty-eight now, the right age, and if she remembered correctly, he also fit the general description.

And he certainly qualified as a man whose sexual behavior put him at risk for HIV.

She read the notes in his file. In the first session he'd come directly from court after his divorce. He'd been tearful at the time, and his request for help seemed genuine. But during the weeks that followed, his sexual swaggering had increasingly dominated the sessions.

The file contained two phone numbers, one for his home, the other for his place of employment, Randolph Bearing. The first connected her to a Chinese restaurant. The second was answered by a Randolph receptionist who told her Donovan had left the firm about two years ago.

With some trepidation, she laid the file on top of her cluttered desk. She sometimes imagined that just beneath the loose-paper surface a secret layer of quicksand existed whose function it was to suck up important documents and make sure they were never seen again.

She stood beside the window, arms wrapped around her midsection, still jittery. Getting a hook into Donovan's name and reeling it in from her subconscious had not dissipated her nervousness. *What's eating you, anyway?*

She padded across the hall and into the nursery. Sylvia pounced out from behind the guitar case and raced up to greet her. Snuggling the kitten against her neck, Cassidy moved to the east window and gazed down at the garage at the far end of her deep lot. She pictured herself trudging out to the squat building, hauling up the left-hand door, sliding into her Toyota. The staticky buzz in her head amped higher.

So that's what this is all about. The fact that I'm planning to drive to the Melrose Park clinic.

She dumped Sylvia on the floor and returned to her bedroom.

No twinges when I drive to Dominick's or Erik's. But soon as I plan a longer expedition, it all starts up again. Looks like I'm scheduled for an anxiety attack anytime I drive outside Oak Park.

Hugging herself, she paced tight circles within the five-foot square of open space between her desk and bed. *Can't not drive. Have to get over this.* She was a therapist. She had treated clients with panic attacks. She should know what to do.

The standard treatment for phobias, which was really what she had here—a driving phobia—was desensitization. That meant gradually exposing herself to the stimulus that precipitated the attack. What she had to do was start driving short distances and build up from there. Today, she would have to grit her teeth and not let the panic stop her. If she didn't, she would end up housebound and hopeless, a therapist trapped by her own anxiety.

Cassidy took a deep breath, aware of feeling slightly calmer now that the decision was made. Jotting down the clinic's address, she headed toward the back door and opened it. A thin layer of footprint-trampled snow covered the stoop, which had been bare the night before. She stood just outside the storm door staring at the stoop and yard. *Too many prints. Should be only Zach's.* Too many on the steps and on the walk between the door and gate. And an extra set, coming and going, curving around the southeast corner of the house and heading into the nine-foot corridor between her place and her neighbor's.

She locked the door and followed the prints into the space between the two houses. They took her to the side door, an entrance directly into the basement. Somebody—Cliff—had first tried the back door, found it locked, next tried the side door, also locked, then turned around and retreated out the gate.

Can't think about it now. Just get in the car and go.

Hurrying to the garage, she eased behind the wheel and backed onto Briar. *So far, so good. Just a short drive to Melrose Park.* Her nerves were buzzing but not to the point of overload. Her desensitization program was underway.

She chugged west to Ridgeland, south to Lake, then west again toward the Melrose Park Health Clinic. Lake Street was the dividing line between north and south Oak Park, and, to a lesser extent, between mansions and bungalows. Zach's lineage and their ilk, the Dear Old Oak Parkers that Helen so envied and resented, lived in national-register homes and mansions in the northwest section of the village.

Crossing Forest Avenue, she entered the quarter-mile strip known as downtown Oak Park, primarily distinguished by empty stores, *For Sale* signs, and clogged traffic. The village had been wrestling for nearly three decades with the revitalization question: How to get people to shop in a commercial area with inconvenient parking and no major stores. So far the one thing Oak Park had confirmed was that the answer lay neither in putting in a mall nor taking one out.

Cassidy stopped behind a line of cars at Harlem Avenue, the border between Oak Park and River Forest, the village's richer, more exclusive western neighbor. As she waited to cross the line and venture outside safe territory, her chest tightened, her heart thumped faster.

Beyond Harlem the traffic thinned out. She pressed the pedal and the car shot forward, her hands adhering tightly to the wheel. Icy worms twitched in her stomach, crept up her spine. Jerking the wheel too sharply, she lunged into the right lane, lightened her foot, and crawled forward. The sky was pale blue, the light sparkling and clear. There was nothing in either the time or place to remind her of a lonely road at night. She focused on taking long, slow breaths and kept driving.

⊠   ⊠   ⊠

Cassidy took a vinyl-cushioned chair that stood against the back wall of the clinic waiting room. A counter in front, behind which people in white uniforms moved briskly, separated patients from staff. She studied the nurses. Nurses were more accessible than doctors, and in her experience, generally pleasant and helpful. She liked nurses. Her gaze bounced from one person to another, then settled on a gray-haired woman with an approachable face who looked to be in her fifties.

Cassidy waited as her designated nurse moved into view behind the counter, called a patient, then exited through the side door. Ten minutes later the woman reappeared, pulled a number of files, and laid them out along the countertop.

Cassidy glided up to the counter. "Could I have a minute of your time? There's something personal I'd like to talk to you about."

Tired blue eyes examined Cassidy through wire-rimmed glasses. The nurse, whose pin said GAIL SHULTY, wrinkled her brow. "Do I know you? If you're trying to sell something, you'll have to talk to the manager."

"What I'm trying to do is locate an ex who ran out on his child support."

The woman's eyes softened. "What makes you think I can help? I'm not aiding or abetting any runaway exes."

"He used to be business manager here. A few months back, when the checks stopped coming, I started trying to track him down. I discovered he'd bailed out of his apartment and disappeared. Name's Ken Leman. When I called the clinic, your receptionist said she'd never heard of him."

A startled look crossed the woman's face, followed by suspicion. "Hey, wait a minute. Leman didn't have any wife. He was single, lived alone, never married. I remember him telling me that."

Cassidy shrugged. "He had a wife twelve years ago. He hung around just long enough to get me pregnant three times in three years, then decided he couldn't handle the responsibility." *Don't lay it on too thick. She could be a friend.*

Gail studied her face as if scanning her brain for truthful ness. Cassidy devoutly hoped that neither her eyes would shift nor her brow break into a sweat. Finally the nurse said, "Well . . . maybe. But it really doesn't matter whether you're his ex or not, 'cause either way, I can't tell you where he is. Nobody here knows anything."

Putting a droop into her neck and a slump into her shoulders, Cassidy gripped the counter. "I guess it was too much to hope for. But could you at least tell me when he left and why?"

Gail glanced around to make sure no one was listening.
"We're not supposed to talk about it."

Cassidy widened her eyes, covering excitement with
surprise. "Why not?"

13

Gran Muffin

"I just told you, I can't talk about it."

Cassidy slumped into an attitude of even greater defeat. Gail's face knotted in a scowl. "You sure you're his ex?"

"Of course I'm sure."

"Well . . . if all you're after is child support, I guess it won't hurt. It's not like there's any big scoop or anything. All I can tell you is, they fired him just about a year ago and nobody knows why. One day this guy from personnel just walks into Leman's office, closes the door, and an hour later he's gone. Not that people haven't been canned around here before. The main difference with Leman was, nobody ever did find out what happened. The next day we got a memo telling us to keep our mouths shut. But there weren't any leaks in personnel so we didn't have anything to talk about anyway."

"There must've been rumors."

Gail shrugged. "Nothing that made any sense."

Ask if he shaved his head, had a ponytail or a flattop. Her mind went blank. She could not think of a single excuse for posing the question. Gail stacked the folders and turned away. Cassidy reached out quickly and touched her wrist. "Thanks so much."

⊠ ⊠ ⊠

On the drive back to Oak Park, her anxiety level rose but did not go over the top. As she crossed Harlem Avenue and entered the village, relief swept over her. Almost home. The buzzing in her brain quieted.

Shaking her head, she began to think about Jenny, the first HIV sufferer she had treated. *Don't know what I'm doing here. Maybe she needs more than standard-issue, support-when-shit-happens therapy.*

Cassidy might not know but she had a good idea where to get the information. Among Oak Park's many groups was an agency called Community Response, an organization serving HIV victims. *Anything in Oak Park we don't have a group for? Probably nobody out picketing to save the Dutch Elm Disease beetles.*

Turning south on Ridgeland, she drove to the agency's Harrison Street office. Half an hour later she emerged with literature regarding available services and some suggestions for treatment provided by a fellow social worker.

⊠ ⊠ ⊠

"I'm surprised your sister wanted you to pick out the kitten." Cassidy spoke to Maggie, who sat beside her on the nursery floor, a cardboard box on her far side. Maggie, also an Oak Park therapist, was Cassidy's longtime best friend.

"She lives in the city and doesn't have a car. Since I was driving down to see her anyway, it makes it easier."

Starshine hunkered between the two women, her eyes fixed on Maggie's every move, tail and ears on red alert. If this stranger were to lift even one threatening finger toward her babes, Mom was ready to take her out.

The kittens were not so wary. Sylvia was chewing her mother's ear. Hobbes raced howling away from Calvin, who pursued his brother from one corner to the other, the two seeming more like low-flying bats than feline quadripods.

Cassidy's brow furrowed. "Did you say your sister already has a cat?"

"She's got this obese, long-haired female name of Jezebel. She wouldn't admit it, but I suspect her main reason for wanting a kitten is to give Big Mama a companion. Sort of a pet for the cat." Maggie was slender and delicate, her oval face framed in soft curls, her voice husky.

"You think she might ignore the kitten?"

"Oh, she'll be all right. So, tell me about their personalities."

Cassidy dragged Sylvia away from Starshine's ear and held her in her palm. "This is the only girl, and she's the real butt-kicker in the crowd. Calico's are always female, you know." She moved Sylvia out to the middle of the room, hoping she would pick on her brothers and give Mom a break. The small calico immediately pounced on Calvin, and

Hobbes wandered over to sniff Maggie's shoe. "This one," Cassidy pointed to Hobbes, "is affectionately known as 'The Mouth,' and the black kitten over there is our cuddler."

Sylvia romped up to attack Hobbes but got distracted and climbed into Maggie's lap instead. Starshine rose instantly to sniff her tiny lookalike.

Maggie scratched behind Sylvia's ears. "Which one's your favorite?"

"Calvin's irresistible when he snuggles in my lap. And I love Sylvia's spirit—she'd take on anybody. And then sometimes I feel like poor Hobbes needs me the most because he has almost no redeeming virtues."

"If they're all your favorite, I guess it doesn't matter which one I take. Anyway, this one picked me, so I guess the decision's made." She held Sylvia aloft and Starshine's ears twitched. "Besides, since I always partner up with women, two females together is what seems right to me."

"You're gonna take Sylvia?" A heaviness lumped in Cassidy's stomach.

Maggie placed the kitten on her shoulder. "So, what's it like living with Zach? Seems like hardly any time at all since you dumped him." Sylvia lashed at the tantalizing silver earring dangling from Maggie's ear.

"Not bad." Cassidy caught the inner lining of her lip between her teeth. "He's mostly housebroken, frequently cleans the whiskers out of the sink, insists on paying more than his share. Actually," she took a deep breath, "I'd have to say I'm fairly hooked."

"C'mon, fess up. Everybody fights about something."

"Oh, well, we quibble all the time. But so far the only real problem is, he keeps trying to take care of me. He canceled my clients after my cousin got shot, then came home early a couple of days to watch over me. It makes me feel weak or something. Like he thinks I can't manage on my own. And the worst of it is, he never lets me do anything in return."

The kitten slid down the front of Maggie's sweater, claws out and snagging. Maggie said, "It's so hard to keep things in balance. I have a tendency to overfunction with Susie, and that pisses her off too."

Yeah, but there's some part of you that likes it when Zach takes over. Wants him to do it more.

Gotta put out a contract on that part.

Maggie grasped Sylvia and dropped her into the box. The kitten bleated pathetic little cries and tried to scale the sides. Starshine jumped into the box, grabbed her offspring by the scruff, and prepared to make a freedom run. Watching Starshine's futile effort, Cassidy felt as if she were in a slow-motion elevator dropping from the top floor to the basement.

Maggie gently removed Starshine, then stood and held the box in her arms so Mom, who circled anxiously below, couldn't attempt any further rescue missions. Cassidy rose also and the two friends faced each other over the top of the kitten carrier.

Maggie juggled the box, freeing a hand to lay on Cassidy's arm. "Losses are always hard. A person, pet, anything."

Following her friend, Cassidy traipsed downstairs and onto the frigid porch, closing the door quickly to keep

Starshine from pursuing her kitten out to the car and down the street. The daylight was almost gone, the temperature close to zero. Once Maggie was in her car, Cassidy scooted back inside. She leaned against the heavy front door and rubbed her arms.

Enormous black eyes stared accusingly.

"I thought you were dying to be rid of them. Pissed because they weren't gone sooner."

Cassidy sank down on the bottom step of the staircase. Starshine, evidently in a forgiving mood, hopped up to sit beside her. Calvin and Hobbes gathered at her feet to untie her laces. *Amazing how two rambunctious, overgrown kittens can seem like such an insufficient number.*

Starshine bounced off the step and trotted toward the kitchen, tail jauntily erect, the mourning period for her lost kitten apparently over. Calvin and Hobbes, highly sensitized to any kitchen-directed movement, zipped ahead. Cassidy, a well-trained cat owner, trailed behind.

Arriving at the McCabe cat-food emporium, Cassidy found Starshine sitting erect on the countertop, Hobbes curled inside the cats' messy bowl, and Calvin stalking a clump of cat fur that drifted across the floor. Cassidy removed the orange kitten from the bowl, wiped globs of food off his fur, then opened a new can.

Standing at the sink to wash out the can for recycling, she stared into rosy-hued darkness, the soft half-light that kept the city aglow from dusk to dawn. *Only five-thirty. I hate the way night comes on so early in winter.* There was something about daylight disappearing before evening began that gave her an eerie feeling, as if she were watching from another dimension as events unfolded without her.

Coming back from her alternative universe, she looked inside the kitchen window a few yards south of hers, the house belonging to Dorothy and Paul Stein and the half dozen children they had adopted from around the world. The Stein kitchen was warm with yellow light, alive with a melee of bodies in assorted sizes and colors. It looked far more appealing than her own house, which felt cold and empty despite the three furry companions that followed her around.

Dorothy Stein's head and shoulders appeared inside the frame as she moved to separate two teenage girls, one of whom had a stranglehold on the other. Gazing at Dorothy's curly head, it occurred to her that her neighbor's window provided a clear view of her own stoop. *Maybe Dorothy saw who made all those footprints this morning.*

Crime was one of Oak Park's biggest problems, and village residents had learned to be keenly aware of anyone who looked like he didn't belong. The Steins were used to clients coming in her rear entrance, but clients didn't try the door, then slink between the houses.

Cassidy tossed the cat food can into the drainer and went upstairs to sit at her desk and dial her neighbor's number.

⊠ ⊠ ⊠

"You happen to see anybody try the back door, then go around to the side door early this morning?"

"There was somebody—a man. He rattled the doorknob a few times, then I got distracted and didn't see what came next. I just assumed he was a client. What was it? Attempted break-in?"

"I'm not sure. You notice what he looked like?"

"He was all bundled up. A honky like us."

"Well, thanks—"

"Now don't try to get away so fast. You've got something going on again, haven't you? I'm beginning to think you're a dangerous person to live next to."

Calvin appeared suddenly and began climbing the leg of her jeans. "If I run into any more evildoers, I'll make sure to warn them not to step over the line onto your property 'cause then they'd be liable for trespass. Oh, and by the way, speaking of crossing the line, I've got two kittens over here who trespass into everything they can get at. Wouldn't you like to do another adoption? Sweet, cuddly kitten this time?"

Dorothy laughed. "Sorry, but we already have our quota of fur and feathers. Two birds, five goldfish, and three hamsters. I'm sure your kittens would love to cuddle with some of the above, but my kids've already had their share of pet funerals."

As she hung up, Cassidy noticed that the answering machine's red light was blinking. Picking up a pen, she punched PLAY.

Gran's voice crackled from the speaker. "Secret agent 000 reporting in. I got all that stuff Zach wanted." She reeled off Mark's address, birthdate, and social security number. "Okay, now here's the good stuff, everything I could get hold of 'bout his hobbies and sexual perversities."

Cassidy tapped her pen against the pad.

"Anyway, he had his own astrologer and psychic. Guess everybody out in California goes in for that junk, but personally, I think they oughtta stick to therapists and leave the rest alone. Now here's the bedroom stuff. He had a thing for bodybuilders, and he liked 'em smooth. He loved putting together outrageous costumes and dressing up, and he also liked nude entertainment, whatever that means. Guess it's just the opposite of dressing up.

"Aren't you just dying to hear how I found all this out? I called his boyfriend and let him run up my phone bill. Now and then I'd throw in a question, and eventually he blabbed everything. So, aren't you glad you let me be your assistant?"

Know the psychiatrist was looking for an ear to bend, but still amazing how much she dug out of him. Boy, would she make one humdinger of a therapist.

Cassidy turned to leave, then remembered she had promised herself to get rid of Kevin's picture. She took it down from its place among her family photos: her mother, grandmother, even one of the father who had left when she was five. In the picture Kevin was tall and gorgeous, arms loose, shoulders broad, head high.

Although she couldn't explain to Zach why she still felt a tiny thread of attachment to her unfaithful, insolvent, Irish-tongued ex, she knew it had something to do with his irrepressible love of life. Being with him had heightened her own sense of aliveness, and that was what had been the hardest to lose. She smiled down at his laughing face, touched her lips lightly to the glass, and carried it out to the trash.

⌗ ⌗ ⌗

When she finished her sessions that night, she joined Zach in front of Mark's notebook. "Gran really came through. She got Bill to tell her all about Mark's 'sexual perversities.' " Plunking into a dinette chair with a cracked vinyl backrest, she relayed the details.

Zach grinned. "We should just send her out to discover Cliff's identity. She'd probably do it."

Starshine rose from her spot next to Zach's right hand and came over to touch noses with Cassidy. A spark zapped between them. The cat jerked away, face clearly offended.

Zach typed in BODYMAN. Nothing happened.

Cassidy folded her arms on the formica table. "I did some field work today. Ken got fired a year ago, about a month before he started seeing me. The day after he left, the clinic distributed a memo directing the staff not to talk about his dismissal, even though nobody had a clue. You think someone might've discovered he had HIV and that's why they dumped him? Like in that movie a few years back?"

"It's a possibility." He typed in NUDGAMES.

"But if he were still asymptomatic, how would anybody find out?"

Zach rubbed the back of his neck. "You'd be amazed how hard it is to keep a secret. Given the leaks I run into, I've come to believe that one of the corollaries to Murphy's Law is, 'damaging information always gets spilled.' As to how it could've happened, Leman might've confided in a colleague, he might've tossed an AZT bottle in the trash. There are all kinds of ways."

"I wish somebody'd spill something in our direction." She shook her head. "And, as if two confounding suspects weren't enough, I've come up with a third. The man I was trying to think of last night. This one's likely to be even more untrackable and untraceable than the others." She told him about her final session with Donovan.

Disgust crossed his face. "You have any clients who *aren't* either sex fiends or the victims thereof?"

"Now wait a minute. Before Cliff, the sexual deviation quotient of my clientload was very small. I have Mira, a current client married to a sex addict, and Donovan, an ex-client who bragged about his conquests. The rest've all been nice, normal people suffering from mild depression, from being in love with Mr. Wrong or not in love with Mr. Right."

"The real question is," he cocked his head, "why would anyone in their right mind want to be a therapist?"

She wrinkled her nose to let him know she did not approve of his attitude. "The real question is, how do we locate this guy after three years?"

"Get a printout from the secretary of state's office of every guy by the name of Henry Donovan."

"You've got some cop friend who'll do that?"

"Emily."

"Oh." Cassidy compressed her lips.

"You don't want me to call Emily?"

How can I object to his calling an old girlfriend when he's been living with Kevin's picture for two months? She sighed. "I don't particularly like the idea but I can't come up with a reasonable case against it."

His eyes narrowed. "You want me to wait and call her from the office?"

"Go ahead, do it now."

He went into the bedroom to make the call, leaving both doors open. She focused on tracing the pattern in the mottled

green formica with her index finger. She would not go stand
in the doorway to listen. She would not check her watch to
see how long he stayed on the phone. After what seemed
like way too much time for a simple request, he returned and
dropped into his chair.

Cassidy cleared her throat. "She say anything about
Mark's shooting?"

Zach met her gaze, his eyes for once providing a glimpse
of what he felt. What she saw in them was concern.

Her throat tightened. "That's a stupid question, isn't it?
The police don't have a thing to go on. We've actually got
a better chance than they do."

He squeezed her hand, then pulled his chair up in front of
the notebook. When he glanced her way again, his blue-gray
eyes had resumed their usual state of detachment. He typed
in DRAGMAN, QUEENBEE, and MUSCLUV. "Okay, it's your
turn. I've run dry."

"Um . . . Smoothnude."

Nothing.

Closing her eyes, she covered her face with her hands and
visualized Mark as a teenager, the age he'd been before his
family left Oak Park. He was such a good-looking kid.
Sleek, blond, radiating health and vitality. He used to say
he'd never grow old, never let bills or jobs or responsibility
distract him from the real purpose of life, which was to have
fun. Tears stung her eyelids. She remembered how she
would call him Peter Pan and he'd leap up and twirl on one
toe like some kind of elfin creature. She brought her hands
down. "Try 'Peter Pan.' "

14

Denial

Zach typed it in, and the image on the screen was replaced by a menu.

"That's it," Zach said. "You got it."

"Oh." She blinked rapidly, pushing away the sadness. "Now what?"

"We get to read his mail." Zach brought up a list of screen names. "This is everybody that's sent e-mail recently." He scrolled though the list. "Most of it's junk, but this one might be interesting." He moved the cursor to *Boytoy re: nite on the town* and pulled up the most recent posting. "Bingo." He found one other incoming message from Boytoy, then accessed two outgoing messages from Mark. "Shit. I can't make a copy without the printer."

"So why don't you move your printer to Oak Park?"

"I'm going to. I just haven't gotten around to it yet."

Cassidy clenched her back teeth. *Sure you are. Soon as you don't need your escape route any more.* She copied the correspondence between Mark and Boytoy on a legal pad, recording the messages in the order in which they were sent.

Mark to Boytoy: Coming to Chicago in a couple weeks. Give you the dates as soon as they're pinned down. Now the truth will out. Am I in for any surprises?

Boytoy to Mark: Only good ones. I'm not worried, are you?

Mark to Boytoy: Flying in next Thurs. You said Thurs nite after your shift at the bar is the best time to hit the clubs. I kept all the info you sent, so I'll just meet you at that place you work. I am REALLY looking forward to having you show me around my old home town.

Boytoy to Mark: I got places you won't find in any guidebook. I'm gonna make sure your nite in Chicago is one you won't forget.

Cassidy said, "With all that sexual innuendo, it sounds more like a cyberdate than an old high school chum." She jiggled the pen between her fingers. "Although it could be an old buddy and they're just being playful."

Zach pushed his chair back, clasped his hands behind his neck, and stretched his legs. "We don't even know if the old friend's straight or gay."

Cassidy's brows pulled together. "Most of his friends must've been straight. Twenty years ago gay teens didn't have any easy way to find each other. But then again, if he did have one gay buddy, the friendship or affair or whatever probably would've been pretty intense. That might explain why they stayed in touch all these years."

"One thing we can do is look at some of the bulletin boards and see if there's a posting under the name 'Boytoy.'" Pulling his chair up to the table, Zach clicked through a series of menus until he found 'Clubs and Interests.' "This one might have a gay board." He scrolled through the list, stopping at 'Gay and Lesbian Interests,' then clicked to another box that identified subjects, authors, and dates. Moments later, the name they were looking for came up. Zach said, "Okay, let's hope Boytoy's got a profile."

Several more clicks and the stats appeared. Boytoy gave his name as 'CK,' his sex as 'gay hunk with taste for variety,' his hobbies as 'hitting the hot spots,' and his personal quote as, 'if you chase the action long enough, sooner or later you're bound to score.' He declined to provide his birthdate or occupation.

Cassidy said, "It's looking more and more like Mark's Thursday night date was a stranger he met through e-mail. But either way, we still don't know if Boytoy had anything to do with the shooting, if Mark heard something on Thursday night he planned to pass along to me, or if there's a connection between Boytoy and Cliff." She sucked in one cheek. "What do you think of those initials? You think maybe 'CK' is 'Cliff Something'?" *In your dreams he'd fall into our laps like that.*

Eyes narrowed, Zach gazed through the dark window. "Nah, I don't think it's gonna be that easy. It's too much of a coincidence, Cliff targeting you to send his victims to, then accidently meeting your cousin through the Internet. But the gay community's pretty tight. It could be what you said before, that this guy picked up rumors about Cliff and passed them on to Mark." He scratched his jaw. "Guessing's not gonna get us anywhere. We need to talk to this guy in person."

"Too bad we don't have the name of that bar. What happened to the old messages, anyway? The computer eat them?"

"Yep, the service deletes stuff after a certain period of time." He grinned. "So it looks like we're gonna have to find Boytoy the same way Mark did."

"Of course, I should've known." She smacked the flat of her hand on the table. "If there's any way of getting yourself into a dicey situation, that's the route you'll take."

"Do I hear a bit of projection going on?"

"Stop using words you don't understand and get on with it." She smiled broadly. "Which apparently means setting up a date with Boytoy."

"Unless you'd rather."

"I'm not his type."

"You could say you have an eight inch—"

Nudging him over, she held both outspread hands a few inches above the keyboard. "You click the cursor, I'll compose the message."

Zach signed off and restarted. "Okay, give me a screen name."

She typed STUDMUFFN.

Clicking on the box beneath the screen name, he said, "Now you need a password."

She wrote AGENT000.

Zach clicked some more and a large box with several lines came up. Inside the box she wrote: I READ YOUR PROFILE. VARIETY AND HOT NITES SOUND GOOD TO ME. I'M 30, PROFESSIONAL, A BODYBUILDER, LOVE TO MAKE IT ON THE CLUB SCENE, AND ALWAYS LOOKING FOR A BIG SCORE. WHY DON'T WE CHECK IT OUT?

✉ ✉ ✉

Cassidy lounged on her living room sofa reading the obituary section of the *Post*. A picture window behind the sofa admitted subdued daylight from the other side of the enclosed porch. Normally, the Oak Park weekly was the only paper she read, having decided long ago that a daily dose of murder and mayhem was hazardous to her mental health.

But today she had a purpose: her own version of the morbid curiosity she decried in others. She wanted to plot Cliff's course, to imagine herself inside his skin as he hunted down victims. Skimming the obits, she searched for women in their fifties, no husband, one surviving daughter with the same last name. *A woman like Jenny, only child from a split family, that's the kind who'd be most vulnerable.*

Letting the paper slide to the floor, she thought through Cliff's approach. He would go to the wake and stand in back to get a feel for how experienced, how confident the daughter might be. He would then proceed to chat up some of the guests, extracting information about the deceased woman and her family.

She pictured a man, his head shaved, hands in the pockets of his heavy coat, watching from the back of the room. Jenny, standing next to the casket, raised her speckled glasses and wiped teary eyes as friends murmured condolences. Then the man, whose face she couldn't see, glided up and said he'd known her mother from church, he was sorry for her loss.

His goal at the wake would be to evaluate the daughter's suitability as a victim. If she passed the test, he would move on to the next phase: observe her house, follow her around, learn her patterns. Then he would set up a second meeting, picking a place that was part of her normal routine, a location where he could step into line behind her and start a conversation. "You're Mrs. Krider's daughter, aren't you? My name's Cliff. I met you at the wake." Cassidy could hear the smooth, easy voice unreeling in her head.

Focusing intently on her mental picture, she tried to sharpen her image of the face, but it remained unclear. Why would anyone set up a mission to make women he'd never met suffer as much as he would have to? He was obviously psychopathic—"antisocial" was the current term—with a strong sadistic bent, but she didn't know if he'd acted on the sadism before or if finding out he had HIV had pushed him over the edge.

Having been married to a womanizer, she'd spent sleepless nights herself worrying about AIDS, and early on with Zach had insisted they both get tested. She tried to envision what it would've been like to hear that she'd come up positive. Running herself through that scenario, all she could imagine was feeling numb. The rage would come later, rage and the urge for vengeance. But even then, the feelings would never be strong enough to push her into action.

Cliff, obviously, was far more disturbed than she, or

anyone she knew. *Not true. I keep forgetting—don't want to remember—Cliff is somebody I know.* He was clearly paranoid, possibly delusional, but not schizophrenic. His behavior was too organized for most forms of mental illness. He undoubtedly had a personality disorder. People with personality disorders possessed an internal spring that bubbled up limitless quantities of black, sulfuric rage. But Cliff's viciousness exceeded anything she had ever encountered with clients, even the most disordered.

She searched her own experience, looking for some parallel to help her understand. She had once been very angry at Zach, so angry she'd wanted to hurt him as much as he'd hurt her. But she would never have wanted to give him AIDS. *What would it be like to have such a driving need for vengeance that I'd delegate stand-ins for the people who'd hurt me and inflict on them the same agony I was facing?*

⊠   ⊠   ⊠

Mira, true to her usual routine, arrived five minutes early for her Saturday session. Her red jump suit and gold pendant provided a striking contrast to her olive skin and razor cut black hair. Her face was more relaxed than usual, and a cheery spark showed in her wide brown eyes.

What happened? She find a way to keep Jake chained to the bedpost?

Mira tangled her thin fingers in her gold chain. "You know how you've been talking about detachment, but I could never stop myself from trying to control Jake? Well, I think I finally got it. This week I was a lot more detached and it was so much better."

Cassidy folded her hands in her lap. "How were you different?"

"Well, for once in his life Jake didn't go out on Sunday night. That's one night he almost always picks himself up and heads for the door. But he stayed home Sunday, so then I started off the week in better spirits."

I ask how she's different. She talks about Jake.

Mira's lips, carefully painted to match her jumpsuit, curved upward. "I made it through the whole week without one snide remark, Jake didn't get angry, and we were actually able to be nice to each other."

"Is that all you want—for him to be nice?" *You can bring home diseases as long as you're nice to me?*

"It was better than that. There were a few times we felt especially close, and one night we even made love. Jake actually went three days straight without taking off on his usual late night jaunts." Her tone was gleeful, as if Jake's staying home were a personal victory.

Cassidy propped her pump on the edge of the wicker table beneath a bushy spray of coleus. "So are you thinking—if you get more detached Jake'll straighten up?"

"I know I should be focusing on myself, not him." She tugged at the pendant. "But isn't it true that if I quit pressuring Jake to stop, the odds're higher he'll do it on his own? I mean, as long as I'm constantly nagging, he resists. So if I'm not pushing, he won't be able to blame his behavior on me anymore. Then eventually he'll have to wake up and see that he's putting his life on the line every time he picks up a hooker."

"Mira, the whole idea of detachment is to stop doing the

very thing you're doing right now. If you're still trying to manipulate Jake, you're not detached."

Mira's triangular face furrowed in a faint scowl. She pulled her slender body up straight. "But he doesn't know what I'm thinking, does he? And anyway, if it works, who cares?"

Cassidy arranged her wine-colored skirt so it draped neatly over her crossed knee, took a deep breath and said, "There's something else we need to talk about. When you first started seeing me, I urged you to get an HIV test yourself and to insist that Jake get tested also. We discussed it a few times, then I let it drop, and now I'm thinking I should've kept on it. You frequently bring up the risk to Jake, but you don't say much about the risk to you."

"What good will it do? Jake's refused, and if I get tested myself, it's not going to change anything." Mira hunched inward. "I mean, if I've got something—if I've got AIDS— why would I want to know? If I found out I had it, I'd just worry all the time. And if I don't have it now, it doesn't mean anything, because as long as I'm with Jake and he's doing two or three prostitutes a week, I could always get it tomorrow." She glanced up, her face defiant. "So what's the point?"

Cassidy said, "The point is, they've got treatments now that can effectively stop the virus."

"You don't have to start the cocktail right at the beginning. If I've got it, I could wait until it turns into AIDS, then get treated."

Would you want to know? When you were with Kevin, you didn't run out to get tested.

*Just because I screwed up is no reason to let Mira off. It's
my job to get her to do better.*

"You've got a question of life and death here, and you
just want to ignore it?" Cassidy's eyes narrowed. "You are
using condoms, aren't you?"

Mira stared stubbornly into her lap.

"You're not? My God, Mira, how could you . . . " When
Cassidy had asked the question earlier, Mira said they were,
but she could have been lying. Cassidy forced herself to
stop, take a deep breath, and speak more calmly. "Just think
how you'd feel if you got HIV and knew you could've
prevented it. You're always angry at Jake for being so self
destructive, but what you're doing is almost as bad."

Mira looked up, the rebellious spark in her eyes slowly
fading. "It's not the same." Her voice slipped into weariness.
"Jake chooses to go out and do all that sexual weirdness. I
may be at risk because I married him, but I'm not doing it
deliberately. There's no way I'd choose to lie awake worrying myself to death like I do every time we have sex." She
twisted the gold band on her finger. "The problem is, I love
my husband and I'm not ready to give up on him. If I demand
condoms, he'll simply stop having sex with me, and then
it'll be all over for us. I wish I could say I don't care, but
that's not true. I can't just let my marriage go. Not yet."

Straightening her back, Cassidy stared at Mira until the
other woman made eye contact. "Doesn't matter how you
feel or if you're ready. Jake Sheffield is not worth dying for."

Neither was Kevin, but that didn't get you to leave.

⊠   ⊠   ⊠

Saturday night Zach announced that he'd made reservations for dinner, so they drove to an upscale steakhouse just off Clark Street on the city's north side. As soon as they were seated, water was poured and a basket of bread arrived.

Having heard about Mira's session on the drive down, Zach picked up a slice of French bread and said, "I can't believe she's letting him screw her without a rubber. The woman oughtta keep a gun under her pillow and be prepared to blow him away if he so much as lays a finger on her."

"Good old denial. The ever popular, it-won't-happen-to-me magical thinking. Amazing the dumb things it allows so-called intelligent people to do." She removed the decoratively folded napkin from her wine glass and spread it across her lap.

"Now that you've hit her over the head with it, you think she'll come to her senses?"

Propping her elbows on the table, Cassidy lowered her chin onto her hands. "Maybe. Probably not. Jake and Mira have developed a joint layer of denial as thick as a rhino's hide. It permits both of them to do what they want without worrying about consequences."

"But don't therapists routinely have to break down denial? Isn't that your job?"

"Considering you're such a heretic, it always surprises me to hear you talk like an insider." Scanning his face, she decided he was merely interested, not trying to give her a hard time. "Sometimes you sound like one of those clients who've seen ten different therapists and have all the moves down pat."

"I told you, I've interviewed more than my share of psychology gurus. As much as you'd like to think otherwise, therapy is not brain surgery. Getting the basics down was no great stretch." He stuffed the rest of the bread into his mouth, managing not to scatter crumbs all over the table the way she usually did.

"What you said about denial—it's not as simple as you think. I have to walk a tightrope between support and empathy on the one hand, and heavy hitting doses of reality on the other. And I'm afraid I screwed up." She took a piece of bread from the basket, broke it in half on her plate, and brushed the crumbs into a pile. "Up until now, I practically ignored the risk. Then I had this brainstorm that Jake might be our HIV carrier, and that motivated me to come down really hard. Maybe too hard. After what I said today, there's a good possibility Mira'll simply quit therapy so she doesn't have to deal with me."

Zach cocked his head. "She's getting laid by a guy who goes to prostitutes and you haven't been on her case about the risk?"

A feeling of heaviness filtered through her chest. "The problem with empathy is, you have to step inside the other person's skin and see things through their eyes. And the better you are at empathy, the easier it is to lose your own perspective. With Mira, my urge to avoid reality lined up with hers because I didn't want to face the fact that she might have HIV any more than she did." *Plus you did the same thing she's doing when you stayed with Kevin.*

"You mean, even therapists do denial? It's not just the poor, ordinary, nonpsychological schlub who occasionally dons rose-colored glasses?"

"I thought you were going to stop being arrogant."

"I forgot." He picked up his menu. "I see our waiter coming. You decide what you want yet?"

A sprightly young man stopped on the other side of the table. Zach ordered prime rib and a bottle of pinot noir. Cassidy ordered chicken fettucini.

When the waiter left, she leaned back in her chair and crossed her arms over her chest. "You know, this place is not exactly in my price range."

"This my punishment for getting arrogant on you?" Zach's eyes were bemused, an indication he was taking the superior stance he sometimes used in an attempt to avoid her complaints.

"You act like we're still dating. You take me to expensive places and pick up the tab, and you dodge all my efforts to develop a plan for sharing expenses. Ever since you moved in, you've just taken over the bills."

"I hate quibbling over money." He drilled the tines of his fork against the tablecloth. "If I can afford it, why not just let me pay? You buy the groceries, I pay the mortgage. You do the laundry, I change the oil, nobody cooks. It all works out."

The waiter brought the wine; Zach tasted; the waiter poured.

Raising her glass, Cassidy gazed into its dark contents. "I don't like it. It makes me feel dependent."

"You? Dependent?"

"You're practically supporting me. You just grab up the bills before I even get the envelopes opened. You're treating me like some helpless little Barbie who can't pay her own way."

"Well, you can't." Pushing his plate back, he folded his arms on the table. "I know, you've almost finished paying off Kevin's taxes, and once that's out of the way you'll be fine. But that's not the issue. The issue is, you see it as demeaning if I throw more money into the pot than you do, and I don't agree. I don't measure anybody's worth in terms of how much they make or spend. And I certainly don't agree that my paying the bills right now makes you dependent. If I were gone tomorrow, you'd still be the same person you've always been."

Right now? Gone tomorrow? What's the message here? She twisted the stem of her glass in slow circles on the table. "Are you saying . . ." she stopped and took a deep breath, "we shouldn't develop a financial plan because the situation's going to change anyway?"

"I don't like keeping score or being tied to some arbitrary agreement, that's all." The waiter arrived with their plates. "Now let's drop the subject and enjoy our meal."

After demolishing a Webster's-Unabridged-sized chunk of meat, Zach sat back. "Your ad's in today's *Free Chicago*, so now we'll see if another Cliff letter turns up on our doorstep. At least I hope it's the doorstep and not the kitchen or bedroom this time."

"You think he might give us his real name?"

"I think he isn't stupid." Zach emptied the bottle and stuck it upside down in the ice bucket. "Which is why I think our job isn't over. We still have no information on your ex-client Donovan, and we're currently out of ideas for pursuing the sex-addict attorney. But Leman—the guy who pays for an hour of therapy to talk about a job he doesn't have—now Leman looks interesting. And since I already scouted out his Rogers Park address, we have the advantage of a known building and a potentially empty apartment."

15

Illegal Entry

"Potentially empty?" She tossed her napkin on the table. "You're not suggesting . . ." She blinked, the meaning coming clear to her. "You're not actually planning to break into Leman's apartment?"

His face closed down.

"Isn't that a felony? Where would you be with the newspaper if you got caught?" He shifted slightly to avoid her eyes. "You look down on other people who slide into denial and get stupid. Isn't this a little denial of your own?"

"I don't think so." He turned toward her, his expression still unreadable. "Chances are a dude like Leman's not gonna be sitting around his sleazebag apartment on a Saturday night. So, if he's not home and doesn't have a deadbolt, I'm going to jimmy the back door, do a quick walk-through, see what's lying around. It's entirely doable. Low-rise building, stairs leading up to the back porch. The kind of transient area where nobody calls the police."

She swallowed the last of her wine and thumped the glass down hard on the table. "I take it I have nothing to say in the matter."

"You can say 'Drive me home,' and I'll drop you off. Or 'I'll sit in the car,' and you can wait while I go up." He gestured to the waiter, who started moving in their direction.

A glint of amusement came into his eyes. *Thinks it's funny, sidelining me in the car.* She shot him an angry look. "If you really didn't want to put me in dangerous situations, you wouldn't be breaking into my client's apartment."

"That's why you're staying in the car."

Like hell I am.

Wait a minute. This is a client. Talk about overstepping boundaries.

There's no way he's leaving me in the car.

✉ ✉ ✉

He parked in the shallow lot between the alley and the brick apartment building. Five individual staircases zigzagged from the ground to porches on the second and third floors. The street light was out. Except for the yellow glow from scattered windows and a whitish aura from snow piles outlining the parking lot, the alley was dense with shadows.

Zach peered through the windshield. "His place is dark, just like I expected."

"How do you know which is Ken's?"

He turned to face her. "I went upstairs and counted doors. He's third floor, second from the end." He nodded toward the building's south edge. "Okay, here's the drill. I'll leave the keys in the ignition and if anybody gives you any trouble, you drive around and park in front. I should be down in, oh—fifteen minutes or so."

"I'm going with you."

Irritation crossed his face. "No you're not."

"You can't force me to stay inside this car."

He glowered from beneath a deeply creased brow for at least thirty seconds. "This is nuts. You're only doing it to prove I can't tell you what to do. When are you gonna outgrow this adolescent rebellion shit?"

Cassidy felt a brief jolt of anger. As soon as it passed, she checked herself to see if it was true. Two different parts were talking in her head. One said, *I'll show him.* Another, louder voice said, *Maybe I'll find something he'd miss.*

She placed a conciliatory hand on his arm. "Okay, I admit I get rebellious when you tell me what to do." *Who wouldn't?* "But I also think we might as well give this our best shot, and two of us'll find more than one. Besides, if there's no danger, why shouldn't I go?"

His mouth pulled back in a tight smile. "When am I gonna learn never to say out loud what I think you should do?"

Interesting description of his drill-sergeant tactics.

They hopped out of the Nissan. Zach opened the trunk and grabbed a flashlight and pry bar. As they crossed the parking strip, Cassidy's boots crunched nuggets of rock salt put down to melt the snow. Zach, jogging two steps ahead, reached Ken's stairway and started up.

Their feet hitting the steps sounded like a string of exploding firecrackers. She pictured all the porch doors flying open and men in ski masks coming out to shoot them.

Arriving at the second story porch, she paused to catch her breath. The doormat-sized porch was heaped with garbage bags, some of which had burst, allowing their innards to spill out like bloated, split-open corpses.

She hurried up to Ken's landing, tidier than the one below, with only one garbage can, its lid firmly in place. Zach had the screen door jammed open and the flashlight fixed on the lock.

"Here's hoping we don't run into a deadbolt." He handed the flashlight to her, then inserted the short end of the pry bar into the crack. Pulling back on the long end, he jammed the frame away from the door and shoved it with his foot. The door creaked open. He stepped inside and switched on the overhead.

The studio apartment contained a king-sized bed made up with a velvet comforter, a student desk, a sagging armchair covered with a handmade afghan, a large screen television, and a tiny formica table. Aside from papers on the desk and dirty ashtrays, the room was remarkably uncluttered.

How does he do it? I've got a whole big house and I can't keep things put away.

Zach moved toward the desk. "You look in the medicine chest. Keep your eye out for AIDS-related meds."

She opened the metal cabinet in the bathroom. The shelves were coated with toothpaste, cough syrup, and other unrecognizable substances. *Yuck. I may not always pick up, but at least my medicine cabinet's clean.* No prescription bottles. She glanced through the waste basket. Nothing of interest. Walking past the galley kitchen, she stopped to check the garbage under the sink. Coffee grounds, french fries, and a grayish slop that gave off a faintly spoiled smell.

"Look at this," Zach said from the desk near the front door.

She crossed to stand beside him. "What is it?"

"Application for a Shell Visa." He pointed to a line on the form. Block letters said THOMAS WEATHERBY. "Phony name."

"But what does it mean? If he'd called himself 'Cliff Connors,' we'd have something." She heard footsteps and a male voice laughing in the hallway. "Oh shit, that's him." Panic swelling in her chest, she strained to listen. The footsteps receded.

"We've gotta get out of here." She tugged at his coat.

"You go on down. I'll be right behind you." Zach's gaze was fixed on an answering machine atop a nightstand on the side of the bed farthest from the door. He headed toward it.

Cassidy started to leave, then turned to scan the room, noticing a closet door she hadn't seen before.

A frail voice came from the answering machine. "This's your old man. When you come on Sunday, bring a bag of White Castles. I don't seem to have the energy for cooking anymore."

She raced to the closet and opened it. Shirts and pants on hangers, a pile of laundry on the floor. Pushing aside the hanging clothes, she peered behind them. A three-foot safe stood at the closet's far end. She pictured a man with shaved head carrying a box into Jenny's house. The back of her neck prickled.

What's he got in there? Pornography collection? Video camera and tapes? Trophies from his victims?

Closing the door, she turned toward Zach, who was bent over the answering machine. "C'mon, let's go."

"Just let me reset it."

She heard footsteps again, this time approaching. A newspaper headline flashed before her: THERAPIST CAUGHT BURGLARIZING CLIENT'S APARTMENT. "That's him. He's coming in." Flying for the back door, she heard Zach clomping behind her, then the scrape of a key in the front door lock. She pounded down the stairs, Zach's feet thudding at her heels. Hitting the ground, she twisted to look up. A man stood on the porch staring down at them. Racing past, Zach grabbed her arm to get her moving again.

As she jumped inside the Nissan, Zach started backing toward the alley. He aimed the car at the street, jammed the gearshift into first, and peeled off.

Stopping at a light, he ran a hand over his face. "I shouldn't have let you go up. I oughtta know by now—I can't tell you what I'm gonna do till it's over and done with."

She took a deep breath and blew out air. "Don't you start running your own investigation behind my back. We've always told each other—" She remembered she was keeping her driving phobia from him. *Secrets. Like acid eating away at the underbelly of the relationship.* "Well, almost everything, and it can't be any other way. Besides, I have every bit as much right to do stupid things as you do."

He chuckled and laid a hand briefly on her knee.

"Ken couldn't tell who we were, could he?" She paused,

then answered her own question. "No, of course not. It was pitch black down there."

"Too bad we worked ourselves into a sweat and all we got for it is more questions."

"Questions?" Shivering, she rubbed her hands under the vent. "Like, what's he doing with a safe in his closet?"

"I wouldn't have expected a safe in a dump like that. People in cheapo apartments usually don't have valuables. They also move a lot, and hauling a safe requires one weightlifter or two ordinary guys like me who don't exercise. I learned this the hard way by helping a buddy carry one up to his apartment."

Zach turned south on Ashland. A blue and white passed, headed the other direction. She pictured the cop car pulling a U-turn, flashing its lights, forcing them to the curb.

Stop that right now. Ken does not have X-ray vision, he did not read the plate number, you are not headed for jail.

She rerouted her mind back to their discussion. "If I were Cliff, I'd want a safe."

"For the videos he takes of his final performance?"

"That, and the trophies. Remember—Jenny said she thought he made off with her pantyhose? And I've also read that sexual sadists usually have extensive pornography collections. If I kept things like that around, I'd want them locked up."

"So, the safe definitely boosts Ken's rating on our suspect list." Zach turned west on Augusta, a boulevard running from the Chicago River through the blighted west side. "Then there's the bogus name on the credit card app. Now that could be nothing more than a survival tactic for a conniver who's been out of work the past year."

"Or it could be business as usual for someone who lives half his life under an alias." She rolled her shoulders to relieve the tension.

"Seems like you really wanna bust Leman."

"I guess seeing his place makes me realize just how much I dislike the man." She grimaced. "Not a great attitude to have toward a client."

Zach glanced her way. "Doesn't he get points for house-keeping? His place's neater than mine ever was."

"But there's that two-hundred-dollar comforter on the bed and the spoiled garbage under the sink." She envisioned Ken's face with its cunning little smile. A faint metallic taste rose in her mouth. "I guess sneakiness puts me off even more than arrogance."

Zach turned a sharp look on her and she suddenly recalled having accused him, at various times, of both.

⊠   ⊠   ⊠

Cassidy whipped the feathered bird above the bed, teasing Calvin, who slipped out from under a section of the Sunday paper and captured it. Zach had gone down for seconds on coffee as part of their Sunday ritual, which consisted of lolling in bed with the kittens, the paper, and extra cups.

Appearing in the doorway, he held a sheet of paper but no coffee. His bronze face had gone a shade darker.

"What's that?" She jerked the bird away from Calvin.

"Another letter."

"Oh shit." Her chest tightened. "It was in the house, wasn't it? He got inside again."

"Conveniently propped against the coffeepot so we wouldn't miss it."

"But how? I poured our first cup an hour ago and it wasn't there then."

Zach sat on his side of the bed and handed her the letter. "You know that side door we never use? He broke out a pane." Starshine rose from the place where she was sleeping, stretched, and climbed into Zach's lap.

"That door's only a few yards from the Stein house. He was really taking a chance."

"He's a thrill seeker. Obviously going for the adrenalin rush." Starshine stared up rapturously as he rubbed her neck.

Cassidy flipped the feathered cat toy in his face. "You mean, the way you add excitement to your life with illegal entry?"

"Read the letter."

DEAR CASSIDY,

SINCE YOU ARE THE CHOSEN RECIPIENT OF MY PER-SONAL HISTORY, I'M PLEASED AT YOUR DESIRE TO KNOW MORE ABOUT ME. ALLOW ME TO BEGIN BY EXPLAINING THE NATURE OF THE MISSION GOD HAS SENT ME ON.

IT WAS GOD'S INTENT THAT MALE AND FEMALE COME TOGETHER TO PROCREATE: THAT A MAN'S SEED BE HANDED DOWN THROUGH THE GENERATIONS. BUT IF WOMEN REFUSE MEN ACCESS TO THEIR BODIES, A MAN'S GOD GIVEN NEEDS CAN DRIVE HIM TO SEEK ALTERNATIVE, LESS NATURAL OUT-LETS.

THE EVIL ONE USES HOMOSEXUALITY TO TEMPT MEN

AWAY FROM GOD. AND GOD HAS SENT HIS PLAGUE DOWN ON
THE HOMOSEXUAL COMMUNITY AS PUNISHMENT. SOME MEN
FREELY CHOOSE TO DESPOIL THEIR BODIES, AND THESE MEN
DESERVE THEIR FATE. OTHERS ARE DRIVEN TO IT BY THE
REPUDIATION OF WOMEN, AND THESE ARE THE MARTYRS.

    IF THESE MARTYRS—MEN WHO YEARN TO FOLLOW
GOD'S NATURAL ORDER BUT ARE TURNED ASIDE BY REJECT-
ING WOMEN—IF THESE MEN MUST SUFFER, THEN SO MUST
THE WOMEN.

    IT IS TO YOU, CASSIDY, THAT I'VE CONFERRED THE
HONOR OF RECORDING MY MISSION. YOU HAVE WISELY CHO-
SEN A REPORTER AS YOUR PARTNER, SOMEONE WHO CAN
ENSURE THE WIDEST POSSIBLE AUDIENCE FOR MY STORY.
YOU ARE NOT IN LEAGUE WITH THE CONSPIRACY AGAINST
MEN. YOU'VE PROVEN YOUR METTLE IN FACING GREAT ODDS.

    MY STORY NOW BELONGS TO THE TWO OF US, AND YOU
MUST TREAT IT WITH THE RESPECT IT DESERVES. THIS MIS-
SION OF MINE—A SHARED MISSION NOW—WILL BIND US
TOGETHER AS WE APPROACH THE FINAL SCENE, A DENOUE-
MENT THAT MAY REQUIRE THE UTMOST COURAGE ON BOTH
OUR PARTS.

                          AFFECTIONATELY,

                              CLIFF

"That's disgusting." Cassidy crumpled the letter and
threw it on the floor.

"Hey, we may need that for the police."

"We can't go to the police because I can't implicate
Jenny."

Hobbes sprang off the bed, grabbed the letter, and
dragged it over to Zach's sneaker in the far corner. The kitten

made a couple of attempts to cram the wadded paper into the shoe, then wandered off.

Zach stood, dumping Starshine off his lap. The cat shot him an offended look and settled next to Cassidy. He retrieved the letter and sat down again. "This guy's both homophobic *and* homosexual."

Cassidy stroked Starshine, aware that she could feel the cat's ribs. "He makes it sound as if he were always getting rejected, but he knew exactly what he was doing when he seduced Jenny. Those rejections he talks about may've happened at an earlier age—maybe he even set them up— and now he's more of a Don Juan. But he focuses on those past rejections as an excuse for his homosexuality. He's definitely got enormous hostility toward both women and gays."

"But not you. He's got you on a pedestal."

"He probably sees women as either good or bad, no middle ground. That's the kind of black and white thinking you find with personality disorders." *No need to mention they're also notorious for flipping, the good person suddenly becoming the anti-Christ.*

"He must've encountered that warm, accepting therapist-presence you put on for clients, so you're on his good side." Zach wiggled his fingers to entice Hobbes.

"It isn't put on."

"Where's all that warmth and acceptance when I wanna spend an evening at the Billy Goat?" She started to answer but he held up a hand to stop her. "Okay, I can understand why he might see you as female perfection, but what's his beef with women like Jenny? They fall all over him, don't they?"

She pressed her thumb and index finger around the tip of her chin. "Maybe it's because they don't jump instantly into bed. Maybe he expects unconditional love, and if he has to work for it, it isn't good enough. A lot of people are hypersensitive and feel rejected if you say 'good morning' in the wrong tone of voice."

"What bothers me is that parting shot about needing courage for the final scene." Tossing his robe on the bed, he dressed in jeans and a new black tee, its red letters proclaiming, BEER: NOT JUST FOR BREAKFAST ANYMORE. "We've gotta have a security system. I'm going to the library to check out different brands in *Consumer Reports*. I'll get the installation started first thing next week."

"Zach, wait. Those things cost thousands of dollars."

"This is not open for discussion." His growly tone warned her to back off.

Cassidy gritted her teeth. *Not even his house and he's just taking over. Hate being pushed around. Why would I even want to be with a commando type like Zach?*

Fetching his shoes from the corner, he said, "Light's blinking. We forgot to check the machine last night." He pushed PLAY.

"This's Kristi. Luke can't wait to see the kittens. But since you're not home . . . So anyway, I'll just have to hold him off till tomorrow."

After Zach left, Starshine stretched out on the bed and cooed for Calvin and Hobbes, who joined her for lunch. As the ever growing kittens chowed down, their mother's eyes gleamed blissfully from her cadaverous face.

"You obviously don't know what's good for you anymore than I do."

Mwat. The scratchy sound radiated contentment.

Cassidy wrapped her arms around her knees. "A security system may be what's best for me, but it sure doesn't make me happy. Zach's about to sink big bucks into this house. So then what happens when he packs his suitcase and he's outta here?"

Starshine began washing Hobbes' face, eliciting a loud squawk from the kitten.

"Then I'll feel obligated, that's what. Zach won't think twice about the money. He's always had it, so it doesn't mean anything to him. But I'll feel lousy if I don't pay him back."

The phone on Zach's nightstand rang. She hesitated. *Jenny called on that line. Could be one of Cliff's women.* She scooted across the bed and picked up.

16

Driving the Expressway

"Is Zach there?" A woman's voice, vaguely familiar.

Where do I know her from? "He's not available. Can I take a message?"

"No, I'll call later."

Cassidy remembered who she was. Her back stiffened. "Emily? Is this about the Donovan plates?"

"I suppose I might as well leave the information with you." A slight note of irritation.

"No, that's all right. I'll have him get back to you."

A short sigh. "You're out of luck. Only five Henry Donovans in the state, none with ages falling between thirty-five and forty-five."

"Thanks." Cassidy sucked in one cheek. "And, uh, Emily? Thanks for calling Zach. After the shooting."

"I'm sorry if I seemed . . . brusque just now. Out of curiosity, what did he tell you about me?"

"Only that you two were involved some time ago." *Doesn't need to hear that I know she tried to get back together.*

"Oh." She sounded relieved. "Zach's okay. You could do worse."

"Except?"

"Well, this is going to sound all wrong coming from me, but . . . he's not one to settle down."

Cassidy let out a brittle laugh. "Don't worry, I'm not picking any wedding china just yet."

"Well, in that case—in the short term he's okay."

"Thanks again for the, um, information."

✉   ✉   ✉

Kristi, Zach's sister-in-law, shook out her wild, crinkly hair and tossed her Evan Picone jacket on the sofa while her six-year-old went tearing through the house yelling, "Where's the kittens?"

As Luke zoomed by, Cassidy captured him in a bear hug. Upon release, he stood facing her, legs apart, hands on hips. "Where's Uncle Zach? Mom said he'd build a snowman with me." A wicked look came over his face. "But I'd rather make snowballs to throw at her and you."

"You're out of luck." Cassidy mirrored the child's emphatic tone and posture. "And if you try throwing snowballs at me, I'll chase you down and wash your face."

"Where's the kittens?" He took off toward the kitchen.

Kristi flashed her gleaming smile. "You're so good with kids. Maybe I ought to leave . . . You could straighten him out for me."

"He's just like the kittens, only bigger and louder. Since I can't manage them, I doubt I'd do any better with Luke."

Whipping into the living room, Luke fell backward, arms outspread, on top of his mother's jacket. "Aren't you through talking yet?"

Creasing her face into an exaggerated frown, Cass said. "No kitten-visiting until you show us you're ready."

He sprang to his feet. "What do I have to do?"

"Be quiet! Kittens disappear—poof!—when loud kids come bursting into their room."

"I'll be just like . . . " He dropped to all fours and began creeping across the floor, "a little mouse."

Cassidy led them up to the nursery, where they sat watching the two kittens play hide and seek around the barbell and guitar. Starshine positioned herself in front of the boy, ears pricked, tail switching. Cassidy jiggled her fingers, luring Hobbes over to stalk her hand, then snatched him up and gave him to Luke.

"Ouch, he scratches." Luke dropped the kitten into his lap. Scampering to the boy's shoulder, Hobbes touched a claw to his ear. "That tickles." Luke giggled. The giggle turned into a sneeze. Hobbes fled across the room. Luke sneezed again.

Cassidy fetched a box of tissues from the bedroom and applied one to the boy's nose. Pushing her hand away, he exploded in another huge sneeze. His eyes had turned red-rimmed and watery; his nose dripped.

Kristi said, "Omigod, he must be allergic."

✉ ✉ ✉

Zach returned and went up to his office to sit in front of the notebook. Cassidy joined him, positioning herself beside Starshine, who had staked out a post on the table at Zach's right hand. From this spot the cat could most easily demand that he take his fingers off the keyboard and place them on her.

Cassidy scratched Starshine's rump, which rose to push against her hand. "Any messages from Boytoy?"

"He picked ours up yesterday but didn't send anything back." Zach clicked off the screen. "All we can do is wait."

She recounted the aborted kitten adoption and the word from Emily about Donovan's plates. "I suppose that means Henry Donovan got himself blown away by a jealous husband or moved out of state. In either case, we can cross him off our list." She frowned. "I guess that's progress."

"But you're not happy about it." Turning sideways in his chair, he draped an arm over the vinyl backrest.

"It doesn't seem finished." She turned toward him to sit face to face, their legs touching. "But I can't think of anything more to do."

Starshine uttered an aggrieved Mror, expressing disapproval of their having redirected their attention from her to each other.

Noting the warmth in Zach's eyes, Cassidy considered not continuing on the track she was headed. But once her brain had started down a particular path, it was as hard to reroute as an express locomotive. "I suppose your day was less of a waste than mine."

"Yep."

"You decided on a security system?" She fingered a rust spot on the table's chrome edging.

"Uh huh."

"Tell me more about this system of yours." Her tone parodied the voice she used with clients.

"ADT. The way it works is, when any entrance is breached a call goes into the security company office, the office alerts the police, and minutes later a dozen cops drive up and nail Cliff. I'll call tomorrow and get things started."

"How much will it cost?" she asked sweetly.

"You know, you like to fight a lot more than I do. Sometimes I think the only reason you wanted me to move in is so you'd have somebody to scrap with besides Starshine."

"That's not true." *Isn't it? If you didn't want to pick fights, why won't you ever leave anything alone?* "I only do it because you make unilateral decisions and I'm left completely out of the loop. I don't even get a vote on whether or not we put a security system into my house."

He grinned. "Unless Starshine learns Robert's Rules of Order, any votes around here are bound to be a stalemate." Pulling her to her feet, he rested his arms on her shoulders. "What say we adjourn to the waterbed?" He planted a kiss on her forehead. "This time, all furry creatures are remanded to the nursery. And that's a nondebateable decision."

⊠ ⊠ ⊠

On Monday, a day with no clients and nothing to distract her from picking away at the investigation, she once again settled on the sofa with the obituary section of the paper.

One obit contained circumstances paralleling Jenny's. The deceased, a fifty-nine-year-old woman named Martha Korski, had only one surviving relative, a daughter with the same last name. The wake would be held Tuesday at a north Chicago funeral home.

Does Cliff follow up on every potential obit? Or is he the linear type—finishes off one victim before starting another? If only I knew what stage he's in now.

She recreated the picture she had visualized before: a visitation room with a man in a heavy coat standing in the back. This time he wasn't bald but had upswept hair and a closely trimmed beard. Straining to bring the image into focus, she was able to glimpse a face. But it was a generic face, an everyman's face that told her nothing about the person inside. Behind that face could be Ken or Jake or Henry. Or someone else she hadn't even thought of.

Will Cliff turn up at tomorrow's wake?

Dumping the paper into the recycling tub, she stared through her kitchen window into the yard two houses south of hers. The Roberts' lived there, a black family with three kids and a stay-at-home mom. The Roberts children, ages three, four, and six, were almost as adorable as the kittens, and Cassidy often watched in fascination as the kids and their dog embodied *happy childhood,* a commodity therapists sometimes ceased to believe in. Observing this family had come to be an anodyne for her work.

Today she saw the two older children lumbering in heavy snowsuits to put the finishing touches on a snowman.

She turned away from the window, too obsessed with the problem of Cliff to enjoy the kids. *How long before he infects another woman? What will it take to get inside his head?*

More information. You need to know more about the head of a psychopath before you can get into it.

She drove to the library, a contemporary stone structure in central Oak Park. Next to the glass doors stood a line of angular metal figures that represented to Cassidy not readers but sentinels: guardians to ensure that this place, which had been her sanctuary since childhood, would always be there to soothe and restore her.

✉ ✉ ✉

At four o'clock, as daylight began to fade, Cassidy sat at her desk reading the book on sexual sadism she had checked out from the library. The phone broke her concentration.

"This is Lou. You remember, Louise Mertz from the party?"

Cassidy cocked her head in surprise. "Oh, yeah. Hi Louise. What can I do for you?"

"There are certain things I think you ought to know." Her voice was cautious. "Our family has a lot of history, some of it not so nice. I guess I'd like for you to have a better sense of what your mother's getting herself into."

Uh oh. The dark side of Roland. "I don't mean to put you off, Louise. I really enjoyed meeting you at the party." *What I remember of it.* "But Mom's the one you should be telling this to."

"Your mother's got this idea we're all against her, which isn't true. Now I have to admit, my sisters can be pretty greedy. But Ron and I—we're not trying to cut her out of the inheritance. However, since she's convinced we're out to stop the wedding, I doubt she'd be willing to hear what I have to say."

"I take it you'd like to fill me in on some of your father's less attractive traits?" *As if what I've seen already were appealing.*

"I realize this probably won't do any good, but I can't get over the feeling that somebody in your family oughtta have this information."

"Do you know what it's like, trying to talk sense into somebody who's in love?" *When I'm in that addled state, I can't even get through to myself.*

"I wish you'd humor me. All I wanna do is provide some background. Once you've got the whole story, I'll be satisfied."

"I suppose I can understand your wanting to tell somebody." *So give her an hour of free therapy. She's gonna be your stepsister.* "Okay, I'll listen." She leaned back and propped her sneakers on the warm radiator beneath the window.

"I'd be a lot more comfortable doing this in person."

"You want to get together? I suppose we can do that." Swiveling around to her desk, she reached for her calendar. *Really oughtta charge her.* "So, you want to set up a time to come here?"

"I was hoping we could meet for dinner in the city. My treat. I don't have a car. Besides, I figured it'd give us a chance to get to know each other."

"Well . . . " Her stomach squirmed at the thought of driving. "My evenings are pretty booked."

"I know it's a lot to ask, but I just can't do it over the

phone. How 'bout drinks instead of dinner? Just an hour after work."

Cassidy heard an urgency in the woman's voice that made it difficult to refuse.

You can't drive into Chicago after dark. You're getting palpitations just thinking about it.

You let this phobia beat you, you'll end up a scared little rabbit, afraid to leave your hole.

Straightening her shoulder, she said, "Tonight's the only evening I have free."

"Great. Then we can get it over with." Louise gave her directions to a north side bar and said she'd meet her at six.

✉ ✉ ✉

Cassidy hunched forward, hands welded to the steering wheel, lips parted to suck in air. She could not rid herself of the idea that icicle worms wriggled in her stomach.

She was on the Eisenhower, a mile east of Oak Park. Even though she'd hit rush hour, the smooth flow of inbound traffic forced her to maintain a fifty mile-per-hour speed.

Can't understand this anxiety. Expressway's lit up like a carnival. All these cars. No bad memories here. She willed herself to keep driving.

The lights and cars disappeared. The entire scene suddenly shifted. She saw a wall of trees on both sides, a narrow band of road, two taillights in the distance. Her right foot slammed the brake. From behind she heard a horn blast, the screech of tires. Her body tensed for an impact, which didn't come.

17

Wake

Cassidy raised a shaky hand to her forehead. *Gotta get back to Oak Park.* Crawling along the shoulder, she continued to the next exit, then proceeded north on Cicero, west on Chicago Avenue.

Back in her bedroom, she worked to get her breathing under control and her voice working correctly, then called the bar where Louise waited. "Sorry I wasn't able to meet you. I had car trouble and just now managed to get home."

"Hey, what a bummer. It's too bad it didn't work out for tonight, but I'm not ready to give up on the idea."

Cassidy swallowed. "After a breakdown like this, I'm not eager to go driving into the city." *Breakdown—that's what it was, all right.*

"Well then, I'll just have to find a way out to Oak Park."

As Cassidy replaced the receiver, Starshine leapt onto the desk, so worn down she seemed barely able to make it to the top.

Lifting the cat onto her chest, Cassidy swung her heels up to the radiator and settled in to provide a restorative cuddle.

Always easier to be the helper than the helpee, isn't it? You jump in fast enough when somebody else is in trouble. But here you've got this major problem of your own, you're not doing anything about it.

Starshine purred, gazing raptly into her eyes.

"This anxiety's turning into a real pain in the ass." Cassidy sighed. "It's almost as if there's some part of me demanding that I talk through the Halloween incident, and when I ignore it, it escalates. It's downright embarrassing—not being able to drive outside of Oak Park." *This keeps up, you're gonna need a long list of excuses for why you can't leave home.*

Cassidy knew she ought to schedule an appointment with her former therapist, Honor Teasdale. Years ago, before becoming a therapist herself, she'd gone into therapy to get help coping with a bad marriage and had stayed through the end of her divorce. Honor had then moved to a small country town, and Cassidy shifted to seeing her on infrequent occasions for supervision only. The big problem with re-upping as a client was that Honor now lived more than an hour's distance from Oak Park.

You need to see Honor. Gotta get rid of this anxiety. And you have too much history with her to start over with somebody new. Long drive or not, you've gotta find some way to get there.

The only way to get there is to drive, which I can't do.

That's not the only reason, a small voice taunted. *You hate admitting you can't fix your own problems. And you don't wanna talk about what you did.*

⊠   ⊠   ⊠

Tuesday morning Cassidy pulled the Sunday paper out of the recycling tub and clipped the Martha Korski obituary. Going to the closet, she rummaged through many years' accumulation of headgear, selecting a helmet-shaped hat that provided maximum coverup. She pinned her hair up in back, pulled the hat down low over her forehead, and went to catch the bus.

The temperature had finally moved above freezing, as evidenced by troughs of half-melted snow along the sidewalks and gutters. To avoid the sludge, Cassidy picked her way down the middle of Briar.

She rode a bus and two els, then walked several blocks, arriving at the funeral home half an hour before the Korski visitation was due to begin. Inside was a foyer with halls leading off in different directions. One hall was lighted. Picking up a pamphlet at the desk, Cassidy planted herself on a straight-backed chair in an unlighted hall ten feet from the entryway.

A thin blonde woman flanked by two suited men entered the foyer from a door marked OFFICE. Although the woman's face showed signs of grieving, she had a youthful, coltish look about her suggesting she didn't lack for male attention. *Too confident. Cliff'd never get anywhere with her.*

The older man said, "I hope you're pleased with the makeup."

The blonde woman reached for the other man's hand. "It's fine. I don't care. No matter how natural, she's still—" The woman and her companion started down the lighted hall. The older man returned to the office.

Soon after that, people began to trickle in. Two women in their fifties. An elderly couple. Three women around the daughter's age. Cassidy shifted in her chair. She was too hot in her wool coat and helmet hat. She couldn't stand to read the pamphlet one more time. She would never make it as a policewoman because one surveillance assignment would push her over the edge.

Twenty minutes later, a man in a trench coat, scarf pulled up over his chin, fedora angled low, walked past. Cassidy hustled after him. Slipping through a door at the back of the visitation room, she sighted her quarry near the front corner of a bank of folding chairs, where he was divesting himself of hat and coat. As she eased closer, she saw that his hair was thin, his chest concave. *Not a day under sixty.*

Two doors opened onto the hallway from either end of the west wall. Half a dozen people clumped around the casket in front. Cassidy took a chair on the east side of the room, a post from which she could watch both doors.

She kept her eyes fixed for a long time but eventually her attention drifted. Sound bites of conversation tugged at her awareness. "I'll never forget the time Marty and me . . . She was always so good about . . . Hey Ralph! What've you been up to, you old . . ."

A young woman rushed down the aisle between the bank of chairs and the east wall. "Fran, I just heard the news," she called to the daughter. "Why didn't you tell me?"

The daughter hurried toward the other woman, her arms wide. "I should've called, I know. I feel terrible . . ."

The two women hugged. The friend had tears streaming down her face. The daughter was sobbing.

Cassidy's scalp suddenly tingled. Her gaze flitted to the entrance at the head of the room. A man wearing a heavy, camel-colored coat, collar pulled up around his ears, hands in pockets, stood in the doorway. He stared straight at her. The moment her eyes touched him, he was gone.

⊠ ⊠ ⊠

That night she said to Zach as she tucked herself under his arm on the waterbed, "If only I'd kept watch on the door. I'm so mad at myself for not getting a better look."

"He familiar at all?"

"I sort of feel like he was, but that could be seeing what I expect to see." She screwed up her face in concentration. "The harder I try to get a picture, the more it blurs."

"Why didn't you tell me you were gonna go wake crashing?"

"I didn't really plan it. I just got this impulse and took off."

His voice turning wry, Zach said, "What was that you said the other day about unilateral decisions?"

⊠ ⊠ ⊠

On Wednesday morning she was sitting in bed when Zach walked in with coffee. He said, "A guy from ADT is gonna show up any minute. He'll look everything over, give me a price, and hand us a contract." He shot her his Clint Eastwood squint. "I want you to sign it. I'll write out the check, but you have to sign the contract."

She stared down at her mug. *Hate having Zach dump so much money into the house.* This from the voice that couldn't stand feeling obligated.

You know he's right, her underdeveloped self-preservation voice kicked in. *We can't let Cliff keep walking in whenever he feels like it.*

She looked up. "Okay."

At eleven o'clock, the time for Ken's regularly scheduled appointment, Cassidy sat at her desk ready to go down if the doorbell should ring but not expecting to hear it. The previous week, when she'd questioned Ken about his little cat smile, she'd guessed he would retaliate by skipping the next session.

Waiting fifteen minutes, she turned to Ken's card in her Rolodex, then jiggled her pen between her fingers. *Could Ken have recognized me when we were racing out of his apartment?*

She tried to picture their escape from Ken's perspective. He had opened the front door as Zach bolted out the back. He might have recognized Zach, which would lead him to her. He might even have identified her directly when he looked down from the porch, since she had been wearing only her jacket and no hat. Her hands got cold thinking about it.

If he had figured it out, wouldn't the police have arrived at her door by now?

Not if he were Cliff.

You're just imagining he knows it was you 'cause you feel so stupid and guilty about the break-in. You predicted this no-show before you even thought of casing his apartment.

She punched up his number and he answered.

"This is Cassidy. I believe you had an appointment today and I'm wondering what happened." She managed to keep her voice cordial, but it wasn't easy.

"I woke up this morning with the flu," he said in a hearty tone. "Guess I fell back asleep."

"So, what would you like to do about rescheduling?"

"I suppose I could come in next week at the same time."

"I'll see you then."

"Take care now."

Didn't sound either sick or sleepy. His tone reminded her of the gotcha smile. *As if he's getting away with something right in front of me.*

She stood and looked through the window beside her desk at the street below. A small child bundled in a shiny blue snowsuit raced toward the corner, its mother dashing along behind. They came from the Roberts' house on the other side of the Steins. Cassidy figured it was the three-year-old girl, youngest of the brood. The child threw herself into the mound of snow at the corner, only to be dug out, brushed off, and dragged home.

Sitting down again, Cassidy placed a legal pad on the desk in front of her in hopes that writing words on paper would clarify her thoughts. "Ken" went at the top of the page.

Starshine ambled into the room, jumped up, sat squarely on the pad, and gave her an intense look.

"So, what do you think? Is Ken Cliff?"

The emaciated cat turned her gaze toward the doorway. *Should feed her.*

Don't let her distract you. Figuring out Ken is more important.

"You'll have to wait a little while. I've gotta get a hold of the dynamics here." *Control. Pretending he's doing therapy when we both know he isn't is a passive-aggressive means of getting control.* "That book I read said sexual sadism is more about power than sex. According to the profile, sadists usually have absentee fathers and domineering mothers."

Purring louder, Starshine extended her delicate pink nose, and Cassidy obliged with a nose-kiss. "You're just buttering me up to get me to feed you." She narrowed her eyes, dredging up the sparse tidbits she had wrested from Ken about his history. "The family was intact. Mild mannered, affectionate dad. Overpowering mom. All his mother ever cared about was looking good in front of the neighbors and browbeating his father."

That's why he goes all out for appearances. Lives in a dump and shops at Nordstrom's. Also where he learned to play gotcha. "I'll bet that's how he handled his mother. Acted like the good son to her face, pulled all kinds of stunts behind her back. And anytime she caught him, he'd do something to zap her, then smile his secretive little smile."

Mwat. Starshine's eyes were turning from green to cold amber, an indication that if Cassidy didn't respond to her soft approach, she was prepared to escalate. She batted Cassidy's hand with her claws.

"Stop that!" Rolling her chair back, Cassidy crossed her arms. "I'm not your food slave. Now just behave yourself and listen."

So how do Ken and Cliff match up? "Okay, I can imagine Ken losing his job because of the HIV. So maybe he came to therapy for support but was too ashamed to talk about the disease, so he made up other stuff instead. He might be so isolated that just interacting with another person for an hour, even if it's bullshit, is better than nothing."

Mrorrr! Starshine's tone was clearly aggrieved.

"I'll feed you when I'm done. So anyway, it could be that this is the first time he's ever felt accepted and nurtured by a woman, which would explain his choosing me to play the role of biographer."

Starshine deliberately rolled a pen off the edge of the desk, then fixed her with a haughty stare.

"Okay, that's it. No intimidation tactics allowed. You'll just have to wait till I'm done thinking this through." She dumped the cat in the hall, slammed the door, and went to stand by the window again. Gazing down into the empty street, she visualized the scene at the wake and put Ken's face on the man in the doorway.

Now wait a minute. You can't make the leap that Ken is Cliff just because his history partially matches the profile for a sexual sadist. Ken's father wasn't absent, remember? And there're countless men with controlling mothers who do not become rapists or killers. Besides, Ken's urge to play gotcha *doesn't exactly jibe with the way Cliff has you idealized.*

Since Cliff had cast her in the role of his biographer, he had no reason to be hostile. He was assuming she would slide right into his scenario. But what would he do if she said *no?*

She shuddered at the thought of what might happen if he decided she also needed punishment.

If you made Cliff angry, he'd want to zap you. And that means he'd have to come out of hiding. If you blew him off, he'd make some kind of move.

You could do it in an ad. She tapped her fist against the oak window frame. *You could tell him he's pathetic, you're not interested. Piss him off enough to provoke a response.*

You oughtta discuss this with Zach. He's not gonna be thrilled at the idea of you using yourself as bait.

If you take a vote, it'll be an impasse, just like he said. Besides, this is your decision. You can't let a man who's only half moved in run your life

She plunked into her chair, brushed cat hair off the legal pad, and wrote out her ad. CLIFF: YOU PICKED THE WRONG WOMAN. I'M NOT FOND OF LOSERS AND I DON'T TREAT PSYCHOPATHS. I SUGGEST YOU LOOK FOR A GOOD PSYCHIA-TRIST AND LEAVE ME ALONE.

Calling the *Free Chicago*, she arranged for the ad to run Saturday.

The phone rang and Louise's voice said, "I figured out how to get to Oak Park." She sounded perkier than in the previous call, more the way she'd been at the party. "Actually, Patrick figured it out for me."

Patrick? Oh yeah, the gay friend who partly redecorated Roland's place.

"He's gonna drive me to his house, which is in Oak Park, and you can meet us there. I know you said you were booked all week, but this won't take more than an hour, so I thought maybe we could do it tomorrow night after you finish seeing clients."

"Thursday? Let's see, I'll be done at eight. I guess I could come over after that."

"Great." Louise gave her the address.

✉ ✉ ✉

Wednesday evening, as Cassidy closed the door behind her seven o'clock client, Zach came into the waiting room and said, "Some woman called to cancel so you're through for the night."

Her mouth compressed in irritation. She would much rather see another client than face telling Zach about her ad.

He turned to go upstairs.

Hurrying after him, she snagged his arm. "Since I'm done early, let's go out."

"Out? Where?"

"We could, um, go to Clancy's like we used to."

On the drive to the pub they had sometimes frequented before Zach moved in, Cassidy pumped him for details on the home invasion story he was writing for the *Post*.

Parking in front of the beer-sign studded window, he said, "When you ask a lot of questions about something you're not really interested in, I start to get uneasy. Is there anything I oughtta be suspicious about?"

"I refuse to answer on the grounds that I don't want to tell you until after the first drink."

As they walked into the drab interior, a pudgy, sixty-something waitress came toward them, her face crinkling in a wide grin. "Haven't seen you two in ages. I was afraid you'd joined all them thin-blooded health nuts, given up booze and grease for jogging."

"If I did any jogging, it'd probably be to the nearest bar." Zach chose a table in the corner. A Frank Sinatra tune played at a sound level soothing to the ear. "We were here about a week ago but you were off."

The waitress took out her pad. "That's Jack Daniels, isn't it? You want any of them crunchy onion rings or maybe a fat, juicy hamburger?"

"Just drinks." Zach said it in his customary way of making decisions for her.

Cassidy kept her mouth shut. She was not about to waste energy fighting over his peremptory order giving when she would need all her resources to defend her own peremptory ad-placing.

The waitress brought their drinks and Zach chugged half of his. "I have to finish this off so I can find out what this latest stunt of yours is that you don't want to tell me about." His eyes narrowed. "Or would I be happier not knowing?"

"Probably." A heavy lump settled in her stomach. "Did you check the e-mail? We get anything back from Boytoy yet?"

One corner of his mouth turned down. "No response.

Maybe you just don't have the right stuff for titillating gay males."

"We've got so damn many loose ends." Wadding her napkin into a tiny ball, she jiggled it in one hand. "Boytoy, Henry Donovan, Jake Sheffield. Leman's the only one we've gotten anywhere with. And it might not be any of these guys. It might be somebody who comes across as totally innocuous."

"Right. Somebody you'd never think of. Like Kevin."

"There isn't an innocuous bone in Kevin's body."

He shrugged. "Let's concentrate on the suspects at hand. Tell me again what you know about Henry Donovan."

"The man with the newspaper." Her eyes followed the waitress as she clomped over to a loner at the bar and leaned close to talk in his ear. "The first time I saw him he was feeling some real pain. No surprise considering he came to my office straight from his divorce."

Zach sat straighter. "You've got his divorce date?"

"Well sure. The date of his first session."

"His ex's name and address are on the decree. I can get a copy from the county clerk's office."

"And she probably knows what happened to him." Cassidy watched as the waitress pulled a stoop-shouldered geezer away from the bar, put his hands into position on her shoulder and waist, then led him into a hip-hop version of a waltz. "Remember Cliff's vehemence about women rejecting him? Now that I think about it, Donovan was pretty pissed that his wife went for a divorce." She ran her fingers up and down the sweaty glass. "And the sexual boasting. No matter how hard I worked to drag him off it, he kept coming back."

"Trying to prove he's straight?" Zach raised his glass, rattled the ice cubes, and slugged down the remainder. He said, his voice severe, "Finish your drink."

She gazed grimly at her half-empty glass. *Confession time. Might as well get it over with. A fast injection of alcohol can't hurt.* She tossed it down. "I called in an ad telling Cliff he's a loser and a psychopath, and I don't want anything to do with him."

Staring at her as if she'd lost her mind, Zach said, "What the hell do you think you're doing? You want your name on his shitlist too?" He reared back, an angry light flaring in his eyes. "That's it, isn't it? You want him to come after you." He smacked his hand on the table. "You've got some half-assed notion of luring him out in the open. Then, when he moves in on you, you're gonna throw your butterfly net over his head. That's what you're doing here, isn't it?"

18

A Return

Cassidy's eyes filled. He was far more outraged than she had expected. She felt incredibly stupid, like a little kid trying to sneak out onto the playing field with a major league team.

Zach stood abruptly. "You think I finally got to the point of living with a woman just to watch her set herself up for HIV? Turn our whole lives into a pill-taking routine? There's no way I'd hang around for that." He threw down a bill, grabbed his coat, and stomped out of the bar.

Cassidy covered her face. A moment later she felt a hand on her shoulder and looked up to see the waitress. The older woman's sympathetic expression made her cringe in embarrassment.

The waitress gave her a comforting pat. "He'll get over

it. You just give him time. The problem with you younger gals is, you wanna talk everything to death. You gotta remember, men don't deal with words. It just irritates 'em."

I'm a therapist—I have to talk everything to death. "I'll try to keep that in mind." Forcing a smile, Cassidy put on her coat and followed Zach out.

He was waiting in the Nissan. They drove home in silence. Stopping at the back door, he said, "You go on in. I need to be alone for a while."

She almost said, *Need to get blitzed, you mean,* but at the last moment realized that in this instance, going on the attack would not be a good strategy. Remembering what the waitress had told her, she behaved in a highly uncharacteristic way: she got out of the car and went inside.

That night she slipped off into a vivid dream in which she awoke to find all Zach's belongings gone from the house. She tried to reach him at the newspaper but the receptionist refused to put her call through. She went to Marina City and was stopped by the doorman, who had orders not to let her in. She finally tracked down Emily, who told her Zach would have her put away if she did not leave him alone.

The alarm shrilled. She opened her eyes to see Zach's blue-robed back leaving the bedroom. By the time he returned with two mugs of coffee, she was sitting up in bed working on her defense.

He handed her the purple mug, his expression unreadable in the hazy light, then sat in the desk chair and swiveled to face her. "Okay, I understand why you did it. If we're gonna be together, I guess I have to learn to live with the fact that once you set your mind on something, you'll go to any lengths to get it."

"Now wait a minute—"

"I know, I can be the same way." He leaned forward, forearms laid across his knees. "But I like to think I don't take it as far as you do. And I'm also sexist enough to assume I'd have a better chance of fending off a six-foot psychopath."

"It won't come to that." She raised her mug.

"We'll see. Anyway, the ad's already in, and if I pull it you'll just find some way around me. The security system's coming in a couple of days but we both know that won't stop him. So now I have to do what I can to protect you."

Some part of her wanted to argue, to insist she could take care of herself. Recognizing the absurdity of that idea, she clamped down on it and nodded.

"There's something else I have to say. If you refuse to cooperate or sabotage my efforts, I'm outta here. I will not stay in this house waiting for some madman to rape you."

Realizing how she would feel if he were at risk, she nodded again.

"I'll be right back." He crossed the hall to his office, then returned and laid his cell phone on the bed beside her. Rolling the chair up close, he waited for her to meet his eyes. "I want this with you wherever you go. Into your office when you do a session. Into the bathroom when you take a pee. If you see anything even slightly suspicious, page me."

Feeling as though she'd turned mute, she nodded once more.

"While I'm out today, I'm gonna run down a pepper gun and the deadliest pocket knife I can find."

She opened her mouth.

He thumped his mug down on the nightstand. "I don't want one word of argument."

"I was just gonna say, why not a gun?"

"A gun's harder to conceal, and if he takes it off you, you've increased his firepower. I thought I'd get a miniature pepper gun and a small knife so you could hide them both in your bra. He'd be less likely to find them than he would a derringer, which you'd have to carry in your waistband. But if you'd feel safer with a gun, I'll get one."

Once before she'd had a gun and it made her feel powerful. But she could quite happily live out the rest of her life without touching one again. "I'll go with the knife."

Standing, he looked down at her. "You mean, you're actually gonna do what I say and not fight me on it?"

"I'm not crazy."

"Really?"

She rose and slid her arms around his neck.

Pulling her up tight, he said, "Okay, then I guess the fight's officially over." He nested his face in her hair.

⊠ ⊠ ⊠

Thursday night, before leaving the house to meet Louise at Patrick's, Cassidy tucked the knife beneath her breast in one bra cup, the pepper gun in the other, packed the phone in her bag, and went out to the garage. The address Louise had given her belonged to a sleek, prairie-school home sitting on its wide lot a gracious distance back from the street.

Guiding her into the living room, Patrick waved his hand broadly. "Well, what do you think? Is there enough of an impact here to offset the impression you got at Roland's?" The minimally furnished room was done in primary colors, relying on a few bold pieces to create its high-energy, audacious effect. An enormous contemporary painting filled with blue and red surrealistic figures against a sunshine-yellow background hung above a raised fireplace flickering with crimson flames.

Louise reposed grandly on a red and blue sofa facing the fire. "I always wear black at Patrick's. It's the only color strong enough to compete in this crayon factory explosion of his."

Accepting Patrick's offer of brandy, Cassidy took a chair next to the sofa and said, "So, Louise, you want me to have the lowdown about your father in hopes that I'll tell all and Mom will call off the wedding."

Louise's large frame was dramatically attired in a long black dress with scarlet collar, her gown easily holding its own against the other colors in the room. "You sound just like my therapist—always looking for ulterior motives."

Patrick fingered his short, dark beard. "You know that's what you want, Louise."

"I probably do hope your mother will leave Roland standing at the altar." Louise draped one arm along the back of the sofa. "I love to see people get what they have coming."

Cassidy waved her brandy snifter. "I don't like getting in the middle of other people's relationships, so I probably won't say anything to Mom."

Patrick got up to poke the fire. "Just let her talk so she can get it out of her system."

"He's right." Louise grinned. "Give me my way and I'm fine." She swirled her brandy. "This probably won't seem like a big deal to you. I mean, compared to physical and sexual abuse, this is probably nothing at all."

"I never make those kinds of comparisons." Cassidy held her glass under her nose, inhaling the potent fumes.

"Okay, so here goes." Louise swallowed some brandy. "When it comes to having everything your own way, I'm a piker next to Roland. If anybody in our family didn't do what he wanted, he'd hammer them with guilt and ridicule until they finally gave in. There were five of us kids in all—the three older girls, then me and Ron. The girls—we always called the three oldest 'the girls' 'cause they came one, two, three in a row—the girls got off pretty easy. He always favored them, especially June."

Patrick returned to the sofa. "And she, of course, turned out the worst of the bunch."

"The rest of us could never get it right." Louise reached for Patrick's hand. "Ron, 'cause Dad expected him to be super macho and he wasn't. Me, 'cause I'd stand up for Mom whenever he went after her. And my mother—well, he was always pissed at her."

Cassidy, who'd been staring hypnotically into the flames, pulled her attention back to Louise. "Why was he so angry at your mother?"

Louise stood and turned her back to the fire, casting a long shadow on the hardwood floor. "Gotta toast the backside." She smoothed down her skirt. "Why was he so angry? I think my father expected Mom to keep him happy, and when any little thing wasn't perfect, it was her fault. But if you were talking to him, he'd come up with this long list of excuses. The top being that after three kids in three years, she didn't wanna make babies anymore. She actually succeeded in holding out against him for a whole decade, during which time he made her life miserable, or so I'm told. That all happened before I was born."

Cassidy asked, "What about the part you remember?"

Louise gracefully twirled her zaftig body, then eased back down on the sofa. "My earliest memories are of Dad screaming at Mom until she crumpled on the floor and put her arms over her head."

Patrick crossed to a blue liquor cabinet on the far side of the room, returned with a decanter, and splashed more brandy into their glasses. "I think people like Roland are every bit as bad as batterers."

Cassidy clenched her back teeth. She hated bullies, particularly male bullies who picked on their wives and children. "Your father was abusing your mother and you were trying to defend her. Tough job for a kid."

"You know what they say." Raising her arm and making a fist, Louise showed off her bicep. "If it doesn't kill you—"

Patrick chuckled, his dark eyes flashing. "This is one woman I'd never want to tangle with."

Louise put a finger to her red lips, shushing him. "Don't interrupt. I've got one more memory. Actually, I've got tons, but if I keep going I'll get too drunk to climb the stairs to my condo. So, last memory. Mother suffered from migraines. When I was twelve they got so bad she couldn't get out of bed for days at a time."

Cassidy winced. "The doctors couldn't do anything?"

"Dad was against doctors," Louise said, her voice disgusted. "Refused to let her see one. All he did was yell at her for being in bed. I can remember him standing over her and screaming when her poor head was already about to split. Finally her brother took her to a doctor and she got some medicine that stopped the headaches. Here she'd been miserable for years and didn't have to be."

"Jesus." Cassidy took a deep drink, shuddering as it went down. "I can see why you had to tell somebody." She swirled her brandy. "Your father sounds like a monster. And there's no way out of it—my mother needs to know." She sighed, picturing her mother's face with its familiar look of disapproval. "Whether she likes it or not." *Likes it? She'd rather eat worms and die than find out her prince is a pig in disguise.* She caught Louise's eyes. "One more thing. Considering what a tyrant your father was, I'm curious how your mother finally got away."

"It was *moi*." Louise pointed to her chest. "But first I need to backtrack. Dad was dead set that the only college bound kid would be the future pres of Mertz Inc. But I was equally dead set that I was gonna get myself a degree and have an income and never, ever be in the spot my poor mother was in."

Patrick said, "That's why she's a fag hag instead of a wife."

"I told you not to interrupt." Louise gave him a stern look. "Anyway, I took out loans to put myself through school so

I was poor for a long time afterward. Then, when I was thirty-one, I bought a two-bedroom condo so at long last I was able to play Indiana Jones and swoop in to rescue Mom from the troll king. But it was kinda sad 'cause she only lived a couple years after that. Here she had herself a whole new life," Louise's chin dropped, "and then it got taken away."

Grasping her hand, Patrick lifted it from the sofa. "Lou took it really hard. Got so bad I had to haul her in to a psychiatrist."

"He did." Louise patted his cheek. "The only thing pulled me through is that I had my two boys taking care of me. Patrick called every day, and Ron piled up enough frequent flyer miles for a trip to the moon." She shook her head. "Poor Ron. Dad's really putting on the screws about his taking over the business."

Patrick said, "He oughtta tell Roland to stick it."

Louise glared. "You don't understand what it's like growing up with a control freak. Every one of us has been programmed to obey. And if we don't, we get swamped with feelings of guilt. Or we get punished."

Patrick kneaded his beard. "You don't."

Louise said, "I don't *obey*. But who says it doesn't make me feel like shit not to? Why do you think I weigh six hundred pounds?"

Patrick snapped back, "Because you have an evolved consciousness and see that fat is beautiful."

Cassidy finished her brandy and set the glass on the floor. "She's right. People get brainwashed from living with a Nazi-style parent. Breaking their hold is always a lot harder than it looks."

Patrick started to rise, the decanter in hand, but Cassidy waved him back down.

Louise gave Cassidy a speculative look. "I'll bet you're a pretty good therapist." She held out her snifter and Patrick poured. "You know, it just might straighten Ron out to have a talk with you."

Cassidy raised a hand to deflect her. "I really can't—"

Patrick laughed. "What're you up to, Lou? This poor woman gets remotely connected to your family, and here you are, trying to drum up free therapy for everybody."

Louise gestured for him to be quiet. "Ron's all mixed up from listening to Dad, and I'm no use 'cause I'm his big sis. But you might get through to him. Now if I could just talk him into . . ."

⋈ ⋈ ⋈

Cassidy trudged upstairs feeling as if she were carrying as many pounds as Louise, her heaviness caused by last night's bad dream, too much fireplace and brandy, and a generalized sense of life's misery.

Following the sound of the television, she found Zach sprawled in his usual place on the bed.

He cut the power and said, "Look what I've got."

Sylvia's head popped up from behind his bent knee.

Cassidy pushed Zach over to his side and plopped down next to him. "What's she doing here?"

Zach chuckled. "She didn't like Maggie's sister's apartment. Or the sister's cat. So she engineered her return." He wrapped a large hand around the kitten's body and held her aloft, her four paws dangling.

"She got sent back? She must've been really bad."

"That she was. A lot like her mother." He sent Cassidy a pointed look. "And grandmother."

Taking Sylvia from him, Cassidy placed the kitten on her shoulder so she could play in her curly, shoulder-length hair. She realized she did not feel as frustrated by the kitten's return as she ought to.

Zach stood, unzipped his jeans, and dumped them in the empty corner with his shoes. "Maggie dropped her off while you were gone. Seems like she ran up a pretty good rap sheet at the sister's apartment. She chased Jezebel—the other cat weighs twenty pounds, mind you—till the poor thing ended up cringing in the closet and mumbling to herself. Then she started an aroma-therapy campaign on the sister. Yesterday, when the sister was at the office, her nose started twitching and she suddenly realized that the dampness on her sweater was not caused by taking it out of the dryer too soon. That's when the official return-verdict came down."

Cassidy laughed.

Zach tossed his shirt on top of his jeans. Removing Sylvia from her shoulder, he shut the kitten in the nursery across the hall, then lay on the bed and pulled Cassidy down on top of him. "Now that we've stopped fighting," he said, his hands reaching under her sweater, "we get to make up."

19

A Cancellation

Friday morning she went downstairs to find Zach and a workman huddled next to the back door.

Installing the force field so nobody can get in. Be better if nobody could get out. I could settle in with my agoraphobia, no more anxiety attacks, maybe even keep myself out of trouble.

After the man left, Zach showed her the ADT stickers in the windows and instructed her on how to operate the panel of buttons by the door. As he left for work, he watched through the window to make sure she punched it on.

Later that morning she sat in her swivel chair and stared out at a leaden sky, the flat, gray light matching her mood. As much as her mother would not want to hear what Louise had said, Cassidy could not avoid telling her.

Infusing her voice with false cheer, she called Helen. "There's something I need to talk to you about. Why don't I pick you up and we can have lunch at Erik's."

She was leaving the bedroom when the phone rang and she picked up. "This is Cassidy McCabe." She heard a click on the other end. *Either a wrong number or somebody who doesn't want to talk to me.* A mild ripple of uneasiness went through her.

Cassidy stood behind her mother in a short line at Erik's Deli, a popular eatery where just about everybody in Oak Park sometimes met for lunch. The line moved forward and a clean-cut, white-aproned youth took their order. Helen asked for an Erik burger and cola. Cassidy, whose stomach was refusing anything but chocolate, requested double-fudge cake and coffee. The young man handed them trays with drinks, silverware, and their order number. Cassidy paid, then led her mother to a small, blond wood table next to the window.

Helen removed her cola from the tray. "Well, dear, Roland and I haven't quite figured out what to do about that legal paper of his, but the wedding's still on, so I guess that's a good sign." Her voice strained for optimism.

Dumping cream and sugar into her coffee, Cassidy noticed that her mother's eyes were worried. *Knows something's up. I probably overdid the good-humor bit.* The same feeling of heaviness came over her that she'd experienced when telling Zach about the ad. *Only difference is Zach insisted on hearing it. Mom's gonna pitch a fit trying to stop me.*

Cassidy said, "What if he waits till the last minute, then threatens to call the whole thing off if you don't sign?"

Helen's face paled beneath her heavy makeup. "Roland wouldn't do that." Her voice sharpened. "I can't think why you'd even want to suggest it. What're you trying to do, get me all upset?" She thrust her straw forcefully into her paper cup.

Another clean-cut teenager set their plates on the table. Cassidy took a small bite of cake, mushing it into thick, chocolate goo in her mouth. "You remember Roland's daughter Louise? She wanted to get together, fill me in on the family history. So I saw her last night."

"Why would you want to hear what that woman has to say? All of his kids, they're all trying to stop him from marrying me." Turning her head abruptly, Helen stared out the window.

She looked back at Cassidy, her faded eyes glinting with anger. "What're you doing, taking her side against me? I guess if you did, that wouldn't be such a big surprise. I mean, the fact that I finally have a man in my life—a successful businessman who really cares about me—doesn't sit too well with you." She bit into her hamburger and chewed defiantly.

Cassidy hunched over her mug. *She actually imagines that I'd begrudge her Roland?* "You think the only reason Louise would want to talk to me is to sabotage the wedding?"

"Why else would she pass on some disgusting story? She doesn't even know you. Roland warned me about Louise. He said she's always had it in for him, he doesn't know why.

Said she might try to feed me some nasty gossip about the past." Helen poked her straw at the ice in her paper cup. "Anyway, whatever it is, I don't want to hear it."

Cassidy stared through the window at two black businessmen in trench coats crossing Oak Park Avenue from the bank entrance on the opposite side. Forcing her eyes back to her mother's frightened face, she lowered her voice, the tone she used with clients. "I guess from your point of view, listening to Louise does seem like a kind of betrayal. But when I agreed to meet with her, I didn't intend to bring any of this back to you. I wouldn't even be mentioning it if I didn't think this was something you really needed to hear."

"Why can't you just be happy for me? Why do you have to try and spoil it?" Tears pooled in the corners of her eyes. "My whole life, I've always been the ordinary one. The one who stayed home and cooked. I watched my mother carry on like an idiot, my sister get all the boyfriends, and even my daughter—my very own daughter—do all sorts of things I'd never think of. But now, for the first time, I have somebody who makes me feel special."

"It's not what—"

"And you can't stand it," Helen rolled on. "You've never been able to keep a man yourself, and you can't stand knowing that I've got somebody who wants to marry me. While all you've got is a reporter hanging around your house until somebody better comes along."

Cassidy blinked back tears of her own. "Mom, that's not true. I do want you to be happy."

Standing, Helen struggled to get her arms into her coat sleeves. Cassidy rose and tried to help, but her mother jerked the garment from her hands and stomped out of the restaurant.

Wednesday night Zach walked out on me, today it's my mother. And I'm the one supposed to help people with relationships.

⊠ ⊠ ⊠

She was hanging her jacket in the closet when the phone started to ring. Another hang-up.

Later that afternoon the phone rang while she was in session. After the client left, she went upstairs to play the message.

"This is Mira. I'm afraid I have to cancel for tomorrow. I'll call next week to explain." Her voice was thick. Cassidy was sure she'd been crying.

She tapped her fingers on the phone. Something was wrong, perhaps something she had precipitated in the last session when she'd pushed Mira to use condoms. *Two hang-ups, then a don't-call-me, I'll-call-you. Bet next spring's crop of dandelions she waited to get the machine so she didn't have to talk to me.*

Your mother's mad, your client's avoiding you. Her mouth clamped in frustration.

Avoiding's not good enough. She dialed Mira's number, but the machine came on and she hung up.

What about Mom? Guilt bubbled up from her bottomless guilt-well. *Okay, kiddo, you've done it again. Made your mother unhappy.* No matter how hard she tried not to, she always ended up being the bad girl. The only way out was to apologize.

Yeah, but this time I'm right. She really oughtta know what kind of guy she's marrying.

You sure there wasn't one little drop of envy mixed in with all those good intentions?

Cassidy winced at the possibility. *Just do it. She's not gonna make any moves—she's enjoying every minute of her martyrdom.*

Cassidy called to apologize and her mother grudgingly accepted.

⊠   ⊠   ⊠

The ringing of the phone gradually penetrated all the fuzzy layers of sleep down to the tiny spark of consciousness that burned like a nightlight when the rest of her was shut down. The waterbed surged, her body briefly bumping the bottom, then she opened her eyes to see Zach's naked figure moving across the darkened room toward her desk. The digital numbers on the bureau said six-fifteen.

"Hello?" Zach's voice was croaky with sleep. "Thanks." He sped through the doorway and down the stairs.

She pulled on her robe and raced after him. As she made the right angle turn in the stairwell, she could see the front door hanging open, feel cold air rolling in. Reaching the entryway, she saw Zach standing in front of the screen door staring toward the street. Her cheeks burned with embarrassment.

"What's going on?"

"Shit." He hurried back inside, nearly colliding with her. "Cliff. He ran out from between the two houses, jumped in his car, and took off. I didn't even get a good enough look to tell if it was the attorney, and I couldn't read the plates."

"What are you doing out there? You haven't got a stitch on."

His head reared back. "I suppose the next thing out of your mouth'll be, 'What will the neighbors think?'"

She grimaced, her cheeks growing hotter. "That's my mother talking, isn't it?" She laid an outspread hand on his chest. "You're freezing. What's the matter with you? You think you're immune to frostbite?" She started back upstairs, tugging his arm to pull him along. "You better get yourself into a hot shower right away."

He followed behind. "Your neighbor saw him heading toward the side door. I doubt that he'd try to break in with that ADT sticker on the window, but I don't like him getting this close. I thought I might be able to grab him if I came around from the front, but by the time I got to the porch he was already in full flight. And I was beginning to wonder if tackling a psycho in my birthday suit was such a great idea."

She leaned against the bedroom doorjamb as Zach released three wildly bouncing kittens from their nursery incarceration. Shaking her head, she said, "I still can't believe you were standing naked in front of all the commuters and dog walkers."

"That bother you?"

"Yes!" Noticing that her feet had gone numb, she retreated into the bedroom and picked up her mauve slippers, moving swiftly to outmaneuver Hobbes, who apparently thought they were floppy creatures in need of killing. She swatted him away and went downstairs.

A short while later Zach joined her in the kitchen, reaching to take the mug she had ready for him. The threadbare black jacket he wore over his black tee reminded her that he was planning to go into the office even though it was Saturday.

She leaned back against the counter. "Here I am, actually awake and it's barely dawn. Why don't I cook you an omelette?"

"Since when do you make jokes so early in the morning?"

She took a swallow of coffee. "I know how to do omelettes."

"I'm sure you do. I just don't want you spoiling me is all."

"You never accept pampering, do you? I wonder why not?"

Putting a finger to his lips, he shook his head. "Not allowed to psychoanalyze me before ten a.m." He stuck four slices of bread into the toaster.

Cassidy bit her bottom lip. "I'm worried about Mira."

"People cancel all the time."

"She was crying on the phone."

"So what do you think's going on?" The toaster harumphed. Zach began applying a quarter-inch layer of butter to each slice.

She frowned at his disregard for fat grams. "I'm afraid my hammering at her about AIDS prompted her to confront Jake. And that would've led to his cranking up both the punishment and the pressure to stop therapy."

Zach carried his toast to the dining room table. "Maybe she'll leave, which'd be all to the good."

Cassidy took the chair kitty-corner from his. "I suppose everyone has their breaking point." *Where was yours? You*

hung in there, no matter what, till Kevin decided to bail.
"But so far her tendency's been to stick like glue."

Disgust crossed Zach's face. "I still don't get it."

Her jaw tightened. "That's because when you run into problems, you leave." She broke off a piece of his toast and nibbled at it, licking butter from the corners of her mouth. "A lot of people are terrified of abandonment, and to them it feels like abandonment even when they leave. What makes it especially difficult is that abusive relationships are even harder to get out of than healthy ones."

"That's nuts."

"What happens is, the abuser punishes the victim whenever she gets out of line, which causes the victim to hand over more and more control. Basically it's an advanced form of bullying. And an essential ingredient is that the abuser isolates the victim and makes her keep everything secret, which is why I'm so afraid Jake'll force Mira to quit therapy."

Talking around a mouthful of toast, Zach said, "That sounds like our boy Jake."

"Whenever Mira confronts Jake about his addiction, he punishes her by withholding affection." She stared out the dining room window into thick, grainy light. "Which is exactly what Cliff did to Jenny. He bullied her into sexual behavior that was way outside her comfort zone."

Zach folded his arms on the table. "So Cliff and Jake use the same tactics."

"It's standard procedure in any abusive relationship. But still, the similarity does add points to Jake's rating as a suspect." She drummed her fingers on the table. "If only we could find out more about him."

"You said Cliff acted out a rape and bondage fantasy with Jenny. If Jake were Cliff, would he try the same thing on hookers?"

She pinched the tip of her chin, mentally reviewing what she had read about sexual sadists. "Yeah, he probably would." She caught his eye. "What are you thinking?"

"Is there any regular time he goes out on the prowl?"

"Let's see . . . " She caught her lip between her teeth. "Mira did say he favors Sunday night around nine."

"If we watched him pick up a hooker, then hung around till he dropped her off, she'd probably be just as happy to sell information as she is to sell her ass."

Cassidy pictured herself wearing a trench coat and flashing a bill at a scantily clad woman. *Only thing missing is Bogart approaching out of a fog.*

Zach said, "This is a real long shot but I think it's worth a try. Didn't you say he lives in a Lake Shore Drive highrise? I'll have to case out the parking garage before Sunday night so we can lock onto his car when he leaves."

The phone rang and she picked up the receiver from the kitchen wall beside the doorway.

"Is Zach there?"

She recognized the voice. "Emily?"

"He didn't answer on his line so I thought I'd try yours."

Cassidy handed the phone to Zach. He listened a moment, then moved into the kitchen so his back was turned and his voice muffled. She sat down again and waited.

He said, "I think she mentioned that name." A beat. "Oh

shit." Two more beats. "Okay, I'll talk to you later." He hung up and came through the doorway, eyes narrowed, face creased with tension.

20

Hooker

"What?" Cassidy's hand went to the base of her throat.

Sitting, Zach said in a gentle voice, "That guy, Patrick something or other, the one you saw the other night. What's his last name?"

"Larkin."

He ran a hand over his face. His eyes moved away, then returned to fasten on hers. He reached across the table, holding out his hand. She placed hers inside it. "Somebody shot him."

"Oh God!"

"The same way your cousin got it. Yesterday after work. Larkin was just coming out of his north side office when this guy in a black ski mask pulled up and nailed him."

Sucking in air, she jerked her hand out of his and hugged

herself. She pictured Patrick waving an arm to show off his colorful living room. "What possible connection could there be between Mark and Patrick?"

She saw the answer in his smoky eyes. Her voice dropped into a rough whisper. "Me. I'm the connection. Two guys, both gay, one shot while he was having lunch with me, the other the day after I visited his house." She started to shiver. "Cliff has a vendetta against gays and women, and now he's started gunning down any gay man I have contact with." She pictured a ski-masked man bursting through their door, machine gun cradled in one arm, flames spitting from the barrel. "Oh shit." Her fingers dug into Zach's forearm. "He's escalating. What if he comes after you?"

He covered her hand with his. "You put your finger on it when you said gays and women. I don't think he's gonna be interested in me."

Taking a deep breath, she rested her chin on her fist. "But how did he know they were gay?"

"He must've seen you with them and figured it out."

Who could've been watching when you were with Mark? Anybody at the party. Or someone who followed you to the restaurant. Not the restaurant—the shooter was all set with the stolen car before you got there.

Zach said, "Emily needs to talk to you. Can you meet her at the station sometime this afternoon?"

Drive into the city? Her mouth went dry. "I can't make it today. I'll give her a call instead. There's not much to tell anyway."

He stared at her as if she'd suddenly turned lunatic on

him, a troubled look coming into his eyes. "This is a police detective working a double homicide."

"I'll call her. We'll figure something out." Feeling as if small jolts of electricity were racing across her skin, she jumped to her feet. "Don't worry. I'll be fine."

He stood also, gripping her upper arms firmly. "You're not fine. How could you be fine? You just heard about another shooting you're involved in." He pulled her into a comforting hug. "I'll stay home today and go with you when you talk to Emily. And don't even try to argue me out of it."

A wave of relief washed over her as she leaned against his chest.

⊠   ⊠   ⊠

Sunday afternoon she carried a basket of clean laundry up from the basement. Reaching the second floor, she noticed that the nursery door was shut. *Zach kitten visiting? But why the closed door? Now that I think about it, he wasn't very talkative during our coffee and newspaper routine.* He'd been his normal self the day before at the police station, friendly with Emily but not bedroom-voice friendly. Then this morning he'd stopped talking.

She set the laundry basket on the bed and began stowing panties and socks in her dresser. *Probably sick of having to prop me up. Shouldn't have let him see I was scared to drive. I hate this whiny, dependent little person I'm turning into.* Five black tees with beer ads plastered across the front went into Zach's bureau.

Crossing to her desk, she found a folded newspaper prominently displayed on top of her piles, the *Free Chicago*, her ad circled in red. CLIFF: YOU PICKED THE WRONG WOMAN. Her chest tightened. *So that's why the door's closed.*

Wanting to push the ad out of her mind, she got rid of the paper, sat in her desk chair, took out Louise's number, then rested her hand on the phone. These kind of calls were never easy. She let two beats go by, then dialed.

"Hello?" A male voice she recognized as Ron's.

"This is Cassidy. I heard about Patrick and called to see how Louise is doing."

"Cassidy?" He sounded pleased. "Louise is asleep right now. She's taking it pretty hard."

Because of me. Patrick was killed because of me. She cleared her throat. "It's good she's got you with her."

"I'm glad she's not alone, but I'm also getting very anxious to return to my own wife, my own house, and my real job."

"Does that mean you've made a decision about taking over the family business?" She twisted the coin-filled wine bottle that rose above the clutter on her desk.

"It means," a note of bitterness crept into his voice, "that dear old Dad can take his plans for my life and stick 'em you know where."

"Well, that sounds nice and definite." She rotated toward the window. Tiny snowflakes swirled in the wind, so light and feathery they looked as if they might stay afloat forever.

"Patrick always gave me a hard time for not taking a stand. Well, now the stand's taken and guess who got me to do it?"

"Your father?"

"Would you believe I've been dithering around for weeks

feeling sorry for the old guy? Actually feeling guilty, for Chrissake? But he finally did something so purely rotten, so purely Roland, it's too much even for me."

She stared into the flurry of powdered-sugar snow. "What'd he do?"

"A few hours after Lou heard the news, this call comes in from Dad. And just get what he said." Dropping into a baritone, he mimicked Roland's voice. "'Now that that fancy dandy you've been hanging on all these years is out of the way, maybe you'll find yourself a real man and settle down like you shoulda done a long time ago.'"

"I can see why you'd want to get out of here."

"As soon as Louise is up to it, I'm gonna make a pitch for her to move to Seattle. The more distance we can put between Roland and us, the better."

Finishing the conversation, Cassidy stood in the doorway to gaze at the closed door across the hall. *Not even sure Zach's in there. He could be on the other side of town for all I know.* Her old house was so large they could wander for hours without crossing paths.

She opened the nursery door and poked her head around it. Zach was seated on the floor, a bag of pistachios beside him. He had Hobbes on his shoulder, Calvin asleep across his arm.

"Can I come in?"

"Suit yourself."

As she settled beside him, Sylvia came racing up from behind the guitar case. "I saw the newspaper. I guess that means you're still pissed about the ad."

"I told you—I'm over it."

"You're not acting like you're over it."

"What do you want me to do? Break out champagne because you've set yourself up to get raped?" Hobbes jumped down, grabbed a pistachio, and scuttled across the room to one of Kevin's old boots that stood beneath the window. The kitten sat up like a squirrel and dropped the nut inside.

Cassidy scooped up Sylvia and held her captive in her lap. "I thought you weren't a brooder."

"A what?"

"When I told you how Kevin used to sulk, you assured me you didn't go in for brooding."

He reached for a pistachio with his left hand to avoid disturbing the sleeping kitten. "Speaking of Kevin, you heard from him lately?"

Her jaw tightened. "What do you want me to do? Call and ask if he's taken to emulating movie stars and raping women?" *When was it Kevin moved out? About six months before Cliff started his campaign. Does that mean anything?*

"How 'bout hitting him up to see if he'd take a kitten or two?" Grinning, Zach held Calvin up on the flat of his hand. "These monsters are no longer bite-sized. What're we gonna do? Keep all three? Take 'em to the pound? Leave 'em in a basket on your grandmother's doorstep?"

She released the struggling Sylvia, who had incised several new track marks on her arm. A picture popped into her head of a trio of tiger-sized cats cornering her in the kitchen and snarling for food.

Zach cracked a pistachio and stuck it in her mouth. "What with all the commotion, I forgot to tell you—I dropped by the county building Friday and looked up Donovan's divorce decree. For once we're in luck. According to directory assistance, his ex is still at the same Albany Park address. Now all we have to do is figure what kind of scam to run, since I assume you'd prefer not to introduce yourself as Henry's former therapist."

"That's a tough one." She gazed through the window at a peaked roof with clouds of snow swirling off the edge like Magic Kingdom fairy dust.

Zach cocked his head. "I could be an old drinking buddy looking to invite him to the closing of our favorite bar."

"Drinking buddy . . . that gives me an idea. How about, I'm a recovering alcoholic and I want to make an amend."

"Amend? As in the old AA twelve-step routine? Even though my denial's kept me from joining up as yet, I do know some of the cliche-ridden jargon."

"So many people are in recovery nowadays, there's a good chance she'll know about amends." Cassidy stood. "Why don't you get me the wife's number while I run downstairs and dig the name of Henry's former employer out of his file."

She returned minutes later to sit at her desk. As she dialed, Zach settled on the waterbed to listen.

"Is this Beth Donovan? Henry's ex-wife?"

"Who is this?" The voice turned cool.

"Please let me explain. I promise, I'm not a telemarketer." *Except where kittens are concerned.* "And I certainly don't want to make any trouble—at least, not anymore than I have already. You see, I'm a recovering alcoholic and I have an amend to make to Henry. Are you familiar at all with AA?"

"Just a little."

"Part of the program is to make amends to people you've wronged." *Like this woman, for instance, whom I'm right this instant trying to con.* "Except you're not supposed to do it if it'd be painful for them, and that's where I'm having a problem. Back when I was drinking I did this thing to Henry, and I haven't seen him since. So the reason I'm calling is to get your input about whether or not it'd be harmful to bring it up now."

"Well, all right. You can tell me."

How could she resist? Gossip about her ex. "This is really embarrassing. It'd be a lot easier if I could come to your house and talk face to face." She drew a face with a squiggly, nervous mouth on a social work newsletter.

"I don't mean to make this any harder, but I'm not sure I should invite a complete stranger into my home."

"My name's Pam Keeler. Henry and I used to work together at Randolph. You can ask if he knows me."

"Well . . . I guess that won't be necessary."

"Any chance we could make it tomorrow night? I'd like to get this over with as soon as possible."

They arranged to meet at eight p.m. Monday night. Cassidy put down the phone and swiveled toward Zach.

"You ever play poker? What were you gonna do if she decided to check you out with Henry first?"

Cassidy's mouth stretched in an uneasy grimace. "I was counting on the fact that most people don't remember names. And from what I know of Henry, there had to be at least one woman at Randolph he'd had a bad experience with."

Zach stood and flexed his shoulders.

She glanced at the window. The light had almost disappeared. "Tonight we follow Jake. Tomorrow we find out about Henry." *And, if Ken shows on Wednesday, I can take a shot at him too.* "This'll be my first time picking up a hooker." She paused, giving him a chance to say "Me too." When he didn't, she asked, "So, when do we need to start watching for the right license plate to pull out of Jake's garage?" She looked again at the snow falling thickly through a gloomy dusk. "Here's hoping he's an all-weather kind of guy."

⊠ ⊠ ⊠

She shuffled around on the back seat of the Nissan to lean against the right door. She would never win any prizes in a waiting contest herself, but Zach, who could trance out for indefinite periods without so much as a twitch, would be a strong contender.

More than two hours had passed since they first saw Jake's BMW leave the underground parking garage. He'd led them south on Lake Shore Drive, west on the Eisenhower. Exiting at Kostner, he'd jogged west to Cicero, then cruised slowly south through an industrial pocket with minimal traffic and no pedestrians.

Cassidy had spotted the woman standing alone on a corner several moments before the pick-up, tiny snowflakes whirling around her in the yellowish glow of the streetlight. Jake's car pulled up, the woman got inside, then the BMW swooped off into the flurries. Circling the block, Zach parked on the side street about ten yards from the hooker's corner.

She shifted to face forward. "This is such a lonely stretch. I was expecting to end up on some trashy, neon-flashing street crammed with adult bookstores and massage parlors."

Leaning against the driver's door, Zach turned to face her. "The town of Cicero's just a couple blocks south of here. Since you don't read the paper, you probably don't know that this street we're on used to be a regular hooker's row. Then, awhile back, the town fathers decided to clean up their little sin city, and the Cicero police started busting the hookers' customers, impounding their cars, and publishing the johns' names in the local paper. Needless to say, business hastened to move outside the Cicero town limits."

She looked at her watch. "They've been gone over an hour. How long does this take, anyway?"

"This is one subject I'm not gonna try and play expert on."

She tapped her knuckles together. "Not an expert . . . but not entirely without experience?"

No response.

"What? A *no comment?* Does that mean you have used prostitutes?"

"That means *none of your business.*"

His voice had taken on a growly edge that told her she'd gone far enough. But since he was stuck in the car and could not walk out, she pressed on. "When people are trying to build a relationship, they shouldn't have secrets." *Except about anxiety attacks and driving.*

"I take the what-you-don't-know-won't-hurt-you position myself."

Remember what the waitress said? Talking just makes

them irritated. Besides, why should you care what he did before he met you? She ground her teeth for a full minute, then asked, "Have you gone to prostitutes?"

"Shit. You never quit, do you?" Turning slightly away, he stared fixedly out the passenger window. "All right, if you really want to know, there were a couple of years right out of college when I was floundering around. During that time I saw hookers on a few occasions—one of the many stupid things I did then."

Cassidy gazed at her hands clasped tightly in her lap. *You satisfied now? You got Zach mad and you found out something you didn't want to hear and don't know what to do with.*

Fifteen minutes passed, then she saw the BMW emerge from the haze. Peering through a gauzy curtain of snow, she watched the woman step out of the car and return to her former post. Cassidy scrunched down on the floor, head propped against the door, so she wouldn't be seen. Zach waited a couple of minutes, then switched on his lights and pulled up to the corner.

From her vantage point she could see only the left side of the car. She heard the passenger door open and a hoarse whisper from the woman, "Hey babe."

Zach said, "How much?"

"Fifty."

"Twenty."

A pause. "Twenty-five."

Zach said, "Okay, get in."

21

Missing Exes

The hooker slid into the front seat and closed the door.

Zach said, "I don't want sex. I just wanna talk."

"You wan' me talk dirty? You maybe wan' me do somethin' while I talk?"

"No, that's not it. Look, first I want to tell you, I'm not a cop."

The hooker's jacket rustled against the seat. *She getting ready to run?*

Zach said, "No, really, I'm not police. I'm investigating somebody, the guy you were just with, but this is strictly private. I just wanna buy information."

"I don' get it." The voice sounded unconvinced.

Cassidy saw Zach twist around. "Look, this is real money. All you have to do is answer some questions. But before I start, my girlfriend's in back. She got down on the floor so you'd think this was a normal pick-up."

Cassidy hauled herself onto the seat. "Hi."

The hooker, face gaunt and hair stringy, gazed at her out of blank eyes. Cassidy flashed an image from the movies of feline creatures flaunting sprayed curls, department-store lashes, and gaudy costumes. This woman was not what she'd expected.

Above the collar of a ratty, fake-fur jacket, her creamed-coffee face was coarse-skinned and cosmetically unimproved. *Evidently, at twenty-five dollars a pop, pretty doesn't come into it.*

"I never seen any pervs like you," the hooker commented indifferently.

Cassidy gave a sympathetic tilt to her head. "I know this must seem strange, but that man who picked you up, he's engaged to my sister and—"

"Sure he is," she mumbled. "I don' care why you're doin' this. You pay, I'll talk."

Zach said, "Tell us exactly what he asked you to do."

"You don' want me talk dirty? Yeah, right." She glanced at Cassidy. "Only, I never seen a woman wanna hear sex talk before." She shrugged. "I don' care, it's your money." She shrugged again. "That guy? He wanted golden showers."

Zach said, "He wanted you to pee on him? Anything else?"

"I peed on him. He jerked off."

Jesus, what a life. So shut down she's more feral animal than human.

Handing her the money, Zach said, "I guess that's it." She opened the car door.

Cassidy grabbed the shoulder of the hooker's scruffy jacket. "Just a minute." She pulled out one of her cards. "I know you're probably not interested, but if you ever want to get off the street, I could put you in touch with some people who'd help."

The woman stared a moment, her flat eyes showing a brief spark of hostility, then got out and returned to her corner.

"That was stupid." Cassidy moved into the front seat.

Zach turned north on Cicero.

"I wish you'd given her the fifty."

"I did. The haggling was only to make it seem legit." They passed two more women standing on corners. "Our guy Jake certainly isn't into dominance with hookers. What do you think? I hate to cross him off—I really liked the asshole for Cliff."

Cassidy moved her head slightly from side to side, considering possibilities. "I read somewhere that men on major power trips sometimes look for sexual humiliation."

"That's weird."

"Actually, it makes a weird kind of sense. Whenever people go too far in one area, such as their public life, they're likely to go to the opposite extreme in a different area, like their sex life. You know, Jimmy Bakker preaching sexual repression and banging his secretary."

Zach glanced at her. "So that means we don't have to write off Jake the asshole attorney just yet?"

"If only we could. But it's possible Jake's mentally

flipped the Madonna-whore dichotomy. Maybe in his warped mind women who practice sexual restraint are the bad girls—the rejectors—so he humiliates them. Whereas women who put out are the good girls, so he gets them to humiliate him."

"So it could be the Cliff persona rapes women like Jenny, and the Jake persona pays to get peed on."

She shook her head slightly. "A psychopath, whose mental wiring is off to begin with, might want to do just about anything. And he could always find a way to rationalize it."

⊠　⊠　⊠

When they returned to the house, Zach found an e-mail message from Boytoy: "Sorry to keep you hanging, but my dance card's been filled. I've finished off the last batch of guys now and got me some empty slots again. If you're still interested, meet me at The Cuckold, corner of Halsted and Hooper, between 9 and 11, this coming Thurs. Just ask for CK, the hunkier of the two guys behind the bar."

This is a guy with an ego the size of Alaska. Actually, he's probably overcompensating, but who cares? The pathetic thing is, people like Mira and me have been known to fall for puffed-up jerks like this.

⊠　⊠　⊠

Cassidy sat in her desk chair, chin propped on one fist, eyeing a Rolodex card with Kevin's name at the top. This was the most recent phone number she had, but considering he'd moved ten times since leaving her house, this one could be out of date also.

Should I do it? Cassidy leaned back and crossed her arms.

Starshine, who'd been sitting on the windowsill, sprang across to her desk and flopped in front of her, the cat's nipples tight and bursting. Reaching to scratch behind the orange ear, Cassidy received a nip on the finger, an admonishment that she'd touched the cat in the wrong place.

"I guess you've got a right to be cranky, considering all three munchkins are still here."

Twisting her head upside down, Starshine stretched out her throat and Cassidy obediently stroked the snowy fur. "I suppose I might as well talk to Kevin, even though it won't do any good. I mean, even if he were Cliff, which he isn't, getting a call from his ex is not likely to elicit a confession." She pictured herself as Sergeant Friday grilling a bemused Kevin under a spotlight in a bare room.

She dialed and a computer voice answered. "The number you are calling has been disconnected."

"Looks like Kev is out of the loop for kitten marketing." She drummed her fingers and Starshine struck her hand to let her know the petting session wasn't officially over.

"Now don't get the idea this means anything. He's constantly changing addresses, one step ahead of the landlord every time." Cassidy rubbed the cat's bony side. "Only reason I called is that I let Zach plant crazy notions. Kevin is as far from Cliff as you can get. Women hardly ever reject him—at least, not until he's messed them over. And besides, he's the most high-spirited, upbeat person I know."

Except for the brooding spells.

Kevin is not Cliff. Don't even think about it.

⊠   ⊠   ⊠

The apartment door opened two inches, the chain that

secured it stretching across the crack. Cassidy could see a slice of Beth Donovan's face. It was eye level with hers and frowning.

"Hi, I'm Pam Keeler." Glancing at Zach who stood beside her, Cassidy grimaced in embarrassment. "Sorry to spring an extra person on you, but I asked my sponsor to come along. Last minute cold feet."

Cassidy's voice came out high and edgy. *Should be nervous, trying to lie my way into this poor woman's house. In my next life I deserve to be a car salesman—no, worse, make that lawyer.*

Beth's frown deepened. "Your sponsor?"

"Zach Moran." He removed his hands from his coat pockets and rested them loosely on his hips. "If you'd like, I can wait in the car."

Cassidy threw Zach a quick look, trying to see him through a stranger's eyes. Except for the scar, his face was ordinary enough, and his bland demeanor tended to put people at ease. But the scar was suspicious. She nibbled her bottom lip. "I don't blame you for not wanting two strangers in your house." Shifting her weight from one foot to the other, she said, "I know I'm being an awful baby about this."

"Well . . . " Unfastening the chain, Beth said in a clear, light voice, "You don't look like home invaders." She pulled the door wide. "I suppose I ought to be more cautious but I don't like having to be afraid all the time."

Zach smiled his laconic smile. "Thanks for not asking me to sit in the car."

"Just make yourselves comfortable." Beth gestured toward a flat-cushioned sofa. Tossing their coats on one end, they sat. The space was uncluttered, its hardwood floors and creamy walls aglow with soft light. Everything was small scale and muted, from the diminutive pastels on the walls to the filmy, daintily patterned curtains covering the windows. The room was hushed, no TV or sound system anywhere in sight.

What's this? A person who can tolerate silence? Cassidy regarded her hostess' pleasant, open face with interest.

Beth picked up a stemmed glass from a teak end table. "I just poured myself some wine. Would you—" Her fingers flew to her mouth. "Oh, I forgot." She let out an easy laugh. "Well, coffee then?"

"Nothing for us, thanks," Zach said in his customary manner of deciding when and what she would drink.

Beth settled into a lightweight armchair across from the sofa. Her slight frame and short, straw-colored hair seemed almost boyish, but the keen blue eyes peering from her elfin face were clearly those of a mature woman. She asked, "So, you want me to help you decide if you should make an amend to Henry, is that right?"

"Let me tell you what happened, then you can give me your opinion. I think I mentioned that Henry and I used to work together at Randolph. Actually, I left the company before your divorce, but I used to stop around sometimes to see my old friends. I'd been divorced myself, so when I heard that you and Henry were splitting, I encouraged him to talk."

Beth smiled slightly. "Encouragement was not something he needed a lot of."

Cassidy twisted her hands together. "I was lonely, and it

felt good to be needed. But considering how much I was drinking, it probably came across to Henry like I was flirting up a storm. Anyway, one night when I'd had way too much to drink, I asked him up to my apartment. What happened after that is pretty much of a blur. All I know for sure is, it did not go well. The next morning I woke up alone feeling sick and ashamed of myself."

Heaving a sigh, she went on, "The worst of it is, I never talked to him again. I refused to take his calls, stopped going to Randolph, just ran away." *You're getting so carried away, you almost believe your own bullshit.* "Henry was so vulnerable right then, and I always worried that my disappearing might've really hurt him. After I got sober, I tried to call him but he wasn't at Randolph anymore and nobody knew how to reach him. I got scared that . . . well, you can guess what I was thinking."

Zach laid his hand on her arm and gave it a squeeze.

Her voice concerned, Beth questioned, "You really don't know what happened that night?"

Cassidy gazed into her lap.

"If it was like most nights of our marriage, nothing happened." Beth's head curved toward her shoulder.

"Nothing?" Cassidy's eyes widened. "You mean, he couldn't do it?"

"The problem started shortly after the wedding. There were a few failed attempts, then he simply stopped trying."

Cassidy said, "But Henry was such a pistol. He always talked like some kind of high-voltage sex machine."

"That was the line he used before we got married." Beth lifted one shoulder in a half shrug. "When I first met him, he was a wild man. Not the kind of person I ever imagined myself with at all. But since I've always been such a good girl, I guess that super-stud act of his had a certain appeal. Then, once we were married, he changed overnight. His mother's one of those smothering, single-parent types, and under those big bad wolf clothes of his, there lurked a scared little mama's boy. He didn't want a wife—he wanted a second mother. Someone to take care of him."

Zach rested his forearms on his knees. "So you finally got sick of playing Mom and kicked his butt out."

"After a lot of therapy." She shook her head. "What made it particularly difficult was his impotence." A look of intense compassion came over her face. "It was like walking out on someone with a serious disease."

Cassidy said, "I suppose he resumed his bad-boy persona after the divorce."

"For a few months, but he couldn't keep it up." Beth smiled. "Strike that last comment—I hate bad puns." She sipped her wine. "At one point, when he was trying to suck me into feeling sorry for him again, he admitted to being terrified that someone might actually take him up on his offer, which is apparently what happened with you. I suspect the real reason he came on so strong was to make sure he got universally rejected. That way he never had to embarrass himself in the bedroom. It really is sad when you think of it—his having to put on this big show just to make himself feel like a man."

"He sure had me fooled." Cassidy moved her head from side to side. "Now that I know the whole story, I think it might be better just to drop it. I gather from the way you're talking he didn't try to kill himself or anything."

"Not Henry. He'd much rather play on people's sympathy."

"But what happened? Has he moved out of state? I've got a cop friend who tried to look up his plates and couldn't find him in the computer."

"He went home to mother." Beth smiled slightly, shaking her head. "She lets him drive her car."

✉ ✉ ✉

Zach started the Nissan's engine. "Is this the same woman who used to tell me she hated to lie?"

"Scary, isn't it?" Cassidy pressed her fingers against her cheek. "I still don't like it, but it doesn't seem quite so bad if I can rationalize it's for a good cause." She sighed. "Looks like we've got another inconclusive situation on our hands."

"You think the reason Henry couldn't get it up is 'cause he's gay?"

"Actually, Beth's story seemed pretty believable to me. If he couldn't do it with that nice wife of his, how would he ever've been able to seduce all those female victims?" She paused. "It's possible the only time he can perform is when he's on his punishing-women crusade, but that's kind of a stretch. He seemed so slimy. I was actually hoping some irate husband had fixed him permanently—in the neutering sense. Then we could cross him off for sure. But now that I know how pathetic he is, I'm stuck feeling sorry for the creep."

✉ ✉ ✉

Cassidy was sitting at her desk when the phone rang. "This is Dale. I'm not sure if you remember me—no wait, how could you not, the way I came barging into your house." Her husky voice seemed tentative.

Probably expecting me to bitch her out. Cassidy pushed snarly, cinnamon hair back from her face. "I was hoping we'd have another chance to talk."

"I clipped your ad a couple of weeks ago but was too embarrassed to call. The way I came at you—that's not how I usually am."

"Actually, I'm glad you did it. Seeing the letter was the first tip-off I had about what was going on."

"I was so sure you and Cliff were in it together. Then I saw your ad, and I started thinking that maybe you really didn't know about him. And if that's true, I owe you an apology."

Cassidy propped both elbows on her desk. "If I were in your place, I might've done the same thing."

"Well, anyway, I wanted to say I was sorry, and since you're taking a survey, I thought I should fill in some more blanks." She went on to say that Cliff had approached her at her mother's wake three and a half years ago; that he had upswept black hair and considered himself a younger version of Al Pacino; that he said he was forty-one and his height was around five-ten.

Shaking her head, Cassidy released a small sigh. "So, how you holding up with all this?"

"I take medication, avoid stress, and hope that maybe someday it'll all go away." She paused. "I think the hardest part is keeping it all a secret. I can't stand the thought of anybody knowing, but at the same time, I go around feeling like I'm living a lie."

Cassidy's throat tightened. "You could get help. You know, a counselor or support group."

Dale laughed. "Now you sound like Cliff's letter." Another pause. "The other reason I called is, I still can't figure out why he's doing it."

"This is a very sick man with a huge amount of anger who's decided that women are to blame for all his problems. Abusers and batterers generally take this point of view, but thank God most of them aren't as crazy or vicious as Cliff."

"But why tell me to see you? Especially if you don't even know him?"

"He's picked me, I'm not sure why, to play Boswell to his Johnson. It's his demented idea that I'm going to broadcast his story to the world. He wants to secure his place in the infamy hall of fame without the discomfort of being caught."

Finishing the conversation, Cassidy swiveled toward the window and propped her purple pumps on the radiator. A bright blue sky behind the bare branches of her corner maple held a false promise of spring. She tapped a pen against the pad of paper in her lap.

Ken was due in ten minutes. Two weeks earlier she'd confronted him because of the odd little smile he wore while talking about rejection, then the following week he'd blown her off. Ken wanted to get away with things. When she let him, he saw it as winning and his *gotcha* smile came out. When she called him on his tricks, he retaliated by missing a session.

Earlier she'd speculated that Cliff, whose letters indicated he had her on a pedestal, would have no reason to punish her. But that was probably wrong. He, like most personality disorders, undoubtedly had a script in his head he wanted her to follow, and whenever she deviated from that script, he would feel a need to zap her. Jenny, who'd tried her damndest to please him, had not succeeded. Cassidy, who had no idea what he expected, had probably been pissing him off on a regular basis.

Jake, the sex addict attorney, did not do rape and bondage with hookers. Donovan was impotent and living with his mother. Ken, who gave her his *gotcha* smile when he won and punished her when he lost, was currently the top contender.

She drew a face with a sly smile on the pad. If Ken were Cliff, what would he do? Skip his appointment and make their next meeting an attack? Show up for his appointment and rape her in her own house? Do a routine appointment now and catch her off guard later?

If she'd told Zach that today was Ken's appointment, he would have stayed home. Telling him would have been the smart thing to do. But instead, she'd set it up so that, if Ken did try an attack, she'd have to throw her butterfly net over his head all by herself.

What're you trying to prove? She bit down hard on her lip. *That you're better at catching bad guys than Zach? That you don't need anyone? What?*

She heard a small voice in the back of her head, "I can do it myself."

She sighed. This was a part of her that had caused trouble

before. A little kid part that insisted she handle everything on her own because it didn't believe she could count on anyone else to come through for her.

"Damn!" She rotated back to the desk. *If I don't get that idiot part under control, Zach's gonna leave for sure. And I wouldn't blame him if he did.*

She left a message on Zach's office voice mail: "I caught myself playing lone gun again, and I want to make an official confession before you get pissed. Ken's appointment is five minutes from now. I have the phone hidden under the coleus leaves, the pepper gun and knife in my bra. One wrong move and I spray his eyes, grab the phone, and run out the door. Call you when it's over."

If you really wanted to repent, you'd tell him about the anxiety attacks.

Reaching under her loose sweater, she touched the two metal objects, one snugly fitted beneath each breast. She stood and checked the mirror. Not a single bulge. She gazed at her reflection. Her body was okay, slender and trim, better than she deserved considering she never did anything more rigorous than biking and a little yoga. It was the part above the neck she despaired of. Cheeks hollowed by anxiety. Deep clefts chiseled between her brows. A near feverish light in her hazel eyes. At her best, she avoided cameras. Now, if a client came in looking the way she did, Cassidy would send her for a psych eval.

Doesn't matter how you look. All that matters is getting the pepper gun in your hand and aiming properly when you need to.

The night before she'd gone outside after dark and practiced. *I hope Ken does show. I hope he's Cliff and he comes after me. If he does it now, I'll be ready with my spray and those penitent words on the machine'll cover my ass with Zach.*

Two minutes later the back doorbell bonged.

✉ ✉ ✉

"Sorry 'bout last week." Behind Ken's neatly styled ginger hair, light from the window angled across the black vinyl sofa, sharply dividing the shaded side on the right from the sunlit side on the left.

Cassidy clasped her hands tightly around her knee. "So, you're all recovered and back to work at the clinic?"

The corners of his mouth curved slightly. "Yes, of course. Why wouldn't I be?" Turning sideways, he half sprawled across the sunny section of the sofa. His light blue eyes caught hers. "Strange thing happened just after our last session. My apartment got broken into."

Holding her breath a beat, she sat absolutely still. *He knows.* "So, how did you feel when that happened?"

"How do you think? Angry. Violated. Betrayed."

Cassidy planted both pumps on the carpet, and pulled herself up straight in her chair. "You know, I think I can understand what you went through. I think I might have the same reaction if I found out a client was misrepresenting himself. One thing's for sure, I'd want to know what he was up to."

The cat smile appeared briefly.

Cassidy said, "You have any idea why somebody might pay a therapist to listen to a bunch of lies?"

"All kinds of reasons."

"Like what?" She watched his face closely. *This guy's so cool, if he were wired to a polygraph his anxiety level'd probably go* down.

"Well, hypothetically speaking, you might have a client who likes to gamble, and this client might get falsely accused of stealing money from his workplace. Especially if he has customers who sometimes pay in cash." Sitting straighter, Ken faced her squarely.

Cassidy observed that his tie and socks matched. "Go on."

"Well, this guy might—we're still speaking hypothetically here—he might get arrested, and his attorney might tell him he's got a chance of avoiding jail time if he makes restitution and goes into therapy for the gambling."

She cocked her head. "So the only reason he's in therapy is to stay out of jail?"

"Let's just say his first priority is to convince the judge that he's seen the error of his ways." The light from the window played against his rugged features. He blinked slowly, his blue eyes warm. "What he needs to get on the judge's good side is a check covering the missing funds and a pile of therapy receipts. To prove he's taken the cure for his little gambling problem, you see."

"Gambling?" She shook her head. "So why wouldn't he ever talk about any of this in therapy?"

Ken gave her his secretive smile.

"Oh, I get it. He didn't want to be in therapy in the first place, so he amused himself by playing games with the therapist." She noticed a glimmer in his eyes that might've been respect.

Doesn't realize receipts won't buy him anything. Judges want reports from therapists, and Ken's not gonna like any report written by me. She smiled inwardly. *Should've spent his money on casino games instead of head games.*

"Well," he drawled, his voice going ironic, "as long as we're having this little heart-to-heart, let me turn it around. Why do you think a therapist might show up with her boyfriend at a client's apartment and go through his stuff?"

22

Studmuffin

Cassidy gave an exaggerated shrug. "I suppose it's possible a therapist might be trying to figure out why the client's turned their sessions into a smoke-and-mirrors show. And then, once she's been in the apartment, she might wonder why this guy, who doesn't appear to have any source of income, would need a safe."

"No source of income?" Ken's head tilted. "This guy's a gambler, remember? When luck's running his way, he brings in some big bills. Now he wouldn't want it in a bank 'cause he doesn't wanna leave a paper trail. And he wouldn't want it under his mattress 'cause people can just walk into his apartment. And he might even be thinking, if he plays his cards right he can build his winnings into a restitution fund."

She glanced at a bird flying across the window behind his head. More false promises.

Ken looked at his watch. "Can I go now, teach?"

"So, why didn't you call the cops?"

"I don't like cops."

She demanded payment for the current and the missed session, then told him she never wanted to see him again.

✉ ✉ ✉

Thursday night, after half an hour's search, Zach scored in his quest for that rarest of finds, a legal parking spot in Chicago's nightlife-crawling northside. He squeezed the Nissan into a tiny space a mere six blocks west of The Cuckold, the establishment where Boytoy tended bar.

"Ever since they changed the policy on towing, parking's been a real bitch," Zach grumbled as he got out of the car. "Used to be every fireplug in town was fair game."

Cassidy, disguised in a blonde wig and bulky, fake fur coat, held her hairpiece straight as she hopped out. She scrambled to catch up with Zach, whose long-legged stride was impossible to match.

"What is this?" She demanded. "You want me to trail along behind like some kind of third-world chattel?"

Slowing, he fell into place beside her. "Sorry, I was thinking about what I'm gonna say."

"So tell me—how are you going to get out of your date with Boytoy?"

He reached for her gloved hand. "After much considera-tion, I've decided to say that I've read Mark's e-mail and if he doesn't tell me everything, I'll hand him over to Emily."

Cassidy halted a moment in surprise. "The truth! I never would've thought of it."

They walked down several blocks crammed with narrow, three-story houses built standing a mere six feet from the sidewalk.

Half a block from Halsted, Cassidy was able to make out The Cuckold's sign on the opposite corner of the intersection. *Recognized me at the wake but the hat wasn't a real disguise. Hope the wig'll be enough.* Pulling Zach to a stop, she asked, "What do you think? If it turns out Boytoy and Cliff are the same, will he know it's me?"

"I told you, I don't think they are. There's nothing that ties them together." Cocking his head, he said, "Maybe the guys in the bar'll think you're in drag." He studied her face. "Nah, queens usually look too good to be true. But why didn't you go for something short and butch?"

"Because Gran's tastes run between Hedy Lamar and Orphan Annie. So, do you think I should change my image? Maybe go blonde and seductive like this hair?"

"Yes, definitely. Sharon Stone would definitely be an improvement."

"Jerk!" She yanked her hand out of his. "You know, I feel really dumb in this long, silky pageboy with bangs in my eyes."

"You could wait outside."

"Did we have a conversation last night about this very topic or am I imagining things?" She resumed walking, her pace slower than before.

Zach took her hand again. "Yeah, I know, you need to eyeball Boytoy in case he's somebody you've seen before."

"In case he's Cliff."

The Cuckold had black windows and a lavender neon sign. Cassidy, who had never been inside a gay bar before, was disappointed not to be able to scope out the interior from the safety of the sidewalk.

"What did Gran think about your borrowing the wig?"

"I had to practically lock her in the closet to keep her from tagging along." They paused in front of the door. "Okay, I go in first, you show up a few minutes later."

She entered a rose-lighted room hung with large-framed, seventeenth century paintings and booming with the kind of music that made her eyelids twitch. A highly polished, carved bar ran the length of one wall. Small tables crowded together in front; gyrating figures marked the dance floor in back. Large male bodies surrounded her. *Men always take up more space. It's not just their size—it's their maleness.*

She scanned the area behind the bar. A man she'd never seen before was pouring wine; another moved rapidly toward a doorway at the bar's far end. She glued her eyes to the retreating figure but could discern nothing beyond his general size and shape.

Perching on a stool, she kept her body turned away from the doorway the man had gone through. The other bartender, who looked to be in his early twenties, stopped in front of her.

"What can I get you?"

Cassidy looked into sparkly brown eyes. "Um, make that chardonnay." He had a sculpted face, a weightlifter's body, and the light, easy movements of a Baryshnikov.

"Sure thing." He set the glass in front of her.

As the bartender moved on, she surveyed the room. *God, I've never seen so many men to die for in one place before. Too bad straight males don't feel such an urge to make themselves gorgeous.*

If they did, you'd really have to be Sharon Stone to compete. Just as well Zach doesn't spend half his life in front of a mirror, or you might be forced to do the same.

Zach came in and sat two stools down from her. She shot him a quick glance, then faced forward to watch out of the corner of her eye. When the Baryshnikov bartender stopped to take his order, Zach said, "I'm looking for CK."

"Me too." The bartender's voice was irritated. "He's supposed to be working—not disappearing and leaving me to handle the whole room by myself."

"Disappearing?" Zach folded his arms on the bar.

"I suppose you're one of those e-mail dates of his. Well, don't take it personally. He left before you came in."

"Maybe he's in the back. Or the john."

Cassidy stared into the doorway at the other end of the bar. *That's where he is.*

Waving at a guy who'd just entered, the bartender said something she couldn't make out. She turned her ear in his direction and picked up the last part. "Leaving in the middle of a shift was a dumb ass thing to do. He'll probably get canned over it."

Shit. He did *see through the disguise. The way he's been watching me, he probably knows exactly how I walk and move.*

Zach asked, "Any idea why he'd take off?"

"Who knows?" The bartender shrugged, his massive

shoulders moving easily under the armless spandex tee. "Part-timers come and go all the time."

Zach placed his hands flat on the bar. "Long as I'm here, why don't you fix me a Jack Daniels and soda."

Allowing her gaze to wander, Cassidy noticed a silver haired fellow eyeing Zach from halfway down the bar. She pictured him blowing in Zach's ear, heard Zach's amused voice say, "Sorry, my tastes run more to Sharon Stone."

What is this Sharon Stone fixation I've developed? Must be from those regrettable minutes I spent looking at myself yesterday.

The bartender placed a drink in front of Zach, who had a bill in his hand but did not offer it up. "What can you tell me about CK?"

"You a cop?"

"Why? You think there's some reason a cop'd be after him?"

The bartender shrugged again. "Just curious."

"I'm a reporter from the *Post*." He laid the bill in front of the bartender. "I need every little detail."

"The only thing about him is he dates e-mail guys from all over the country, then brags about the hot sex." The bartender shook his head. "Can you believe it, in this day and age? But these older guys, they just don't get it." He glanced briefly at Zach, the color rising in his cheeks.

"No problem, son," Zach drawled, his voice deepening.

"Anyway," the bartender started wiping down the polished wood in front of him, "CK thinks he's hot shit 'cause he works out sometimes and gets a steady stream of new faces off the Internet. He's got no idea how ridiculous he looks to guys my age." He gazed down the bar. "Hey, I've got all these customers to take care of."

Zach pulled out another bill. "Come back soon as you can."

When the bartender returned, Zach had his spiral notepad out. "What does he look like?"

"Nothing special." The bartender shrugged. "About six foot, maybe a hundred and eighty. Firm enough, I guess, but not really buffed. Brownish hair, wears it a little too long. Clothes are out of date."

Zach handed over the second bill. "I need his phone number and address."

"Yeah, I needed it a couple weeks ago myself." One corner of his mouth pulled down. "He gave us a phony number. The boss should've fired his ass back then, but decent part-timers are hard to come by."

⌧ ⌧ ⌧

"Will you slow down?" Cassidy grabbed Zach's hand and jerked him to a stop. "Are you racing ahead to avoid talking about the fact that we just missed Cliff by two seconds? Or that it was stupid to think he wouldn't recognize me in a blonde wig?"

Under the yellow streetlight, the lines in Zach's face stood out harshly. "I'm mad at myself is all. You said Boytoy might be Cliff, and I didn't take you seriously. I kept thinking they couldn't be one and the same because we don't have anything that connects both you and Mark to Cliff."

He jammed his hands into his pockets. "Well, it's obvious that something *does* connect them, we just don't know what it is. If I hadn't just dismissed the whole idea, I'd've realized that, considering how Cliff's been in and out of our house, practically dogging your footsteps, there's no way either one of us could've fooled him with some simple disguise. I just wish to God I'd been more careful, that's all."

Should've figured it out. Should've been more careful. I told him it might be Cliff. What he should've done is listen.

⊠ ⊠ ⊠

The next morning Cassidy was in the nursery sweeping up spilled litter, her hands moving quickly to evade Sylvia's fishhook claws, when the phone rang. She answered in the bedroom.

"Oh Cass, everything has turned around and all because of you." Mira's voice fairly sang with excitement.

Cassidy slid into the desk chair. "What happened?"

"You remember how you told me Jake wasn't worth dying for? Well, I was really pissed at the time, but I couldn't get your words out of my mind, and I ended up in this major funk. So in the middle of the week I asked Jake if he'd get tested, only I said it in this whiny sort of way. You can imagine what his reaction was."

"He got angry?" Cassidy heard growling from the hall. Swiveling toward the doorway, she saw Starshine march into the room, ears back, tail swishing.

"He said if I were thinner and sexier, if I knew how to give him what he wanted, he wouldn't need to look elsewhere."

Cassidy pictured the stringy-haired prostitute Jake had hired to pee on him. "Yeah, right."

"That's when I called to cancel. I was ready to give up on therapy, myself, everything."

As Starshine curled herself on the bed, Sylvia climbed the comforter and launched herself at Mom.

"I guess canceling that session was my version of hitting bottom." Mira's voice dropped. "Afterward I got really mad—at Jake, for once, instead of myself. The words 'nobody's worth dying for' kept running through my head like a mantra. Then, Sunday night when he went out, something clicked and I started to see everything in a different light."

"What was different?"

"I hate to admit it, but I used to think that Jake was somebody really special. Then, Sunday night, I suddenly saw him for what he was—just an insecure jerk with a puny little penis. A guy in need of constant reassurance. The only reason I ever thought he was so great is that he kept telling me he was. So I packed my bags and went to a motel."

"And that's what caused the turnaround?" *When the pursuer stops pursuing, the distancer sometimes becomes a little lost puppy.* Cassidy stared at two nearly identical calicoes, one big, one small, wrestling on the bed.

"A couple days later he was begging me to meet him for dinner. He admitted that every time he acts out, he feels sick and ashamed afterward. And that his being so mean to me was only a coverup so I wouldn't find out how bad he really feels about himself."

Right. He had to act like a jerk so you wouldn't guess that he feels like one. "So what happens now?"

"We both went in to get tested. The results'll be in later today, and of course I'm scared, but somehow I have this feeling it's going to be okay. Jake's started Sex Addicts

Anonymous, and I'd like to come in for my regular session tomorrow."

Cassidy agreed and they hung up.

Starshine stood over Sylvia, sinking her teeth into the kitten's throat. Screeching, Sylvia jumped out of reach, then dropped into her stalking mode, ready to start all over again. Mom sprang to the top of the television and glared down at her offspring.

Cassidy spoke to Starshine, who refused to acknowledge her existence. "You mean, even mothers have their limits? I hate to tell you, but you appear to be on the verge of becoming permanently offended. Curmudgeonly for the rest of your nine lives."

She called Zach and filled him in on Jake's transformation.

He said, "If Jake took the test, I'd have to guess he doesn't already know he's got it."

"Me too."

"Shit. I was still hoping to bust the asshole. So where does that leave us? Anybody we can resurrect or are we pretty much at the end of our list?"

"Donovan's living with his mother, Ken's trying to stay out of jail, and Jake's twelve-stepping. It's probably somebody we never even thought of." Envisioning the back of the disappearing bartender, she wished she could turn him around and look into his face.

⊠   ⊠   ⊠

Clipping two comic strips, a BUCKETS and a SYLVIA, Cassidy carried them down to add to her refrigerator collection. Although she had little use for the news, she regularly read several cartoons, considering them to be a major art form as well as high satire. She'd lamented the retirement of CALVIN AND HOBBES, and often insisted she could learn everything she needed to know from DOONESBURY.

The back doorbell rang announcing Jenny's arrival. When the woman's large frame was settled on the sofa, Cassidy crossed her legs and said, "I'd like to hear more about the AIDS. I know you don't want to see a doctor right now, but I really wish you'd consider getting treatment."

"Please don't try to change my mind." Jenny let out a nervous laugh. "I'll go when I start to get sick, but not now."

"Well, okay, if you're really certain." Cassidy pressed her fist beneath her chin. "Can you tell me what it's like, knowing you have HIV?"

Jenny brushed at the tiny crumbs of foam surrounding the black tape on the sofa. "After that last night, when Cliff stuck me with his needle, I went for months either angry or crying." Her watery eyes filled and she raised her speckled frames to wipe them. "Some days I'd wake up and be mad just because the sky was blue. Other days I went around hating people on the street 'cause they could just live their lives without worrying. But eventually, I don't exactly know how it happened, I got tired of being mad all the time and the anger just sort of went out of me."

"How're you feeling now?"

"Sometimes I can just focus on today and push the sickness out of my mind. But now and then I have to go ahead and think about the AIDS or else I lie awake all night imagining I've started with the fever and chills. What works best is, if I just let myself go sometimes—just worry it to death," she laughed dryly. "Then I can put it away for a while."

Cassidy nodded. "Makes sense to me. But what do you worry about the most?"

"Being alone." She grasped one of her sandy curls and gave it a sharp tug. "Sometimes I get really upset about the fact that I was always there for my mother, but when I get sick there won't be anybody there for me."

"You don't have to get sick. You could take the cocktail."

"I don't wanna go on, year after year, trying to keep track of all those pills when there's nothing to live for anyway."

"They have volunteers who visit people with AIDS. But you probably wish you had somebody who'd be like you were with your mother."

"Well, I suppose I shouldn't complain." She let go with a bitter laugh. "But now that we're talking about being alone, there's something I wanted to ask. You know those kitten pictures on the bulletin board?" Her gray eyes turned pleading. "Well, I wondered if you might be willing to let me have one of 'em?"

Did I just hallucinate that those words came out of her mouth? "As a matter of fact, I do have a few kittens I wouldn't mind parting with."

"The problem is, I'm not sure if I oughtta do it. I mean, it doesn't seem fair to the kitten, since I'm probably gonna skip the treatment and just let myself get sick."

"So what would you do with your cat if you got sick?"

"Guess I'd have to find him another home. Anyway, sometimes I get real lonely, and I thought a kitten might be some company."

Uncrossing her legs, Cassidy leaned forward. "As a matter of fact, cats can be very companionable. Especially if they get lots of affection." *This is therapy. Leave the kitten-marketing out of it.*

"So you think it'd be all right for me to have one?"

"I think you'd be a great cat mom."

"You remember the kitten that made all that fuss the last time I was here? He's the one I really want."

Cassidy blinked in surprise. "You want Hobbes?"

"You said he made noise to get attention, and I thought that was really something. You see, I always wanted attention, but I never had the courage to yell about it."

23

Margaritas and Truth Telling

Cassidy was headed upstairs after Mira's session when Starshine accosted her in the kitchen. Looking like a Holocaust survivor, the cat bumped her ankles and bit her knee, ruining yet another pair of pantyhose.

"Your communication style's getting more antisocial by the day," Cassidy remarked cheerfully. "I suppose starvation has that effect."

At the first whir of the can opener, Calvin and Sylvia came zipping through the doorway to jump their mother. Starshine let out a thunderous growl and smacked both kittens repeatedly until they raced squealing from the kitchen. The cat sprang to the counter, shot her human a cantankerous look, and buried her face in the bowl that Cassidy hastened to place in front of her.

"Motherhood's ruining your disposition for sure."

The phone rang. Cassidy leaned against the dining room doorjamb to listen to her mother.

"I'm having this little problem with Roland, dear, and I need your help." An exasperated sigh. "I never used to understand why you wanted to bother with relationships. I always thought having a man in your life made everything worse." A brief laugh. "Now I'm beginning to think I wasn't so far off after all."

"What's the problem?" Cassidy watched through the dining room window as a woman jogged past on Briar.

"You know how Roland's always had the idea that his son's gotta take over the business?" Helen sounded personally aggrieved. "Well, now Ron says he won't do it. Says he's going back to Seattle, that's flat. And Roland's simply having a fit."

"So how do you think I can help?"

"Well, dear, I need you to tell me what to say to get Roland to stop being so mad."

"Uh, I don't think you can stop anybody from being mad."

"But there must be something I can do. He just goes on and on, and I'm at the point where I can't stand to hear another word."

Getting a taste of the real Roland. "You might try saying you don't want to discuss it anymore."

"Really, Cass, I can't see how that would help. What I

need is a way to get him to stop making his kids so important. Personally, I wish they'd all move to the ends of the earth."

"Sorry, I can't help you with that one." Cassidy drifted into the kitchen and started to read cartoons.

"I thought therapists were supposed to know all about things like that." Another small sigh. "Oh well, I guess there's nothing you can do with a man like Roland who has to have everything his own way."

A smug little I-tried-to-tell-you feeling spread through Cassidy's chest.

Helen clicked her tongue. "Well, dear, there's one other thing. When I called your grandmother yesterday she sounded a little down but I couldn't get her to tell me what it was. Maybe you should talk to her."

Hanging up, Cassidy glanced at Starshine, who stared down from the top of the refrigerator. The wild look in the cat's huge, dilated pupils seemed to be sending a telepathic message: "If you don't get those voracious little thugs out of the house now, I'll never be your friend again."

Cassidy hooked her thumbs into her waistband. "Before now, whenever we discussed your children's leaving, I always picked up this little hint of ambivalence. But yesterday you bit Hobbes' ear just before Jenny put him in the box, and then you stalked out of the room when he started screeching. Your urge for survival, like Mira's, seems finally to have won out over your heart and mammaries."

She turned back to the phone and dialed her grandmother. "I just finished talking to Mom, and she says you're not your usual chipper self. So what's up? And don't try to squirm out of it, 'cause I'm not letting you off till you tell me."

"I didn't want to get into it with Helen since she's already got her hands full with that fiancé of hers." Gran's tone was flat, like sparkling water that's been sitting too long. "You know, Cass, your mother's not as strong as we are. From the time she was little, she always needed more than her sister did."

"So, what's going on?" *God, hope it's not her health. Gran's not allowed to change. Couldn't bear it if anything happened to her.*

"It's Mark's mother, Dottie. You remember she moved down to Florida. Well, I've had the sense of something wrong for months now, only I couldn't pry it out of her. But the situation's gotten worse, so now she finally had to let me know."

"What is it?"

"I hate to tell you." Gran's voice broke. "It's hard even to say the word."

"Cancer?"

"She's been fighting it for quite awhile. Always thought she'd lick it. But now it's in her liver."

"Oh Gran, I'm so sorry."

"Mark originally planned to wait till summer for his Chicago trip, but then he moved it up 'cause of his mother's illness. He had it in mind to get Helen and Dottie back together again. Dot says he always blamed himself for that big fight they had about his being gay. So after his mother's sickness got so bad, he was bound and determined he was gonna get the two of them to make up. Only he never got the chance."

"That's it!" Cassidy thumped her forehead. "That's why

he wanted to talk to me. His partner said it was a message from somebody else, and that must've been a message from Dottie that she wanted to make peace with Mom. His reason for the lunch had nothing to do with his getting killed."

"It never occurred to me, but now that you say it, I can see you're right. I wish I could stay on the case with you and Zach, but after losing Mark and finding out about Dottie's cancer, I just don't have the heart for it. I've gotta get my tail down to Florida as fast as I can."

✉ ✉ ✉

Zach said, "I'm gonna have a margarita. How 'bout you?"

Margaritas have more alcohol than wine. And Cliff's out there, just waiting to pounce. Can't afford to be fuzzy-headed.

One margarita will not a lost weekend make.

"Okay, a small one. And the botanas grande."

They were in a corner booth at La Majada, an Oak Park restaurant tucked away on Harrison. Eight o'clock on Saturday night and the place was humming. A guitarist stopped to sing for a couple at another table. Cassidy could not make out the words but the smooth sound of his voice reminded her of warm brandy. A smiling, brown-skinned waiter took their order.

Zach asked, "So, how'd it go with Mira today?"

"The good news is, their tests came up negative. Aside from that, she enjoyed the session a lot more than I did." Cassidy screwed up her mouth in frustration. "Mira spent the hour rhapsodizing about how wonderful everything's going to be now that Jake's seen the light. And I spent the hour doing my damndest not to utter gloomy predictions about backsliding."

"Sudden conversion like Jake's—I'd give it two months at the most."

The waiter brought their drinks. Cassidy took a swallow, her mouth turning icy, and felt the margarita's coldness roll toward her stomach.

Zach folded his arms on the table. "I keep thinking about our defunct suspect list, wondering if we missed anything. Not having my computer makes it hard to keep track of all the details."

But can't bring your computer to my house 'cause that'd make it seem like you're actually living there. She filled her mouth with chips to keep the words from jumping out.

Zach cocked his head slightly. "Why do you get that look on your face every time I mention my computer?"

"Why is your computer still at Marina City?"

His eyes narrowed. "You pissed 'cause I haven't emptied out the condo?"

She drew in a long breath through clenched teeth. "No, I'm pissed because it's obvious that you're only camping out at my house. And that the minute you start to feel crowded, you'll pack your two suitcases, three boxes, and beat a hasty retreat. What's really got me pissed is the fact that you never talk about it—you just leave me guessing."

The waiter brought their dinners: a plate of bite-sized tacos, nachos, and tostadas for her, chicken smothered in mole for Zach. Her stomach told her it was not accepting food at the moment so she took another pull at her drink.

"The reason I haven't talked about it is, there's nothing

to say." He leaned forward. "Most of the time I like living with you. The only time I don't is when you put ads in the paper without telling me or scowl when I have one more drink than you think I should."

Her stomach relented. She jammed a miniature taco into her mouth. *You only pretend to like salads. There's actually a secret junk food addict lurking inside that pops out whenever it smells real food.*

A strand of hair fell across her cheek. She tucked it behind her ear and said, "Then why haven't you moved the rest of your stuff?"

"Procrastination. I'm constantly hammered by deadlines at work, so when there aren't any I tend to let things go."

"Oh." She devoured two nachos. "I kept remembering what you told me about getting suffocated with that other woman. And I just figured that sooner or later, you'd feel the same with me. Or you'd get sick of my being so dependent all the time."

"Look, do me a favor and don't do therapy on our relationship." His forehead creased in irritation. "What I get mad about is just the opposite. Every time I want to do anything for you, you fight me."

"Oh." Dropping a small tostada back on her plate, she scrubbed her greasy fingers with the napkin. *Exactly what he's been saying all along. You're so damned scared he's gonna leave, your guard's been a mile high ever since he moved in. The stuff self-fulfilling prophecies are made of.*

She sipped slowly. *Zach's been straight about things from day one. It's you keeping secrets. Not talking about the anxiety. Clinging to your lifelong belief that you've always*

*got to maintain this facade of being strong and independent
or nobody'll ever love you.*

Picturing Starshine in her lap, she reflected on how
clearly the calico communicated whenever she wanted food,
attention, petting. And how good it felt to be needed by her
cat. It came to Cassidy as an epiphany that being needy on
occasion might not be all bad.

She carefully set her empty glass on the white tablecloth.
"I think I'll have another margarita." When the drink arrived, she took a healthy chug and said, "There's something
I have to tell you." She went on to recount her panic attack
on the way to the party, her overindulgence while she was
there, and the subsequent episodes whenever she tried to
drive outside Oak Park.

Pushing back from the table, Zach gave her a long look.
"And the reason you didn't tell me is, you wanna act like
you've got it all together, then zing me whenever I drink too
much or don't tell you about Emily?"

"Um . . . something like that."

"The really scary thing is how much we both like to have
the upper hand." He laid his palm on her arm. "Okay, so
you've got this problem with anxiety. What do you have to
do to fix it?"

"I think I need to go back into therapy and face up to those
shootings. That's not the standard treatment, but that's what
my gut's telling me to do."

"So why haven't you done it?"

"Because my therapist moved out to Woodridge and I
don't want to start over with somebody new. Because I'd

never make it driving that far." *Because you don't want to get help and you don't want to talk about what happened.*

"I'll take you."

"I thought you didn't approve of therapy."

"Just not for me. It's fine for everybody else."

"Well, you can't. It's too far. It'd take hours to get there and back, and there's no telling how many weeks it might be before I'm finished."

His face tightened in disgust. Scanning the room, he beckoned to their waiter.

"Okay, I'll go."

Although it was past nine when they returned to the house, she called Honor and set up an appointment for the following Tuesday.

✉ ✉ ✉

Cassidy sat on the nursery floor, Calvin snuggling under her chin, Sylvia untying her shoelaces. Starshine hunkered atop the pile of boxes, her eyes cold amber. Cassidy realized the calico had refused all petting advances for days. *What if she hates me for the rest of her life 'cause I didn't get rid of the kittens fast enough?*

Stepping into the nursery, Zach said in his burry, bedroom voice, "I've got some calls to make, but afterward maybe we can settle in with some wine and that new CD player I bought."

A warm, interior smile flowed through her. Amazing how all the edginess she'd been feeling toward him was gone now that her secrets were out and she knew he wasn't planning his escape.

Minutes later she heard his voice on the phone from the

makeshift office on the other side of the wall. The front doorbell rang. She glanced at the darkness outside. Seven o'clock Sunday evening, and the daylight was long gone. Feeling a twitch in her stomach, she told herself that with Zach in the house nobody was likely to bother her. She scooted downstairs, flipped on the outside light, and peered through the small window in the oak door across the width of the enclosed porch.

Two black children she recognized as Carrie and Chip Roberts stood on the other side of the screen. Darnella Roberts, holding the small girl she had seen jump into a pile of snow the other day, was standing behind them.

Cassidy opened the screen door. "What a surprise. Why don't you come on in?"

"We wanna see the kittens," Carrie, the six-year-old, announced as she marched past Cassidy.

Chip, the younger brother, followed his sister into the living room. "Mrs. Stein said you'd maybe let us have one."

Darnella stopped on the porch. "We were at Dorothy's and she mentioned the kittens. Well, the kids here weren't about to give me any rest till I let them come over to see if you had any left."

Cassidy blinked. "Is this for real? You're not just saying this so you can watch me do cartwheels, then fall on the floor laughing when you tell me it's only a joke?"

Darnella chuckled. "That mean you're not going to require character references?"

"The kittens are upstairs," Cassidy said. "You can leave your coats on the sofa while we go up."

Carrie removed her own jacket, then unzipped her

brother's. Tiny braids sprouted from her scalp. She had wide-set, almond eyes in an angular, high-cheekboned face.

"Are they girls or boys?" Carrie asked. She grabbed Chip's baseball cap off his head as he struggled out of his jacket. Darnella snagged the cap and replaced it on the boy's head.

"The black one's male, the calico's female." Cassidy started up the staircase, the two children crowding behind her. The phone rang twice, then stopped.

In the nursery Cassidy gestured toward the scuffed hardwood floor. "You have to sit quietly or the kittens'll hide."

Maintaining a tight grip on the three-year-old, Darnella assumed an Indian style position on the floor. Carrie and Chip slid downward, their backs against the wall.

Chip said, "We know all about cats. We had one once."

Sylvia peeked out from behind the guitar case, then raced over to duck inside the tunnel formed by Cassidy's bent knees. Calvin strolled up to sniff Chip's shoe. Atop the pile of boxes, Starshine pointedly turned her back, assuming her humans-don't-exist pose.

Cassidy placed Calvin in Chip's lap, setting off a wild peal of boyish giggles. She asked, "What about your dog? How will he take to having a kitten in the house?" She pictured the small dustmop dog she'd seen romping with the children last summer.

Darnella said, "He's cool with cats."

Here's hoping he doesn't end up trembling in the closet like that tubby Jezebel-cat Sylvia worked over.

"Well kids," Darnella said, "you wanna take one of these critters home?"

They responded in unison, Chip clamoring for the boy, Carrie for the girl.

"Maybe you should take both," Cassidy suggested helpfully.

"Aren't you the sly one?" Darnella responded.

"Yes both!"

"Let's take both!"

Darnella sighed. "Won't Daddy be surprised."

Zach joined them in the nursery. Discovering that they intended to depopulate the house of kittens, he offered to hunt up a box.

Thumping down from her perch, Starshine gave a cursory lick to Sylvia, a nip to Calvin, then sauntered out of the room, not to be seen again until the house was rid of both neighbors and kittens.

⊠ ⊠ ⊠

Cassidy sat on the bed. "You ready for music and wine?"

Pulling his hand out of his jeans pocket, Zach gazed at the array of keys in his palm. "Unfortunately, we're gonna have to postpone our Dionysian adventures for an hour or so. Some maintenance guy at Marina City called to tell me there's water dripping through the ceiling of the place beneath mine. He can't find the key to my unit, so I've gotta go down and let him in."

A jittery feeling started in her stomach. "How long you think it'll take?"

"If you're nervous about staying alone, you can come with me."

First you were scared to drive, now you're scared to stay

home. What's next? You gonna take to your bed for the rest of your life?

"I'm fine." She glanced away, then made eye contact again. "No, wait. I'm not fine. I made a pact with myself to stop playing Invincible Woman. I'm a little anxious but there's no reason to be. I'm gonna lock the door, turn on the security system, and keep the cell phone glued to my right hand. And in addition, I've been wearing the pepper gun and knife in my bra every day just to make certain I never forget."

"You sure you're okay?"

"I'm sure."

⌖   ⌖   ⌖

Fifteen minutes later Cassidy was settled on the waterbed, her shoes off, a mystery in her lap. Starshine sprang onto the bed, sent her a meaningful look, and sank a fang into her big toe. Cassidy made a grab but Starshine jumped down, trotted into the hall, and telegraphed a second meaningful look.

"Not bad. You waited almost an hour to begin your official post-motherhood, fattening up stage." She pulled on her sneakers. "I'd say you have a fine sense of decorum." She grabbed the cell phone, hustled downstairs, and fed Starshine at her favorite place on the counter.

Her stomach full, the cat stood on all fours and made fervent body contact, bumping with her head, wriggling with her torso, the entire display accompanied by a raucous purr.

"I can't believe it." Cassidy scratched the calico's jaw. "If I didn't know cats were incapable of gratitude, I'd say you were thanking me for getting the kids out of the house."

Starshine took tiny, mincing steps and flexed her paws. "Oh, I get it. You're buttering me up to make sure I don't ever let any of 'em back in."

The phone rang. She glanced through her window into the house next door. For once, none of the multiple occupants was in the kitchen. Her chest tightened ever so slightly. Her left hand folded around the cell phone. Her right hand reached for the receiver.

24

Driving Chicago Avenue

"We've been waiting for you to come downstairs." A male voice pitched unnaturally high. Cassidy knew instantly that it was Cliff talking in a falsetto so she wouldn't recognize him. A metal band closed around her lungs.

He said, "I saw the cat jump up and thought I'd give you a minute to feed it. But you really shouldn't allow animals on the counter, you know. It's not sanitary."

Trying to sound like a good guy. Wants everybody to like him.

Switching off the kitchen and dining room lights, she stepped up next to the teak table and peered out the window. He'd have to be on the opposite side of Briar to see as far as Starshine's feeding station. A dark sedan, someone sitting in back with the dome light on, had a direct bead on her kitchen.

"Can you identify the woman in that car across the street?"

Suddenly she knew who it was. "Oh God! It can't be!"

His voice turned gentle. "I think you understand the situation now."

She felt as if she'd been punched in the stomach.

"Now turn the lights back on so I can see you." She did. "I'm going to give you directions, then you're going to drive to the place I tell you and we'll meet you there."

Anxiety crackled in her head. "What? Why do I have to drive? Why not ride with you?"

His comforting tone continued. "Because I said so. Now don't ask questions."

"But I don't understand. Why not just let me follow you there?"

Irritation crept into his voice. "I know how conniving you can be. If you're behind me, you might try to signal a cop or run me off the road. Now write down the directions on that pad you've got there."

The pad lay on a small counter beneath the phone. Moving into the kitchen where he couldn't see her, she put down the cell phone and picked up a pencil. "Okay."

"Take Chicago Avenue west to River Road, then north to Irving." He dictated several more turns. "You'll be in this industrial park. When you get to Walnut, there'll be a large, two-story building on the northwest corner. Pull into the lot, park in the space closest to the door, and wait in your car. You got that?"

She struggled to take in air. "What are you going to do to my mother?"

"You follow my instructions to the letter, she'll be fine."

Cassidy clutched the cell phone, hoping to page Zach while still shielded from Cliff's view. "Is that it?"

"Step back into the doorway so I can see you." She did. "Once you hang up, you have exactly twenty seconds to get out the door. If you make one additional phone call, if you take one second too long, I'll drive away. And I'll hurt your mother."

The metal band tightened across her chest.

"Now get in your car and go to the place I told you."

"I will."

"Hang up now."

She raced to the closet. Pulling her handbag off the shelf, she buried the phone in the bottom. She took out her keys, scrambled into her jacket, stuffed the directions in her pocket, and ran to the garage.

Hauling up the garage door, she heard a footstep land behind her. Her whole body jumped. A man in a black ski mask had just come around the corner from the alley. He said in his falsetto voice, "Go on inside the garage."

She slipped into the narrow space between the car and wall, her heart pounding.

"Now turn around." He spoke agreeably, as if giving dance instructions.

Taking her bag, he rummaged through it. He wore a black raincoat, black pants, and black tennis shoes. His hands were uncovered but gave no hint to his identity. He removed the cell phone from her bag, shoved it in his pocket, and tossed the bag aside. Stripping off her jacket, he checked the pockets, then patted her down. She gritted her teeth as he slid his hand over the outside of her sweatshirt, briefly felt her breasts, ran a finger around the inside of her waistband.

Thank God his metal detector didn't go off. Or his hand into my bra.

He stepped back. "I expected a gun. But if you had one, I'd've taken it away, and then I'd be even more annoyed than I am already. You know, it's a real pleasure to deal with someone more on my level than the women I usually consort with."

"Now what?" Her voice sounded quavery. She wanted to stand up to him but the anxiety sluicing through her system had taken too much out of her.

"Proceed with your instructions." He started toward his own car.

Rolling part way down the block, she stopped next to the sedan and gazed into her mother's frightened face. Helen's mouth was open, her eyes bulging. From the way she held her shoulders, Cassidy could tell her hands were tied behind her. She mouthed, "I love you, Mom," then drove toward Chicago Avenue.

✉   ✉   ✉

Heading west on Chicago across the two-mile stretch that comprised the village, she felt a staticky buzz building in her brain. Her gaze passed blindly over gracious, expensive homes, well-tended yards, lawns patched with snow now that the temperature had dropped down into the twenties again.

She crossed Harlem and started into River Forest, her

stomach lurching as the anxiety amped higher. Her frame seemed welded in place, muscles so rigid she could move neither her hands from the wheel nor her foot from the accelerator. In some distant corner of her mind, she realized she was pressing too hard, the car hurtling too fast, everything zooming forward at the same hyper speed as the thoughts racing in her head.

Noticing a stop sign up ahead, she knew that she was rocketing toward it but could not get her brain to telegraph the message that would lift her foot off the accelerator.

Flying past the untrafficked corner, she saw a major intersection about a mile in front of her. Clenching her teeth, she made a massive effort to get her cortex to snap off the neurons that would move her foot from the accelerator to the brake. Suddenly, as if transported to another planet, she saw a wall of trees on both sides, a lonely road ahead, two taillights in the distance. The southwestern forest preserve. As soon as she identified it, the image evaporated and she was back on Chicago Avenue, the red light coming up fast.

Concentrating on her foot, she hammered it onto the brake. The car jerked to a stop, her head whipping backward. She opened her mouth, sucked in air, and began shaking all over.

If I don't get out of the car this minute, I'll die.

If you do get out, your mother'll die.

Gotta make this panic go away. My heart's gonna burn up, my lungs collapse, my brain explode.

No way to stop an anxiety attack. You've just gotta drive on through it.

✉ ✉ ✉

She crawled from block to block and finally arrived at her destination. Turning into a brightly lit parking lot, she stopped in front of a steel door in an industrial-style building.

Using the small amount of control she had left, she pried her hands from the steering wheel, rested her head against the side window, and listened to the storm popping inside her skull.

A dark sedan pulled up about six spaces to the left. Consumed by internal static, Cassidy watched with detachment as Cliff stepped out, removed Helen from the back, and walked her toward the Toyota. His left hand gripped her mother's arm; his right held a gun. Cassidy opened the car door, put one foot on the ground, and pushed out. Lurching forward, she stumbled, caught herself, then stood upright.

"Cass!" Her mother's voice jolted her back. Helen tried to twist away from Cliff but he held her in place. "Let go of me, can't you see she almost fell out of the car?" Helen stretched out toward Cassidy. "Are you sick? What's the matter?" Cliff and Helen, her mother dressed only in sweater and slacks, halted two yards away.

Cassidy opened her mouth to say she was fine but an internal voice stopped her. *You're not supposed to do that anymore.* Feeling as if she'd drunk truth serum, she said, "I had an anxiety attack driving over and I'm a little shaky."

"You're playing some kind of trick." Cliff's falsetto sounded irritated. "Now go inside that building."

Still feeling woozy, Cassidy kept her eyes down, one hand on the wall, and went where she was told: up a flight of stairs, down a hall, into a large corner office.

Cliff came through the door behind her, Helen in tow, and flipped on the ceiling light. Pointing toward a swivel chair placed about a yard out from the wall opposite the door, he said to Cassidy, "Sit there."

He guided Helen to its companion standing about four feet to the right of Cassidy's and put her in it. Cassidy was relieved to see that he did not treat her mother with unnecessary roughness. A rectangular table occupied the middle of the room. Cliff tossed his raincoat on the table, then pulled off a coil of rope he had slung over his shoulder and threw it on top of his coat.

Helen fidgeted in her chair. "What are you going to do?"

Hearing her mother's scared, pleading tone, Cassidy felt tears sting the back of her eyelids.

Cliff moved behind Helen's backrest. "I'm going to tie you into this chair, and if all goes well, Cassidy will drive you home when this is over, no harm done."

Cassidy watched as he undid the original bond and retied Helen to the chair frame. The eyeholes in the ski mask revealed blue irises that seemed familiar, but the strangeness of the covered face and falsetto voice threw her off. *Wouldn't bother with the mask unless he intends to let us go. I've gotta figure out who this creep is so I can nail him afterward.* But the crackle in her head, now diminished to a low buzz, was still making it hard to think.

Perching on the table about two yards from her chair, Cliff said to Cassidy, "You sit quietly and don't make any trouble, I won't tie you up just yet."

"Why Mom and not me?"

"You'll be moving soon. Then I'll use the rope." His hand

slid across the blond tabletop. Through the hole in the mask she saw his mouth widen. *Don't have to see his face to know there's a big, fat, lecherous grin plastered across it.* The metal band across her chest twisted a couple of knots tighter.

Cliff reached into his coat pocket and took out her phone. "Hello Zach? This is Cliff. You're probably wondering where Cassidy's disappeared to about now."

Cassidy blurted, "How'd you know Zach would be gone?" *The maintenance man.* "You're the one who sent him off to Marina City, aren't you?"

His mouth moved; she knew he was smiling again.

He spoke into the phone. "That's right, I've got her here." A pause. "There's no reason to get all upset. She's just sitting here next to her mother behaving herself better than usual. So here's what we're gonna do. I'll give you directions and you'll drive on out and meet us." He repeated his instructions.

"I don't think you need to talk to her. I know that's what they do in the movies, but I'm gonna pass on that little piece of melodrama. Now this offer I've made does have a couple of restrictions. First, if I don't see your Nissan parked beside her Toyota in twenty minutes, all three of us'll be gone when you get here. Second, if there're any cops, I will regretfully have to kill them both. You can understand my position here, can't you, Zach?" He put down the phone.

Cassidy shook her head. The spaciness was nearly gone, her thoughts focused and clear again. "Why'd you call Zach?"

"You don't need to know that now. In the next twenty minutes, I want to make sure you're fully briefed. So, what would you like to hear about me?" He rested his gun in his lap.

Don't let him know you're practically back to normal. Make it seem worse than it is. Maybe you can try fainting or something. Bending forward, she dropped her head into her hands. "I'm sorry, I can't help it. I'm still so dizzy."

"You're just trying to get away with something."

Helen turned to stare at her. "No she's not. I can tell. There's something really wrong."

"Yeah, I'll bet. Now sit up and listen to what I'm about to tell you."

Straightening, she slumped against the backrest. *What's he after—Academy Award, most bizarre story of the year? Still thinking I'll be his stand-in on Oprah and tell all?* Fear rippled through her. *Maybe planning to hold Mom hostage till he gets his air time. Gotta try the pepper gun. But better to wait till Zach's here for backup.*

"Okay, you listening now?" Cliff flexed his shoulders. "When I was young, I had a special relationship with God. I prayed every day, and I could always hear God's voice in my head answering. Then one night he showed me a vision of the new world order He's planned for the next millennium. But before this new order can come to pass, mankind has to be purged. All the sinners—the homosexuals, the prostitutes, the drug users—they all have to be destroyed to make way for God's kingdom. So he sent down His plague to eradicate them."

Making her voice sincere, she said, "And He needed you to help him move things along."

"My task was to herald in the new regime, just as John

the Baptist prepared the way for the Messiah. But before I could proceed, I had to be tested—like Jesus being tempted in the garden. So when I entered adolescence, I suddenly found myself having these powerful impulses to violate God's natural order. It was almost as if I'd developed this separate personality, as if there were two parts at war inside me."

"A good part and a bad part." *This is the good part talking about how he and God are all buddy-buddy. Then, when it's time to tie me down, the bad part'll step in.* She rubbed her arms against a sudden chill. *Good guy Cliff never has to soil his hands—he just sends in his evil twin to do the dirty work.*

"The good side desperately wanted to obey God's law, but the other side, the demonic side, kept pulling me toward an unnatural lifestyle." His left hand gripped the table's edge. "If I'd only been able to establish a normal relationship with a virtuous woman, I could have overcome those other urges. For years I tried pursuing a succession of different girls, but they all refused to help me in my battle for purity. And if the truth be known, most of them weren't so pure themselves."

"So the bad side won," she said, wanting to hurry him along. *Oh God, I hope he's not gonna use Mom to make me go public with this delusional bilge. If that's his plan, why'd he say she could go home with me? And why call Zach?*

He turned the gun over in his hands. "I was able to hold out until I fell under the spell of this beautiful young man who'd chosen homosexuality as a lifestyle. I knew the path he'd taken was wrong, but he was so gentle and kind, our love was so strong, I couldn't withstand the pull." His voice turned sad. "Not a day goes by even now that I don't miss him."

"What happened?"

"He thought he was lucky, thought he'd always come out a winner. He went through life with the same sense of immortality Mark had. But they were both wrong. My beautiful lover died of AIDS. And Mark's dead because I shot him."

Cassidy peered intently at the black mask. Something clicked in her head. A picture emerged in her mind of the face behind it. "I still don't understand—why kill Mark?"

"I shouldn't have told him." He gazed out the window.

"Told him what?"

"About the HIV. I thought he'd be sympathetic." His voice turned aggrieved. "Wouldn't you think he'd show some compassion?"

Dropping her head, she pressed her fingertips to her forehead as if she felt weak. "What did Mark do?"

"This look of shock came over his face and he said, 'What about all those men you meet online? You tested positive and you're having sex with these guys?' Then he got up and left."

"That's why you killed him?"

The falsetto speeded up. "He should've been more understanding. He's the one who always had all the luck."

Always? How far back do they go?

"Just because I caught it and he didn't is no reason I should have to give up sex." His voice turned bitter. "All these people, they have no sense of God's plan, but they're the ones who get the money, power, sex. Why shouldn't I?"

It's okay to kill people 'cause life's not fair?

"After Mark walked out, I knew he had to be punished, and I must say, I came up with a very clever way of doing it. I called on Sunday, just as if nothing had happened, and when I asked about his plans, he mentioned the lunch with you. So I told him to sit next to the window 'cause I'd be driving past the restaurant and we could wave good-bye."

"I'm really fading in and out." Wrapping her arms beneath her breasts, she slumped even lower. "But there's one other thing. Patrick."

"When I shot Mark, it was a real rush. I found out I liked it, at least the bad side did, and I could see I had quite a talent for it too. Even the good side had to admit the logic—that if God wanted to punish homosexuals, killing them directly would move the plan along faster." He glanced at his watch. "We need to stop now. I have to be ready."

Ready for what? A picture snapped into her mind: Zach walking through the doorway. *Oh God! He's going to kill Zach so I have to explain everything and then the story'll be all over the news.*

Cliff stood, picked up the rope, and stretched a length of it in front of him. He said, his voice gentle again, "I need you to undress now."

Helen cried, "Oh no, oh please, don't do that to her."

Cassidy sat motionless, not even breathing, for three beats, then she inhaled deeply and doubled over. "Oh shit, I'm gonna faint." Sliding her left hand under her sweatshirt, she grabbed the two metal objects tucked beneath her breasts. She transferred the pepper gun to her right hand and tried to get a fix on Cliff, who had started backing rapidly away from her. By the time she pulled the trigger, he was standing in the doorway.

"Goddamnit." Coughing, he rubbed at his mask-covered face, then said in a voice that was not a falsetto, a voice that matched the picture in her head, "I told you you should've tied her up."

If I try to spray him again, he'll go out in the hall. If I try to go after him he'll shoot me.

Cassidy jammed the pepper gun into her waistband, dashed to her mother's chair, and began sawing the rope with the knife.

"You barely touched me." Cliff spoke in the falsetto again. "I'll be over this in no time, and now you've forced me to add on another punishment. I was going to let your mother go, but now I'll have to kill her to teach you a lesson."

Helen moaned.

Oh shit, oh shit. Maybe if I beg and plead, I can talk him out of shooting her. Cassidy pressed the knife into her mother's hand and scooted back to her chair.

"I'm sorry, so sorry. I know it was wrong of me." She threw the pepper gun onto the floor. "Please don't hurt my mother. From now on I'll do whatever you say."

"We'll see. If you make me really happy, I might spare her." He went to the window and gazed at the parking lot below. "We're running out of time. This damn spray is slowing me down." He wiped his arm across the eyeholes in his mask. "Now get on the table. I want you on your stomach with your arms and legs spread-eagled. I'll have to cut your clothes away later."

Cassidy's teeth locked shut and her body went cold with fear. For a moment she couldn't respond, then a strangled gasp from her mother reminded her of what would happen if she didn't. She rose and got onto the table in a series of tense, ragged movements.

Cliff tied her hands and feet to the four corners, then took up a post beside the window. Gulping air, she shut her eyes against the waves of humiliation flashing through her. *Oh God, I'd rather die.* Time passed with aching slowness. Driven by the sense that she had to calm herself for her mother and Zach, she worked to get her breathing under control.

Finally she heard the falsetto voice, "He's here." Cliff opened the door wide, then flattened himself against the wall, the gun extended in both hands.

Yanking at the ropes, Cassidy flailed and twisted in her attempt to get the best possible view of the hallway. She realized Cliff had set it up so that the sightline ran from the table to the stairwell, which meant Zach would see her spotlighted under the office fixture as soon as he came upstairs.

"Struggling's not going to do you any good." Cliff whispered. "You can be a good girl and take your mother home with you or make trouble and lose both of them."

She stopped thrashing. Her throat thickened in despair. *Jesus, if only he'd shoot me first, then I wouldn't have to watch.*

Footsteps sounded faintly on the stairs. Her mother sniffled behind her. Sweat popped out on Cassidy's brow. Zach emerged from the stairwell a good twenty yards from the office doorway and started down the unlighted corridor. She could not see his face but knew exactly how it would look, the eyes narrowed in concentration, the mouth firmly set. He walked with an easy, measured stride, arms loose at his sides, taking time to plan his approach. He would be picturing the room, gauging Cliff's position, rehearsing his moves. As he came closer, she saw the gun in his right hand.

If only I hadn't fought you so much. Or gotten us into this mess in the first place. And why, oh why, didn't I ever tell you how beautiful you are? Or how much I love you?

Zach was ten feet away when Cassidy heard a bustle of movement behind her. Helen shouted, "You can't do this." Cassidy twisted to see her mother throw herself at Cliff. Turning away from the door, Cliff punched her in the face. She staggered back, then grabbed his arm and jabbed the pocketknife into the side of his neck, drawing blood. Zach stepped into the doorway.

Holding Helen off with one hand, Cliff fired at Zach and missed.

Zach stood, legs apart, and took aim. "Get down *now!*"

Helen dived to the floor. Zach pulled the trigger. Cliff crashed backward, bounced against the wall, and dropped to the ground, the gun skittering out of his hand. Blood bubbled up from a hole in his chest. Screaming, Helen crawled away from the body.

"Omigod!" Cassidy rasped, her stomach heaving at the coppery smell of blood. Cliff lay still, his body twisted at an unnatural angle. *Dead or unconscious.*

Zach scooped up the gun, then fixed his eyes on her face.

She sucked in air. "I'm fine. Do Mom first. She's all bloody."

He lifted Helen to her feet. Both hands and one cheek were smeared with crimson. Grabbing her arm, he said, "C'mon, we've gotta get you cleaned up."

She pulled away and stood staring at the body.

He gripped her arm again. "We've gotta get this blood off."

"Well, you don't have to be so rough about it," Helen complained as he dragged her toward the door. "The only thing wrong is, I hurt my back when I fell. This is just a little blood I got on me when I cut him with the knife."

Leaving her mother in the restroom, Zach returned to cut Cassidy loose. She got off the table and forced herself to gaze down at the body. *Zach had to do it. No other way.* She asked, "How bad does it look with Mom?"

"I didn't see any lesions. Odds are she'll be fine."

"Well," Cassidy released a deep sigh, "we've finally got Cliff. How's he doing? Still breathing?"

Zach crouched beside him. "Unfortunately, he's probably gonna live. Doesn't look like I hit any vital organs."

"I don't know why I was surprised to see you with a gun. I should've known you'd be planning for something like this."

Standing, he draped an arm across her shoulders. "Since I'm not wearing gloves, I don't want to take off his mask. But I think it's pretty obvious who we've got here."

"Obvious?" Reaching for the hand that lay on her shoulder, she rubbed his fingers against her cheek.

"Didn't you see that MERTZ ENTERPRISES plaque downstairs?' This must be the heir apparent, the guy who told his old man to fuck off."

Shaking her head, Cassidy said, "I didn't see anything. I was too busy trying not to fall on my face. And he used a falsetto so I wasn't able to recognize the voice. But I think the reason Cliff picked this building is because he used to work here, and Roland Mertz is one of a long list of people he has it in for. I think Cliff is both Mark's old friend *and* his e-mail buddy—that these two guys are one and the same—and that when Mark said his aunt Helen was marrying this rich Mertz guy, it reminded Cliff he had one more person he needed to punish."

"Bringing us here is punishing Roland?"

"Cliff figured we'd zero in on Ron, and even though the police'd eliminate him when they discovered he wasn't positive, having a shooting at the Mertz building and his son implicated would certainly create a few waves for his ex-boss."

"So who is it? And how'd you make him? His eyes give him away? Or have you turned psychic?"

"As my gambling client might say, I'm betting on Ken. I got the first inkling when he used words like *bet, odds,* and *lucky.* Then later, when his bad side popped out, it was Ken's voice. The final piece fell into place when you told me this is the Mertz building. That's when I remembered Ken mentioning he once managed a warehouse and the old man was a tyrant. It's gotta be Roland he worked for."

Hearing a gasp from the body, she felt an urge to raise the mask so he could breathe more easily. *Remember all those women.* She hardened herself and continued, "If I were a gambler myself, I'd lay money that CK from the bar is Clifford Kenneth Connors, and that Cliff's the paranoid, religious zealot, and Ken the bad boy who gets around Cliff the same way he used to get around his mother."

25

Driving to Woodridge

Cassidy gazed out the Nissan window at long, unbroken stretches of mottled brown and yellow—bare dirt, dead grass—with occasional rumpled throw-rugs of grayish snow tucked into the shadows. It was Tuesday afternoon. After driving west on the Eisenhower, Zach exited onto a country road that meandered in a southwesterly direction toward Woodridge, the small town where Cassidy's therapist lived.

He glanced her way. "So, how you doing? You ready to tell your shrink all about this controlling guy you've picked up with who keeps interfering in your attempts to get yourself killed?"

"Actually, I'm not certain I need to see Honor after all. I

took the car out yesterday and did fine. I think forcing myself to keep going on that drive to the Mertz factory may have done the trick. Implosion techniques are one of the standard phobia treatments, you know."

"Implosion? I love it when you talk dirty like that." His jaw tightened. "You trying to weasel out of therapy?"

She sighed. "I realize I still need to talk about the shootings."

He patted her knee, his way of saying *That's a good girl.*

She decided that, since he was driving her all the way to Woodridge, she would not get prickly about it, even though his tendency to patronize was one of the things she liked least about him.

He asked, "How's your mother?"

"Hysterical, but who can blame her?" She bit her lip. "I thought Jenny was overreacting when she refused to get tested. But now that it's my own mother, I'm terrified. We've still got a couple of agonizing days before the test results come back."

"Yeah, well, I think it's gonna be okay." Zach punched on the radio, changing from a rock to a light music station, the one she played in her waiting room. "When the night has been too lonely" flowed through the speakers.

Zach said, "By the way, I found out how Ken managed to break into the factory, and it was very ingenious. He used a fire extinguisher to force air through a crack in the door, and the pressurized stream of carbon dioxide set off the security system. He triggered the alarm about a dozen times over the weekend, so Roland finally decided the system was malfunctioning and turned it off. I have to say I'm impressed."

"Ken's impressive in a lot of ways, none of them good." Her teeth gritted briefly. "I went to visit him this morning at Cook County Hospital and he filled in all the holes. He certainly doesn't mind talking about himself, but that's part of his narcissism. He's convinced that if everybody knows his story, he'll finally get the recognition he deserves."

"So, what holes did you get filled in?"

"You know how you kept saying it was too much of a coincidence that Cliff'd picked me to be his biographer, then just happened to run across my cousin on the Internet? Well, it turns out there is a connection. Cliff was Mark's old friend, the one I dimly remembered. Back in high school he knew me through Mark. That was when he was getting rejected by all those girls, and apparently I was nicer than most of the others, probably 'cause he never asked me out. So Cliff and Mark stayed in contact—it was Cliff who got Mark started with e-mail guys—and a while back Mark mentioned that I'd gone into private practice. Then, when Cliff needed a therapist, he remembered I'd always been nice and looked me up."

"Shit! It was right there in front of me. I can't believe I missed it."

Should I tell him he's getting arrogant again?

A moment passed, then Zach said, "Any other holes?"

"Patrick." A feeling of sadness filtered through her. "Ken got such a high out of shooting Mark it led to a whole new mission. The night I went to Patrick's, he tagged along. Since one of his many obsessive urges was to learn every little detail about me, he followed up the next day by doing research on Patrick. And lo and behold, he found out that Patrick was not only gay, he was also connected to the Mertz family. Cliff by then had generalized his hatred to the entire Mertz clan on the basis that they had money and power and he didn't, so he saw Patrick as an ideal target. Little did he know he was doing the old man a favor."

Zach shook his head. "Speaking of Roland, where do the wedding plans stand?"

"Mom says they're 'in limbo,' although I suspect that's a face-saving euphemism on her part. I believe Roland actually turned purple when he heard about Mom jumping Cliff. He claims to be upset about the AIDS risk. My take on it is, Roland doesn't like her showing all that gumption and also figures no fiancée of his has any business endangering herself for a mere daughter."

They passed an ENTERING WOODRIDGE sign.

"Ironic, isn't it?" Cassidy remarked. "Here we did everything we could to stop Cliff, and the upshot is, he gets his story on the ten o'clock news. He got what he wanted after all."

"Yeah, but he was planning to watch from the comfort of his living room." Zach scratched his jaw. "One other thing I've been meaning to ask—what kind of nut do we have here exactly? You mentioned his bad side coming out and speaking in Ken's voice. Is he a genuine-article multiple? The sort of thing I've never quite believed in?"

"It's possible, but I doubt it. I think he just had two strongly competing urges. One side wanted to be a good boy and keep God happy. The other wanted to have gay sex and play gotcha. The way he managed the internal conflict was to disown those traits he didn't approve of and label them his Ken side."

Zach's thick brows drew together. "If he's not a multiple, then what? He's clearly a psychopath, but what kind?"

"Most people with psychological problems don't fit into neat little boxes. My guess is that it started with denial, plus a lot of rage, and just kept growing till it became a full-blown paranoid delusion. He had this conflict—religiosity versus homosexuality—so he denied that he was homosexual and blamed his gay urges on Ken. Then he denied that he was responsible for his behavior and blamed it on women for rejecting him. And finally he denied that he had a sadistic urge to hurt people and blamed the whole thing on God for sending him on his crusade. Add a large dose of obsessiveness and narcissistic personality disorder and you end up with a lunatic like Cliff—a mixed breed."

He stopped at a traffic light. "What about his story that he got arrested for stealing money and had to go into therapy?"

"All true. When he was talking his head off at the hospital, he particularly went into detail about this Adonis-like hunk—the great love of his life. This is the guy who thought he was lucky but died of AIDS. Seems like the hunk was a compulsive gambler and his last name was Leman. Since Ken felt like they were married, it's not surprising that he took on the guy's last name, as well as the gambling addiction and the disease."

"Falling in love certainly can be dangerous."

Cassidy gave him a sharp look, not sure whether or not

to take the comment personally, but his expression was bland, with no sign of the amused superiority he displayed when he wanted to zap her.

Zach said, "The only other thing is, where'd he hide his computer? We didn't see any sign of it in that dump of his."

"He kept it at his father's place. Given the poor security, he didn't want anything valuable in his apartment."

Cassidy directed him to turn left, then pointed to a rustic wooden cottage. "That's Honor's place there."

He pulled up in front.

Unbuckling her seatbelt, she turned to face him. "There's something I want to say and I have to do it fast before I lose my nerve." She laid her hand on his thigh. "You and I usually don't go in for a lot of mushy talk, but when I was on that table watching you walk toward me, I was so sorry I'd never said the words." Pausing, she took a deep breath. "I really do love you, you know."

"Yeah, I know." Zach leaned over and kissed her lightly on the lips. "Me too."

The Eclaire series
by Sophie Dunbar
Behind Eclaire's Doors
Redneck Riviera
A Bad Hair Day
Shiveree

Dunbar brings New Orleans and the South alive in this acclaimed series featuring sleuthing couple Claire and Dan Claiborne. Claire's upscale hair salon, Eclaire, attracts some mighty deadly clients from time to time and Claire's penchant for being in the wrong place at the right time places her squarely in the midst of murder and mayhem!

"Mysteries don't get more fun than this!" —*L.A. Times*

"Delightfully irreverent, slightly wacky, and sizzlingly sexy." —*Sunday Magazine, Baton Rouge*

"Makes the pulse pound—for several reasons. May there be many more of these ribald, racy romps."
—*Washington Times*